STAFF DOMINION: A RELIC HUNTER THRILLER

Treasures of the Ark #1

NEENA ROTH

So Moses spoke to the Israelites, and their leaders gave him twelve staffs, one for the leader of each of their ancestral tribes, and Aaron's staff was among them.

—Numbers 17:6 (NIV)

PROLOGUE

KNEPH, EGYPT—THREE DAYS AGO

Children froze mid-play to watch him stride down the street. Dust bulged around each step, like a man riding in on a storm. Their young years didn't shield them from the purpose surrounding him—his destiny. Wariness filled their eyes and fear propelled them home to the safety of their parents' arms. But they'd soon see his true power and clamor for his favor.

He remembered this village, had played here as a child. And now Kneph would play a key part in revealing his true destiny. The one destined to be his at birth, yet denied him.

Until now. Because he possessed the staff of Aaron.

Its power pulsed through him, beckoning him for release, driving him to find the one who needed what it had to offer. The staff knew his desire, fed his need, just as he fed the staff's. Each time he wielded its power, they became more united...inseparable.

A woman darted out of a small house and stood in the doorway like a barricade. Didn't she understand? Didn't she know he came to save her son?

"Where is he?" Even he could hear the force in his voice that caused her fear to grow. He said it again, softer this time the growing vibration of the staff. His heart beat louder in his chest like a cacophony of war drums.

He pushed the woman aside. A young boy lay on a cot. His sickly pallor matched the pale covering over his slight form. Sunken eyes surrounded by dark circles stared back. Death huddled near.

The living force of the staff pulsed in tune with the man's heartbeat. So close, so close...

He stood in the middle of the simple house, surrounded by power. His senses overloaded.

The woman ran to her son, a soft cry slipped from her trembling lips. She shook her head as she grabbed the boy and held him against her. Terror filled her eyes.

The room shifted and jarred into a juxtaposed reality. The woman's form doubled then blurred. As her two parts reunited, her expression spewed cruel accusations from a familiar face from his past.

He slammed his eyes shut, head turned away. Blinking, he dared to look again. Not real. Lies. He would not listen to the falsehoods of the past attacking him.

The woman appeared as before, fear-ridden and still clutching the boy, her lips moving as she spoke into his ear. Words of comfort most likely. Surely she must see that he held the promise of life for her child.

This was his destiny. His time. He focused his mind.

The power vibrated down his body to his feet. He knelt, fingers outstretched to the child. Doubts regarding his purpose attacked him again, but determination grew stronger. Resolute, he pushed the fabric aside laid his hand on the boy's chest.

Light burst out from the staff in a familiar yet silent explosion. Just as before, but the power unleashed each time seemed to increase. Just as it did now.

Fear tried to overtake him as he felt himself start to lose control. He grasped the staff with both hands. Power rumbled up his arms and shoulders in a violent torrent. The force of the staff stretched beyond his mind and control. He squinted his eyes against the blinding light as a roar filled his ears to a deafening pitch until he realized his own scream had melded with it.

The surge stopped, like a flick of some supernatural switch.

He gasped and fell to his knees.

Darkness, filth, unworthy...

No, this can't be. His destiny said otherwise. He'd fought to regain dominance but failed. He released the staff—released his feeble attempt to control its power. Now lifeless, it lay on the ground, taunting him with temptation.

An eerie stillness reached his ears and tormented his soul. Had he failed again? He lifted the staff from the ground and rose to his feet. He stood in the doorway. Outside, bodies lay everywhere. Children no longer played.

He turned around to look behind him. The boy crouched next to the inert form of his mother, no longer sickly, but healed. Full of life.

And fear.

"I'm sorry." He clutched the staff to his chest, determined to continue trying until he got it right.

Sometimes destiny came with a price.

His would be blood.

CHAPTER ONE

EL-MINYA, EGYPT

Nichole Strauss tossed her work gloves into the back of the pickup truck and smacked her hands against her jeans. A cloud of dust floated from her hips, joining the powdery coating on her boots. One more night in a tent and then back to Cairo and a hot shower.

Just in time for lunch. Her stomach growled as a confirmation.

Despite their meager resources, she admired how these people endured. Somehow their semi-nomadic lifestyle had kept them alive for generations. Until recent months. Drought now threatened their very existence. That, and the growing communities crowding access to the Nile. She prayed the well they just drilled would be the answer to their needs without diminishing their traditions. Thanks to the Strauss Foundation's partnership with Jaensen Investment Group, the people here would soon see desert land converted to large-scale farming.

And if the new investors came on board for the Clean Water & Farm Project, they'd have a solid infrastructure started by this time next year. Which reminded her—she better call Robin tonight and see where things were on that end. Plans needed to be made and contracts signed.

Twenty yards away, Jerad shook hands with the foreman. Both held the satisfied look of a goal accomplished. Half a dozen local workers stood nearby, smiling and laughing. The first gurgle of water never ceased to evoke joy and triumph. Her father would've been proud. The melancholy she carried over his death had become a constant companion over the last year. At least now she could think of him without breaking into a torrent of tears.

Jerad left the group, heading in her direction. She loved his swagger and easy smile. Contracting for the Strauss Foundation suited him. And her. As their official, on-staff environmental scientist, Jerad Nebal's skills, coupled with her archeological expertise, presented a unique safety factor that most countries found trustworthy. The Strauss Foundation had never received so many requests for aid as they had in the last six months.

Nichole snagged her engagement ring from her pocket and put it back on her finger. Perched on the tailgate, she admired how the modest diamond twinkled in the late afternoon sun.

"You're gonna lose that thing if you keep carrying it around." Jerad leaned against the side of the truck next to her.

She reached out and ran her fingers through his hair above his ear. The sunlight gave his nearly black hair silk-like sheen. "I waited five years for this ring. What makes you think I'll let it out of my sight?"

Holding her hand, he kissed her finger by the ring before pressing dusty lips to hers. The smell of dirt and sweat coated him, but she didn't mind. The degenerative nature of Jerad's seizures made every moment matter. The aftereffects of Soren Umberber's poison may still be wreaking havoc with their lives, but nothing would separate them again. She'd see to that.

His smile faded to a look of puzzlement as he stared at something over her shoulder. She twisted around to get a better view. A sandy plume approached from the distance. Much too small for a dust storm, but certainly large enough for a vehicle. The brown, swirling mass mixed with the vibration of a rumbling motor drew closer. A Jeep emerged from the cloud of dust.

Nichole shielded her eyes from the lowering sun. "Please tell me this isn't another one of those hecklers."

"Don't worry about it. The well's finished." He glanced at the small group of children nearby, their play poor camouflage for the intense curiosity feeding their bravery. "You'd think we'd just installed a swimming pool."

"Can you imagine what they'd do if they saw one?"

A shout came from the direction of the newly completed well. The Jeep edged away from the workers and continued toward them. Nichole hopped to the ground. "I bet you a steak dinner it's a reporter."

"Good thing we're not in India right now, cuz you're gonna lose."

Even with the intended humor of his words, his serious tone stopped her short. What did he sense that she couldn't see? She picked up her pace when she recognized the black clothing of the two men climbing out of the dirt-coated Jeep.

Nichole didn't break her stride until she barreled into Achem Mizrahi's outstretched arms. "Never expected to see you here." Memories of her father flooded her in an instant. In her mind, Achem and her father had become inseparable in some ways.

She stepped back, frowning. "Why *are* you here?"

A concerned smile broke Achem's stern features as he gestured to the man with him. "You remember Liran Dakarai, my second-in-command?"

The young man's face seemed familiar despite her reluctant recall of their last encounter with Soren Umberger. Thankfully any damage Soren's genetically modified superseed caused had been reversed or prevented, and the Strauss Foundation hadn't suffered by association when Umberger-Broadman Biotechnology declared bankruptcy.

And the *Natsar* had receded back into anonymity with the gold manna jar in their possession, never to cause the world harm again.

She hoped so anyway. Maybe one day the manna jar could be used for good. Maybe even the Ark too.

"Yes. Good to see you again, Liran."

Hands behind his back, he nodded at her with a hint of a smile that didn't quite reach his dark eyes. His apparent shyness and wavy, dark brown hair gave him an almost boyish appearance. He had to be younger than she and Jerad.

Jerad shook each of the men's hands. "Glad to see you both, but I don't get the feeling you two came for a social visit."

An inquisitive expression draped the Achem's face. "I see you still have the discerning gift the jar left you."

"Yes, among other things." He shot a glance at Nichole.

Nichole locked stares with Jerad as she entwined her fingers with his.

Achem moved closer. "No change?"

Jerad pursued his lips and shook his head.

Nichole squeezed his hand. "We're going to see a doctor in New York next month. I'm sure he can help." She detested seeing the doubt in Jerad's eyes whenever she mentioned their trip.

He let go of her hand. "So, what brings you our way? Interested in learning how to drill a well?"

"A noble cause, to say the least, but unfortunately we've come to warn you." Liran's quiet demeanor did nothing to diminish the deep rumble of his voice, which in light of his youthful appearance, took her by surprise.

He hadn't spoken when they'd met briefly in the midst of the turmoil last year. No way she'd forget a deep and melodic voice like his with just a lilt of the Egyptian cadence she'd grown accustomed to.

She darted her gaze between the two men. "Warn us about what?"

This time Achem spoke. "There's been a plague outbreak in the next village. We knew you were here and wanted to make sure you weren't planning anything in the area."

Jerad frowned. "Bubonic?"

"No, they don't know for sure, only that there have been several outbreaks in the last six months in outlying areas and it's more deadly than anything they've seen."

Nichole took a step closer to them. "I appreciate the warning, but why are you two involved?"

Liran looked to Achem as an unspoken dialogue flitted between them.

Achem's eyes seemed to darken, contrasting even more with his near-white hair. "There's rumors of a man coming into these communities just before the outbreaks."

Jerad shrugged. "It's just been our regular crew here. You think this man is the one spreading the disease?"

"Not him directly, but what he carries. A staff." Achem pulled his shoulders back, giving him a taller appearance as if to carry the gravity of what he was sharing.

The heat of the day did nothing to stop the chill running down her body. Her vision of Achem holding the staff had haunted her dreams more frequently in recent weeks. Along with the other dream of a mystery man on a stage and drums beating in the background. "A staff? You think it's the...?"

Achem nodded. "Yes, the staff of Aaron."

"If you're right, then why? What does he have to gain? Is he just killing people for fun?" Her words tumbled out with the force of the injustice she felt hitting the core of her being.

"We weren't sure until this last incident. Something different happened. A young boy who was dying not only survived but appears to be healed. We're on our way to investigate."

"Where?" Jerad tossed his gloves into the back of their truck.

"A small Coptic village called Kneph."

Jerad furrowed his brow. "Can we come with you?"

Achem took a couple steps closer to Jerad. His eyes glittered like a man driven to a higher purpose. "The manna jar had the power of provision. The staff could very well have a special power of its own."

Nichole lowered her chin as her gaze focused to a narrow pinpoint on Achem. "Like what?"

"Healing. The staff of Aaron has many mysteries surrounding it, some true, some not. We will soon find out." His gaze now shifted and settled on Jerad.

A pregnant silence followed Achem's words and flooded the space between them. Nichole's shriveling hope jolted to new life. Could this be why the dreams had intensified? Did she dare to hope God would do such a thing for Jerad? Heal him?

Jerad clasped her hand and searched her face. An inner battle waged behind his green eyes. "We could head out early. Be there by mid-morning and still get back to the hotel according to plan."

She tucked her doubts into a deep crevice for later review. Jerad clearly needed to do this. She wanted this. "Let's do it."

"I must warn you, I have no idea what we may be walking into." Achem's remark brought all focus back to him.

Puzzled in expression, Liran closed the gap between him and Achem. "Then why—

Achem jerked his arm out, palm flat, signaling Liran to silence.

The volley between them made her antsy. She'd known Achem long enough to understand how deeply his wisdom connected to his faith. Yet, the obvious discord between him and Liran—did Achem doubt his choice of second-in-command?

Jerad's shoulders visibly relaxed. "Must be stronger than that to bring you all this way." He gestured toward the village behind them. "Our camp is on the other side. There's room if you two want to bunk here for the night."

"Your hospitality honors us. We'll head out first thing in the morning." Achem bowed his head, then walked toward his Jeep. Liran strode next to him, body stiff. No doubt an argument brewed there.

Jerad faced her. "I wouldn't call a dusty tent much in the way of hospitality."

"Doesn't matter. Hospitality is deeply steeped in Judaism."

He trailed a finger down her cheek and sported a grin that lit up his green eyes. "I don't want to get your hopes up."

Nichole didn't need heightened perceptions to see through his guise. Jerad never could hide his worry. She still struggled to believe, but how could she add her doubts to his? He needed her strength right now. "I'd slap you upside the head right now if it wouldn't rattle your brains more than they already are."

He chuckled at her remark, but then his expression turned serious. "I know you're afraid to hope, Nikki."

Couldn't she keep anything to herself? She took two steps toward the truck, then stopped. "Don't do that. Just let me be here for you...for a change."

He didn't answer. Just stared at her before nodding.

She forced a smile she didn't feel and retreated to the truck. Tears pricked her eyes. With every step, she berated herself for getting upset. But if she didn't walk away, he'd see the fear she kept hidden in a deeper, darker place.

The one that made her want to run and never look back.

THE JEEP BOUNCED OVER THE ANCIENT ROAD. THEY'D LEFT CAMP hours ago and would soon be within sighting distance of the small village of Kneph. Achem checked the rearview mirror again to confirm that Nichole and Jerad still followed. A dust tail swirled behind the vehicle like a maddened tornado, forcing them to keep some distance.

Liran braced one hand on the cracked dash and gripped the top of the window frame with the other. He'd said little to nothing the entire morning.

"What troubles you?" Achem shifted his scrutiny from the rearview mirror to do a quick study of Liran's face. The sun glared through the open window, bringing his profile into sharp definition. His dark brown hair curled in sweaty ringlets at his forehead and temples. Moisture glistened above his defined lips. A blend of

Egyptian and South African parentage gave a more refined exotic appearance to his features.

"Nothing."

Achem knew better. "You remember playing there as a child, don't you? You and your brother were always welcome."

No response. Liran pinched his dark brows together. "Vaguely. But that was a long time ago. People change."

The subtle message in Liran's last words hit deep in Achem's spirit. He resisted the urge to push Liran to explain, knowing full well the subject of his older brother would be met with scrutiny. But his spirit also told him to be on guard, because he sensed Liran held something back since his return from his recent sabbatical.

Achem returned his attention to the road and zigzagged between two gazelle-sized craters. Liran's older brother leaving the *Natsar* had been difficult for all of them. The signs had been there, that something had changed his Eben, But God had given him peace and reassurance about their future. But he couldn't help but wonder if Eben's departure had thrust Liran into the position of second-in-command too soon. The young man had much to learn still.

But what choice did Achem have? His time grew short. God had shown him as much. The position of *Natsar* leader came to him at an early age as well, but not nearly as young as Liran's twenty-nine years. The man still had much to learn before he took command of the *Natsar*—the Keepers.

"Events don't choose the people, Yahweh does." He prayed Liran would catch the subtext of his reply as he steered the vehicle around another rut large enough to swallow an elephant calf.

"What about the people of Kneph? If the staff of Aaron has resurfaced, how do we explain that Yahweh did not *choose* for this to happen to them?"

Achem didn't miss Liran's emphasis. "The people of Kneph will understand they were not under judgment but the victims of evil." The small Coptic community had chosen their name carefully decades ago. Translated from Hebrew, *Kneph* meant *spirit*. They chose to identify themselves by their beliefs. "Think about how the manna jar affected those who hungered after its power."

Liran pursed his lips in thought. "The darkness in their hearts attempted to control its power for their own gain, but Yahweh intervened."

Achem nodded, appreciating that Liran showed the glimmerings of deep wisdom. Perhaps he'd learned more in the past year than Achem had given him credit. "Yahweh's plan is never a reaction to circumstances, Liran. Quite the opposite. I pray one day you will understand how far-reaching and well-designed the will of Yahweh is."

"Do you think it's part of His plan to involve them?" He gestured over his shoulder at Jerad and Nichole's jeep.

"I'm beginning to think so, yes."

Liran remained silent for a moment before turning in his seat to face him. "The risk seems too high, Achem. Forgive me if I offend you, but I must be honest."

Achem pulled his gaze from the road long enough to take in Liran's concerned expression."Of course, Liran. I wouldn't expect anything less from you."

Eventually, Liran would come to understand God's timing was anything he wanted it to be and usually beyond one's understanding in the middle of it. This area of Liran's training frustrated Achem most. Ultimately, God would be the one to make this clear to his protégé.

Achem returned his focus on what lay ahead. "Ultimately, we must learn to trust that Yahweh is always present and working, regardless of what we think we know or see."

Liran stayed silent as he settled back into his seat.

Achem would leave further discussions to God's prompting, despite the urgency growing within him. He, too, had to trust that God worked in the silence to prepare Liran for the duties he would soon shoulder.

The future of the *Natsar* had never appeared so uncertain.

❦

Despite the sun beating through the truck's windshield, the steering wheel felt like ice in his grip. Jerad flexed his hands, careful not to give Nikki any clue to this latest symptom. She'd pounce on him quicker than a lioness on the hunt if she knew his brain had started to cross signals. The doctor warned them this might happen.

The fine line between peace and causing her worry had shifted to gray and fuzzy lately.

Her signals, on the other hand, told him to tread with great care. She hadn't said much the rest of the evening and still had her emotions closed off this morning. But he didn't miss the telltale circles under her soulful hazel eyes or the way she kept her chin tucked. Even the dusting of freckles across her nose and cheeks seemed faded in weariness. She may think she could handle the burden of his illness, but Jerad had his doubts.

She'd lost so much already. And the one-year anniversary of her father's death—murder—was just weeks away. He had it in his ability to protect her from false hope, and he planned to exert that power at all cost.

Jerad couldn't stand the thought of his last days on earth making her miserable. He glanced at her, taking in the subtle curve of her neck, the strands of blonde hair blowing loose from her ponytail, and the delicate pursing of her lips, which she did when she was stressed. "You gonna tell me why you're still so peeved?"

She faced the window—silent.

"Nikki, come on. I know you're scared. You don't have to protect me." He'd never seen anyone's head spin so fast. Any quicker, and she'd be headless.

Her mouth hanging open added a nice touch to the daggers shooting out of her eyes. "Jerad Nebal, I can't believe you just said that to me. As I recall, yesterday you were the one trying to protect me. And don't think I didn't notice what you were doing with your hands." She gestured to the steering wheel.

He let the breath he'd been holding out in a loud exhale. "That's different. I just don't want to see you get hurt."

"So you think protecting me from the truth will help?"

The punch hit him low and hard. Hard enough to open his eyes and show him where he went wrong. He stared at the rooster tail of dust swirling behind Achem and Liran's Jeep. Jerad had messed things up royally this time. "You're right. I'm sorry. I shouldn't have kept it from you."

She turned sideways. "No, you shouldn't have. I can handle this, Jerad. I want it all, good or bad."

"Point taken."

In the distance, a growing cloud of smoke peaked above the haze of their trek. Achem's Jeep picked up speed. Jerad pressed the accelerator. "I think things just got worse."

Nichole watched the horizon. "I'm afraid to even guess."

Neither spoke during the last ten minutes of the journey to what Jerad assumed to be their destination. By the time he pulled up, only the charred remains of primitive houses blackened the ground like shadows of what they used to be. Dust and ash floated in the air.

Achem and Liran climbed out of their Jeep and headed toward a group of men standing near the dying blaze.

The smell of burning flesh filled the air. Jerad rushed to Nikki's open door. "You sure you want to do this?"

She appeared somewhat agitated, but not fearful as she had when they'd run into the funeral pyre in India. She gave him a slight smile and got out. "It's okay. I've made peace with how Mom died."

Pulling the gator he wore up over his mouth, Liran approached one of the four men tending the fire. A steady stream of Arabic passed between him and the man wearing a bandana. The red and black cloth shifted up-and-down as he answered Liran's questions.

Achem responded to Jerad's inquisitive look with a shake of his head. "We'll know soon enough."

Jerad nodded but held his position next to Nikki. He couldn't help noticing the way Liran took control of the situation. Why did Achem seem to be holding back from his position as *Natsar* leader? By Jerad's estimate, the man had years of service left. Based on Achem's reaction to Liran the day before, perhaps the man felt his protégé would take years to train.

Grim in expression, Liran headed back. He trained his attention on Achem like a lieutenant about to give a report. "They're burning the entire village to stop the plague from spreading."

Achem's brows rose, but he remained silent, almost lost in thought. "Survivors?"

"One boy. He's with relatives in a village not far from here."

"And the staff?" Jerad had to ask. Had to know if hope had just slipped into oblivion again.

Liran slid his gaze from Achem to meet Jerad's. "They said we should ask the boy."

"The boy?" Nikki stared at the men before turning to Achem. "Why the boy?"

Liran shrugged. "They won't say anything more."

Achem turned toward the Jeep. "Then our journey continues."

Jerad stopped him. "Is it worth the risk?"

"You tell me." Achem waited for him to answer.

He glanced at Nikki. The first vestiges of hope had already settled into her hazel eyes. They'd come this far. "Let's go."

They took a side road in worse condition than the main route. The truck bounced as viciously as the concern jousting his thoughts. "Nikki, I don't want you—"

"Don't."

His knuckles turned white on the steering wheel.

Her voice barely carried over the rattle of the truck. "Let me hope, Jerad."

They both knew the future looked bleak, and she'd barely surfaced from her father's murder. How could he love her without adding more pain to her life? "Okay."

If he had more time...more time to be with Nikki. They made a great team. In grief over his sister's death, he'd mistaken his own self-hatred as justification to blame Nikki for Leah's suicide instead of building a life with her. So many years wasted...he'd do just about anything for a second chance to have that future with her.

Anything.

❧

As they drove up to the village, a small group of men, leathered by the sun and lean bodies familiar with work and hunger, gathered to greet them. Yet Liran sensed residual darkness here, a shadow of what, or who had passed in their midst. He slipped out of the jeep before it came to a full stop and greeted them in Arabic. The men seemed more than willing to answer his questions. He glanced over his shoulder once to make eye contact with Achem, who remained with Jerad and Nichole.

He'd expected Achem to join him and also interview the men. However, more often than not Achem seemed to be standing back and allowing him to control situations. Liran understood the process, but he'd yet to make peace with it. In his mind, there was still a chance his brother could return, despite what Achem believed. Blood didn't give up on blood.

Liran left the men and strode to where the others waited. "They said a stranger showed up with the boy and left him at the edge of the village. He disappeared before they could speak with him."

One of the older men pointed to a small house near the end of the dirt street and then headed that direction. They followed him to the doorway where he turned around and spoke to them. "*Ahlan wa Sahlan.*"

Liran glanced at Nichole and Jerad. "He's welcoming us into his home."

His tall height required him to duck his head through the small doorway. The house appeared crude on the outside but cozy and clean on the inside, notwithstanding the dirt floor. Two small windows let in enough light to keep the one-room house from appearing dreary. Pieces of brightly colored fabrics hung on the mud-brick walls.

At the far side of the room, an old woman sat in an aged wooden chair scarred with use. A boy who looked no more than eight played with two battered toy cars near her feet, making engine and screeching sounds to match a car chase.

Keeping his head ducked, Liran moved farther into the room to allow the others to enter the small main area. He stood back, waiting for Achem to speak to the boy, but he signaled for Liran to do so. With a nod, he crouched near the child and took in the boy's tousled hair and pink cheeks. Speaking in Arabic, he spoke first to the woman. "Has the boy said anything about what happened?"

"Just bits and pieces. He cries for his mother most of the time."

"Anything about the stranger?"

The woman's eyes darted to her husband. Her hand trembled slightly in her lap. "Only that he carried death." Her lips and words trembled with fear.

The older man came near and put his hand on the woman's shoulder. "He also said the stranger told him he was healed."

Liran fixed his gaze on the old man. "Healed? Of the plague?"

He shrugged. "When I ask the boy more, he starts to cry again."

"What's his name?"

"Umi."

Liran hunkered lower and tried to catch the boy's attention, but he kept his head down. Liran held his hand out for one of the cars, motioning that he wanted to play too. With a hint of a smile, Umi handed him one of the cars.

Liran pushed the toy after the boy's to continue the chase. "Umi, can you tell me what happened? Please."

Umi's car lost a wheel but he said nothing.

"Was the stranger sick too?"

Umi shook his head. "He was very fierce."

Liran glanced at Achem, but he kept his eyes on the boy. Liran gently took the car from Umi and reattached the wheel. "Umi, do you know why you didn't get sick too?"

Umi shrugged. "I was already sick. The doctor said there was nothing else they could do but send me home. Mama cried."

As he handed the toy back, Liran studied the boy for any sign of disease or illness, but he appeared healthy. "But you aren't now, are you?"

"No. No more pain." Umi lifted his head. Dark lashes blinked, giving a quick glimpse of the boy hiding inside. He reached out and touched the *Natsar* emblem pinned to Liran's collar. "Mama said to tell you."

Prickles ran through Liran's neck and shoulders. The boy's mother must have described the *Natsar* emblem, a cross surrounded by the Star of David. He moved his head closer to the child. "Tell me what, Umi?"

The boy looked up and for the first time met Liran's gaze. The toy cars forgotten, he began to weep. The woman lifted him from the floor to her lap. A soft flow of conciliatory words passed from her lips. He squirmed, growing more agitated. She stroked his cheek, but he appeared inconsolable.

The boy continued to stare at Liran, his cries diminishing to a whimper. Fear defined his expression as if he watched a nightmare revealing itself in the light of day.

Careful to hide his concern, Liran rose. The darkness he sensed earlier seemed to grow heavier, like a dankness seeping into the room. Achem approached the older man, removing the pin from his collar. "Bring the boy to Cairo if you have need. Any of the Coptic churches will know how to reach us. Understand?"

The old man nodded and pocketed the emblem.

Achem moved back toward the boy and positioned his body between Umi and Liran. "What did your mother tell you, Umi?"

Instinct made Liran want to move from behind to see the boy again, but his gut told him to remain still.

Achem's voice took a soft cadence as he remained crouched

over the boy. “Umi, your mother gave you a very important mission. Do you understand?”

Umi’s crying diminished. “Yes.”

“Good. Then finish your mission. What did your mother want you to tell me?”

The boy’s voice trembled. “The staff lives.”

CHAPTER TWO

JERUSALEM, TWO WEEKS LATER

In the first light of morning, the Mount of Olives perched above an urbanized sprawl like an ancient relic freshly revealed from the depths of darkest night. Trees pebbled its modest crest. Rows of gravestones covered most of the hillside. The sight never ceased to bring a sense of awe to Liran. Though out of his way, he often took this particular route back to his office at Archaeological Consultants Group, which also housed *Natsar* headquarters in the lower levels, just for the view. And the solitude.

He relished the brief times he had in this place. With Jerad and Nichole on their way back to the States and no solid leads as to the whereabouts of the staff, he had time to think and work on the excavations in the city as he fulfilled his day job as an archeologist. Achem worked daily, reaching out to various contacts all over the world for some new intel on the plague and its mystery man. So far, Egypt and its surrounding areas had managed to contain the outbreaks deemed as unusual and isolated.

Muffled voices came from behind him. He glanced over his shoulder. A tourist group.

Oblivious to Liran's presence, the guide continued her running dialogue as she pointed at the mountain view overlooking the Kidron Valley. "According to Jewish tradition, the Messiah will appear here and bring the dead back to life. Therefore, the hillside has become the holiest cemetery." A hush fell over the crowd.

Liran left the group to their explorations. Several eyed his dust-coated cargo pants and shoes from working at one of the excavation sites. For a moment he wondered what they would think if they knew of the *Natsar*—the Keepers called to hunt, conceal, and protect the ancient relics of Yahweh. And that he would one day lead their organization.

Images of Steve Rogers wearing the star on his chest made him chuckle to himself as he pictured the star of David surrounding a cross on his. But his humor quickly turned into a much heavier weight in his chest. Would he be able to handle such responsibility? Picturing Yahweh's temple restored was easily imagined, but accomplishing such a feat required more talent and ability than that of a mere man. Yet when he allowed his mind to wander...

Teach me to rely on your strength and timing, Yahweh.

His prayer never changed. He waited expectantly, as Achem always told him to, but how would he know the difference between his own strength and Yahweh's? The question plagued him night and day.

He hiked up the path and continued along the stone walk. The hillside drew his gaze back to the gravesites. What would that day be like—the Messiah's return? As a Messianic Jew, he believed Christ already came. So many others still waited for His first coming. And the Muslims believed Him only a prophet. How could one reconcile such differences?

His phone vibrated in the side pocket of his pants. Liran stared at the screen. The sight of his brother Eben's name churned fresh hope—and fear—into the pit of his stomach.

He prayed for wisdom. Perhaps this time he could finally persuade his brother to return. "*Shalom, achi.*" *Peace, my brother.*

"I hear you're back in the city."

"Yes, for now at least. The excavations are progressing—"

"Why do you waste your time there?" Eben gave a frustrated laugh.

Liran paused on a set of stone steps leading down to the lower level and to the small building that housed the offices of the Archeological Consultants Group, which served the Institute of Archeology and at times consulted with the Israel Antiquities Authority. In other words, his day job.

By night, so to speak, they operated in secrecy to fulfill their mission—find and preserve the ancient relics. The unknown catacombs beneath the building had held the true allure to the location, giving the *Natsar* a secure place to operate and secure their finds from falling into the wrong hands.

"It's not a waste. This is our history—our connection to Yahweh's temple."

"Of the past. Not the future. I told you that when we met last month. Achem has contaminated your mind with deceptions and false beliefs."

The last year had done little to change his brother's cynicism. Neither had Liran's visit during his sabbatical. Why did he continue to hope for his brother's return to the *Natsar* and his rightful place as its future leader? "Eben, come back and see for yourself. Make peace with Achem. Your place is here, *achi*."

As was his brother's dream for unity. Did he still believe he could unite all faiths? Liran hadn't the courage to ask during his recent visit.

"You know I can't. Achem has decided I'm not good enough for his precious *Natsar*. You, on the other hand, seem to be his perfect replacement. And mine."

Perfect replacement? Hardly. Liran seemed to agitate Achem more than help. No, he was no more than a second choice—the next best choice to his brother.

"I'm not so sure." He cringed. When would he learn to think before blurting out his first thought? Besides, speaking his doubts to his brother would only bring more discord and break the already tenuous connection they'd formed a month ago after almost a year of complete silence.

"Whom do you doubt, *achi*? Yourself or Achem?"

Liran ducked behind a wall of cascading vines and followed the path down to a door. The smell of dirt and moss infiltrated his nose. "I believe in what the *Natsar* stands for."

"I didn't say the *Natsar*." Satisfaction edged his question. "I know you're struggling. I could see it when we were together. You don't completely agree with Achem's plans for the Ark and its elements—"

"Enough!" Liran inhaled deeply, willing his heart to slow to a normal beat. "I never should have shared any of that with you. I just thought—"

"Thought I'd come running back if you painted a pretty enough picture? No, the *Natsar* isn't my future, and I pray it won't be yours. Be on guard, Liran. Things are about to change. I prefer not to see my brother on the wrong side."

"What are you—?"

"*Kol tov, achi.*" *Be well, my brother.*

The connection ended. Liran stared at his phone. He'd only tried to help make a way for peace. Now he had the distinct feeling he just unleashed a war.

Achem closed his eyes and lifted his thoughts upward. The cool stone of the cement bench warmed under his body heat. Water gurgled softly from a spring in the far corner of the garden. Birds chirping delighted his ears like a song sent from Yahweh. The fragrances of eucalyptus and grass filled his nose, a sweet reminder of childhood. He'd spent many a day with his father and grandfather in this courtyard behind the main offices of the consulting firm. And only a select few of those who knew of the *Natsar* and helped their cause had knowledge of what the lower levels held.

From the air, the grounds appeared as part of an estate located on the far east side of the City of David. A steep slope concealed the bulk of their facilities underground. All thanks to a silent benefactor.

Only in the garden did he find real peace though. Here, he could almost feel the hand of God reaching down from heaven. But even as he prayed, the serenity he usually found eluded him today.

Current circumstances had pushed Achem to the verge of worry. Something he hadn't done in a very long time. None of his contacts had heard anything regarding a mysterious man wielding a staff. The plague outbreaks had stopped as well. It was as if the man and the staff had ceased to exist. Yet he sensed an evil at work unlike anything he'd previously witnessed, which only confirmed his growing suspicions.

Time was running out.

He'd given the old man the *Natsar* emblem in the hopes it would serve them in the future. If the boy revealed more, the man could use the token to reach Achem through one of the Coptic churches in Cairo.

His thoughts returned to the boy's reaction upon seeing Liran. Achem replayed it over and over again in his mind, unable to set aside this presentiment of some dark connection. Which led him to further reflect upon Liran's reclusiveness since his return from his sabbatical. Had something happened during his time away? Yahweh hadn't revealed anything to him regarding Liran, and he suspected certain unseen events had yet to play out.

Footsteps crunching on stone broke his concentration. Achem kept his eyes closed, certain the interloper was Liran. Another test to see if the young man understood the gravity of the position destined to be his? Or perhaps Achem simply longed for more time in solitude. He could discern neither through the agitation of his spirit.

He remained still.

Liran inhaled and then cleared his throat softly.

Achem opened his eyes. The tendril of order he'd captured remained, though a poor representation of what he desired. He lifted a brow at his impatient protégé.

Liran bowed slightly then straightened. Shoulders back and chin jutted just so—curiosity and stubbornness rolled into one neat angle. "You wanted to know when we received word from our contact in Cairo."

Again, Achem wondered at Yahweh's choice for his replacement. Liran still struggled with his future role as leader of the *Natsar* and his guilt for being chosen over his brother. Achem couldn't reveal what God kept hidden. Trust needed to be learned. "What have they discovered?"

"Just as the boy said, they sent him home when the treatments failed. His cancer had progressed too far."

Achem rubbed a finger under his lip. "Yet now he is perfectly well."

"Yes, a full remission." Liran paused, his brows pinched together. "What other explanation could there be?"

Achem dropped his hand and straightened his back against the bench. "He was healed."

"By who, this stranger?" Liran's frown deepened the cleft under his nose, making his lips appear fuller with his frown. Or was it a smirk?

"The staff of Aaron." Achem studied Liran's reaction.

He stood motionless, more silent than the trees lacking an afternoon breeze.

Obviously, Achem would have to prod him for what lurked behind the scenes of his thoughtful eyes. "Does the idea seem impossible to you?"

"No, but it doesn't make sense."

"Why not?"

"What purpose does it serve?"

"The boy was healed. A life was saved. As well as his destiny."

"But at the cost of over two dozen others. What of their lives and destinies?" Liran's expression contorted to one of almost...pain.

That was the compassion Achem had been waiting to see emerge in Liran. "An excellent question. Perhaps the lesson learned from the manna jar applies here as well. Power held with impure motives can't be released in purity."

"Then the objects of the Ark can never be revealed."

"Not even to help someone, like Jerad Nebal?" Achem raised a brow in question.

Gaze hardened, Liran lifted his chin. "You would still risk bringing an outsider into this?"

Such pride. Just like...no, he wouldn't compare. Liran passed Yahweh's examination, just as David had in the Old Testament. Achem would trust God on the outcome.

He rose and squared off in front of Liran. Fifty-eight years—twenty as *Natsar* leader—now stood eye-to-eye with his almost thirty-year-old soon-to-be replacement. "As I have said in the past, I don't presume to know the will of Yahweh. I simply prepare to act in whichever direction He sends me." Achem smiled. "Do you wish to challenge my judgment on this?"

A grin tugged at the corner of Liran's mouth. "Do I look like a fool?"

"Always full of questions, just like your father." Achem strolled toward the inner chamber, patting Liran on the back as they entered the shelter of the breezeway.

Liran grimaced. "I can barely remember his face."

"Look in the mirror. You appear much as he did at this age."

Head down, Liran paused near the double doorway and remained silent. Shadows obscured his face.

Achem sensed his brooding mood had more to do with the guilt still eating at him. Only regret brought a man to such a place. He rested his palm over Liran's heart. "Yahweh saw what lay within each of you, Liran, and made His choice. You cannot hold yourself accountable, my son."

His head shot up. "Yet my brother does. I thought by now he would have accepted Yahweh's will and returned."

"We've discussed this before. Pride can drive a man away indefinitely but never out of Yahweh's reach. Have faith." Achem entered the doorway of the main area, intent on returning to his office.

Liran called after him, "Sometimes I think he will never return."

Achem stopped and turned. He hated to see Liran's hope dashed, but he could never lead without understanding anyone, even those he loved, was capable of evil. "You could be right. The question is, what will you do if he does?"

CHAPTER THREE

SAN FRANCISCO, CALIFORNIA

Shouts of the surrounding people grew to a deafening pitch. Nichole stood, transfixed by the figure on stage. His amplified words fed the crowd's excitement. He crossed from one side of the stage to the other, menacing and magnetic all at once. Every step in her direction thrust her agitation to a higher level; until fear stole her breath.

She turned to Jerad—tried to call his name, but the growing excitement of the audience drowned out her voice. Only the man with the mic had the power to be heard. The closer he came, the more he seemed to tower over her, Jerad, and a burgeoning crowd of frenzied spectators.

Her knees weakened. The glare of the stage lights expanded to an ethereal glow as she struggled to fill her lungs with air. The image of the man grew sharper with macabre detail. He held a wooden staff almost as long as he was tall. A branch covered in delicate white flowers protruded up toward his head and shrouded his face. And as she watched, another branch sprouted on the opposite side and began to bloom as well.

What little light remained over the audience moved toward the man, as if sucked into a vortex and stripped of any will, just like those surrounding her. The darkness left in its place grew and slipped around her, swallowing her whole.

Nichole gasped, sucking in oxygen like an addict greedy for a fix. She shoved the blankets away as she fumbled to turn on the lamp on her nightstand. Light flooded the room, dispelling the darkness of her nightmare. She perched on the edge of the bed, heart pounding and sweat-drenched.

The dreams came every night since their return from Egypt. Before, the images visited once in a while, like a vague memory and nothing more than a repeat of the last vision she'd had while in the presence of the manna jar. But now the dream had changed, filling her with a foreboding that something major was about to slam her world. She'd chalked it up to what she witnessed while in Egypt. Somehow her brain had put the man on stage from her previous vision together with the mystery man wielding the staff that was rumored to be the source of the plague outbreaks.

She retreated to an overstuffed chair in her living room, taking note of the first glimmer of light peeking through the narrow slats of her blinds. A soft mew came from her feet. Chester rubbed against her legs. She ran her hand from the cat's head to his tail, enjoying the feel of his soft, and finally matte-free, rust-brown fur. She never succeeded in getting that old coot Henry to come to the shelter. Not even with the promise that he could bring his beloved cat. He'd passed in the cold of the night, leaving his cardboard home and furry friend behind. At least now Chester had a warm place to spend the rest of his days.

But even Chester's friendly presence didn't disperse her lingering unease, and sitting in a dark apartment would only hold her thoughts captive in a grim replay of her nightmare. She returned to her bedroom and slipped on her bathing suit and robe before grabbing her goggles and a towel from the closet. As he made a beeline for the door, she shoved her cell phone into her pocket. With his random seizures, Jerad might need her.

Though the chill of the morning air pimpled her skin, the heated pool wrapped her like a warm blanket. She held her breath, went under, and swam the length of the pool before breaking the surface with a gasp. Nothing like an adrenaline rush to clear the cobwebs.

Every lap forced the puzzling imagery farther away but did nothing to eliminate the threat she sensed coming. Maybe she should tell Jerad about the nightmares. Or perhaps Achem? All of them shared the part of the vision involving the staff, but only she'd seen the mysterious man preaching on stage.

Holding the budding branch...

Or could she just chalk it up to an overactive imagination and be done with the whole thing. Nichole ignored the burn in her thighs and stroked harder; as if each lap brought her closer to sanity and farther from her tormenting thoughts. Could she not find a moment's peace?

A cramp stopped her near the steps. She worked her foot up and down until her calf muscle relaxed again. The cold air felt like ice against her wet skin and made her teeth chatter. She dried off quickly and cocooned herself in the hooded robe.

Loath to return to her apartment, Nichole sat in a pool chair, hugging her knees to her chest. A shiver ran between her shoulder blades and down her back. In the distance, a sleepy sunrise teased the hilltops. A rarity at this hour. The peak of Mount Diablo usually floated above a wall of fog that imprisoned the Golden Gate Bridge.

She dropped her chin and prayed—what she should've done to begin with. Why did she always forget to pray these days?

Ever since Dad died—

Nichole checked the time on her iPhone. Jerad's flight to Denver didn't leave for another forty-five minutes. She could still reach him at this point, if he hadn't turned his phone off yet. But should she? He seemed determined to find out if this man, Stone Abrams, could accomplish what Jerad's doctors said was impossible...and desperate hope kept her from asking too many questions.

She touched the screen to bring up his name and tapped his cell number. With each ring, she debated canceling the call. Trusting Jerad seemed to always come with a price.

"You're up early." The sound of his voice warmed her insides.

"I was swimming laps."

"This early?"

"I couldn't go back to sleep."

"Something going on I need to know about?" The timbre of his voice deepened with his concern.

Should she tell him? She clenched her eyes shut and barreled through. "Just a bad dream. Not a big deal." She cringed at the way her voice broke.

"Nikki, tell me."

She sighed. "Remember the last vision?"

He chuckled. "I remember getting knocked off my feet and something to do with Achem holding the staff."

"Do you remember me mentioning I saw a man preaching on a stage?"

Silence stretched only a moment but seemed too long. Had they lost connection?

"Jerad?"

"I'm here. Sorry. That whole day's still a blur."

He did sound tired. Had his seizures increased?"Are you all right?"

"Yeah, finish what you were saying."

She took a deep breath. "That part of the vision started showing up in my dreams a few months ago but not often. Now it's every night. But something is different."

"Are we talking dream here or nightmare?"

"That's the thing I can't make sense of. Nothing *appears* threatening in the dream, but it's like I know something is very wrong."

"Give yourself a break. Life finally calmed down for us. Don't go looking for trouble."

His remark made her bristle, but maybe he was right. Had she grown so accustomed to the turmoil that when it didn't exist, she fabricated something to fill the slot?

"Nikki?"

"Sorry, I was just thinking."

The rumble of his soft laugh broke the tension. "Good, I thought maybe you were ticked at me for that last statement."

"Oh, don't think you'll get off easy for that one." She tilted her head to the side and smiled. The man knew how to keep her heart pounding.

He sighed before chuckling again.

"Call me when you're done with your meeting. I want to know if this guy thinks he can help you."

"Maybe I'll just send you an e-mail."

She laughed at his playful tone. "Afraid of me now, are ya?"

His voice turned soft, yet deep and intimate. "Not on your life."

Warmth traveled over her cheeks and down over her shoulders. Comforting and smoldering all at once. How did he do that?

"Don't worry, Nikki. Everything's going to be fine."

His words brought unexpected comfort. Maybe she was over-analyzing things. "Okay. See you soon." She hated saying goodbye. "I miss you."

"I miss you too."

Nichole headed back to her apartment. At least she went back with the beginnings of a smile, thanks to Jerad. In the light of day, the whole thing seemed silly. Like he suggested, she'd quit expecting doom and start hoping for a future with him. Nothing lurked around the corner.

She almost believed it.

HE'D COMPLETELY FORGOTTEN ABOUT THAT PART OF HER VISION. Could there be a connection? Jerad shoved his cell phone into his computer backpack. Nikki's call tempted him to cancel his trip and go home. Agreeing to meet with a man claiming to be a faith healer was either insane or desperate. Or both. But traditional medicine had done nothing except give him a stay of execution.

But a faith healer? He'd heard of healing ministries where they prayed with a person and sometimes people were even healed, but Stone Abrams presented himself with the title of "faith healer."

Maybe he should've explained more about his meeting to Nikki. She had seemed so hopeful when he told her about it that he'd let her think Stone was more of a holistic practitioner. Even after their phone conversation, Jerad still didn't understand the full realm of the man's self-proclaimed abilities.

Or perhaps his desperation kept him from exploring further and finding out the man was a hack.

A voice crackled over the intercom system, barely discernible above the hum of activity in the airport and the vibrations of planes landing and taking off. He slung the backpack over his shoulder and grabbed his carry-on, weaving through a sudden barrage of foot traffic. A woman passed him, munching on a soft pretzel as she walked. His stomach rumbled at the doughy, buttery scent coming from the nearby food vendor.

"Mr. Nebal?"

Jerad turned toward his caller but didn't stop moving. He'd rather talk to the person at the pretzel stand.

A man who looked like he just stepped off the cover of GQ blinked at him through black-rimmed, rectangular glasses. The stranger matched his stride to keep up with him. "Jerad Nebal?"

"Yes. Can I help you?" Jerad did a mental inventory of the last half-dozen inspections he'd done across the globe. The man didn't look like a disgruntled plant manager recently fired. Or one of the many environmental scientists he'd lectured within past years. Determined to uphold the codes he represented, Jerad had dealt with them all at one time or another. But plant managers didn't make enough money for the duds this guy wore. Neither did most environmental scientists. He had the patched jeans to prove it.

"I represent a group of antiquities collectors determined to protect relics. I believe you're in contact with a man by the name of Achem Mizrahi?" The man's bearing bespoke of a very expensive education.

Jerad stopped so fast the stranger wound up two strides ahead of him before realizing and turning around. Hearing Achem's name from a complete stranger did weird things to Jerad's insides.

"I thought the name might get your attention." Equal in height yet average in stature, the man posed no threat, but his words packed a wallop.

"What do you want?"

As the man closed the gap, he extended a packet to Jerad.

He stared at the manila envelope. No way the contents boded well. How did he get out of this snag? "I'm sorry, my flight's about to leave. I really don't have time for this."

"Mr. Nebal, you need to read the documents in this envelope."

"Perhaps you think so, but I don't." Never mind the pretzel. Jerad sidestepped the man and headed for security. A line snaked from the checkpoint and wove through a maze of stanchions. So much for a quick escape. And here he thought he'd have an uneventful trip.

"Then am I to assume you're not concerned how your involvement with the *Natsar* could tear down the Strauss Foundation just by association?"

Jerad stopped, dropped his carry-on, and faced his pursuer again. How and what did this guy know about the *Natsar*? He looped his thumbs in his jeans pockets and lifted his chin. "What exactly do you want from me?"

The man adjusted his glasses from the left side as he continued to hold out the envelope. "Nichole Strauss has already lost her parents to the negligence of this group. I'd think you'd be more concerned for your fiancée's well-being."

This bozo knew entirely too much, and that set him on the verge of strangling someone—namely the nitwit with the envelope and smug expression. He'd had seen enough like that to last him a lifetime after his lethal association with Soren Umberger.

Could this be what this was, a final farewell from Umberger's grave? "Is this in any way related to Umberger?"

Not even a blink. "No, I assure you, it's not." He looked over the top rim of his glasses while extending the packet to Jerad. "Mr.

Nebal, this can't be avoided. Not unless you wish to do unnecessary harm to Ms. Strauss."

Eyes narrowed, Jerad took a step closer. The envelope poked him in the chest, but that just strengthened his resolve to ignore it. "Are you threatening me?"

"On the contrary, I'm trying to help. I'd hate to see the name of Gabriel Strauss slandered. As I'm sure will happen when we release this information to the press." He glanced down at the packet and lifted it higher.

Jerad clenched his jaw with a deep inhale. "When?"

"At the end of the week, unless you contact me with your consent. My business card's inside."

"My consent for what?" Jerad grabbed the envelope.

The man spun on his heel and strode away without a backward glance.

Checking his watch, Jerad spun around and stared at the dwindling security line. He could go after the guy and miss his plane. But he'd miss his meeting with Stone Abrams.

With a growl, he shoved the packet into his bag. Once through security, he made a dash for his gate and wound up the last one boarding the plane. He pulled out his cell phone and debated calling Nikki. What could he tell her? Some Joe Schmo in a designer suit and glasses accosted him with a manila envelope? He put his phone in airplane mode and slipped it back into his pocket.

The contents of the envelope weighed on his mind like a ticking bomb. To see her father's name and everything he'd built defamed would break Nikki's heart. Jerad found his seat and pulled out the envelope before stowing his bag in the overhead bin. Once settled in by the window, he kept the envelope on his lap. Airline magazines never looked so appealing.

He slipped the quarter-inch stack of documents out, shielding them from the passenger next to him. An overhead shot of him and Nikki in a dark alley in Malta sat on top. An eerie glow emanated from the box they held and illuminated their shocked faces. The angle of the photo displayed the shape of the manna jar to perfection. He shoved the photo to the bottom.

A business card fell to his lap. Jerad snatched up the rectangular card and nearly laughed out loud.

Artemis Tombs.

Had the man's name thrust him into the world of collecting artifacts of the dead, or had he changed it to create an air of mystery? No wonder he hadn't introduced himself. Jerad wouldn't have heard a word after that because of his own laughter.

The company name and logo covered the top of the card. Just two words.

The Collective.

Next to the distinct lettering sat a circular logo, more like a thick, swirling line that thinned as it spiraled to the center and ended in the shape of an eye. Very clever, actually. But he'd never heard of them. Had Achem?

He flipped through the other items. A newspaper article from Malta, relating the death of two unidentified bodies found in an alley. He almost felt the gun digging into his forehead at the memory of their encounter with the thugs in Malta.

The next piece made him laugh. A sworn statement from Jeremiah Lentz, Master Artifact Authenticator—the title alone was ridiculous—stating he'd witnessed and *authenticated* the golden manna jar. Yeah, right. How'd he do that from a prison cell? Once he and Nikki had returned from Malta, she'd stowed the jar in the Strauss Foundation safe until the day Umberger wrapped his evil intentions around it. Lentz never even saw the thing.

Several more documents followed affirming or confirming the existence of the jar. Most Jerad hadn't even heard of, except for one. Dr. Isaac Pembry, a leading authority on Holyland, Egyptian, and Near Eastern art and antiquities. And Nikki's former mentor. How would she take finding out her old teacher worked for the other side? Based on the fond way Nikki had spoken of Dr. Pembry during college, Jerad couldn't imagine what would persuade the good doctor to fall in league with such a group.

Maybe Pembry didn't realize what the Collective had planned to do with his documents.

The last item nailed whatever disregard he had to the floor—a sworn affidavit confirming the *Natsar* had found and possessed the Ark of the Covenant. Jerad held the document closer to study the signatures. Though dated almost twenty years ago, Dr. Pembry's scrawl on the witness line matched the other document he'd signed, confirming the validity of the jar, but the other signature left him cold despite the stifling warmth of a plane left on the tarmac too long. Talk about the past coming back to haunt a person.

The declarant—Gabriel Strauss.

CHAPTER FOUR

DENVER, COLORADO

He had to be crazy. Or just plain nuts.

Jerad stared across the white tablecloth at the empty seat opposite him. Desperation was a more likely catalyst. Didn't matter. Every way he twisted it, he still came up with no logical reason for agreeing to meet a complete stranger claiming he could heal Jerad.

He fumbled with a dish containing eleven packets of sugar—ten since the waitress had refilled his iced tea. A set of salt-and-pepper shakers stood like soldiers on watch, and two bundles of silverware rolled in white cloth napkins blended into a matching tablecloth. He diverted his attention to the bustle of the outdoor cafe, the occasional clatter of plates, and the aroma of Mexican cuisine unsuccessfully tempting his stomach.

Jerad checked his watch. Fifteen more minutes. He could still make a run for it, but one question kept him in his seat.

Could Stone Abrams really heal him?

Jerad had asked himself that question for the last two weeks. He hadn't found a lot of history on Stone when he searched online. And most of what he did stumble upon had only recently been shared. He did appear to have a growing reputation as a healing evangelist though. That much he'd confirmed by watching multiple YouTube videos of the man that churches all over the country had posted. The messages usually ended with a ministry time where people lined up to have the man pray for them. Most of the videos ended at that point.

But not all.

Some showed people getting healed. If they were legit...

He should leave. Since Nikki told him about her nightmare, the peculiar feeling in his gut hadn't left. Either his stomach knew something he didn't, or he still hadn't recovered from the sub-par airline snack he'd forked over ten bucks for.

If he left now, he could catch the next flight back to San Francisco, send Stone Abrams a nice apology e-mail, and forget he'd ever considered such a crazy idea. All in time to have dinner with Nikki.

Besides, Stone had called him. Jerad couldn't figure that one out. How did the man even know who he was, let alone his condition? Granted, the whole debacle last year had made some headlines, but he'd kept information about his condition a secret only a select and trustworthy few knew about.

He shoved the chair back. Metal screeched against the cement. He stood and turned, barreling into a man about his height with the build of a soldier and dark brown wavy hair that brushed this collar. Tanned or of foreign descent, Jerad couldn't tell.

"Sorry." Jerad stepped back before redirecting his steps.

"Jerad Nebal?"

He stopped. Great. The guy showed up early. How could he escape now? "Yeah, that's me."

"Stone Abrams." He extended his hand, flashing two perfect rows of very white teeth. "I see you were already waiting for me. I like to arrive early as well. I find that works best."

Jerad shook his hand. "How so?"

"If I come on time, I wind up dining alone sometimes. I guess people have second thoughts." He lifted his brows in question.

Jerad chuckled, hoping his embarrassment didn't show on his face in any shade of pink or red. "So, why me? I've never met you, yet you know I'm...sick?"

"Let's just say we have a mutual...friend." Stone gestured at the table. "Shall we?"

Who could they possibly have in common? Jerad glanced at the exit leading to the sidewalk—and freedom—then back to Stone. What did he have to lose? He took his seat and leaned back in his chair.

Stone sat then leaned forward. "I know what you must be thinking."

"Do you?"

"You have doubts, concerns. That's natural." Stone shrugged as he glance to the side.

Until he figured this guy out, Jerad would keep his concerns to himself. "Go on."

"You're not sure why you agreed to come. You're not even convinced I can heal people, let alone help you." Stone's gaze grew more serious. "I'll also take a gamble and say there's a woman in your life, perhaps your wife, and she doesn't know you're here or what you're really doing."

The guilty lump in the back of Jerad's throat shook hands with the turmoil in his gut. "Fiancée and she knows I'm here."

"Really? That's fascinating." He sat back slowly, brows bunched as if lost in thought.

Jerad waited to see what the enigma called Stone Abrams would do next. He could still get up and walk.

Stone's smile returned. "Still want to leave? I won't be offended if you do."

Did Nikki feel this way when he sensed her emotions? Kind of creepy, like a book not only read but memorized. Maybe this guy had more meat to him than a reputation. "I'll stay, thanks."

"Good." He gestured at Jerad. "Then fill me in."

"I thought you already knew."

"I only have a cursory understanding. What's your diagnosis?"

"Mild seizures, at the moment. Side effect of a genetically engineered poison." Jerad lifted his hands to show the mild shaking that had become his norm. "Degenerative. No cure. Doctor says the seizures will get worse until I either die or turn into a vegetable."

Stone nodded. "What about your faith?"

Jerad snickered and sat back. "I believe in God, if that's what you mean. I wouldn't be here otherwise."

"Oh, I've healed many an atheist."

"Really?"

"You'd be surprised. Sometimes they're the easiest because they're not caught up in the rules."

The waitress brought a glass of water for Stone and two menus. "Be right back for your orders, gentlemen."

"No hurry." Stone set his menu aside.

"Rules? Are there rules to this?"

Stones shrugged. "Not really. I call them guidelines."

Jerad said nothing more and focused on Stone, a clever technique he'd learned as an environmental inspector that usually forced the other person to speak out of discomfort. He'd learned some very juicy tidbits in the past using such strategy.

But Stone stared him down. How did someone get that comfortable in his own skin—to remain silent in the presence of a stranger and stare back? And with a smile? Always smiling. Jerad squirmed. He'd let Stone have this one. "So what happens next?"

"You tell me." Stone clasped his fingers in front of him.

Jerad's urge to bolt intensified, but curiosity kept him rooted to his seat. "Nope, ball's still in your court."

Was that a flicker of frustration or did Stone's smile just slip a notch? "Okay, if you truly want to pursue this, I have some requirements."

"The guidelines." Groaning inwardly, Jerad waited for the inevitable bottom line.

"No, requirements. Let's not bother with guidelines just yet."

"Okay, shoot."

"One, come to one of my conferences first, so you can see me in action." Stone pulled a postcard from his pocket and handed it over. "Sacramento isn't that far from San Francisco. I'll be there next weekend."

Jerad studied the event information listed to the right of a professional-looking photo of Stone, along with one of him on a stage. The man had upped his game.

Nikki's dream...

The discomfort in Jerad's stomach threw the lump back up into his throat. Had to be a coincidence, right?

"And two, you should bring your fiancée so you two can talk about it and decide if you really want to pursue this."

Bring Nikki? Maybe death was a better option after all. The lump in his throat might as well strangle him. If he could make a connection between her dream and Stone, she would too. Even if it were a coincidence.

Or was it?

He took a deep breath and exhaled slowly. "I didn't realize you did such a presentation."

"We're living in a postmodern culture. If I'm to reach the younger generation, I have to relate on many levels. It's time to do things differently."

"Interesting."

Stone laughed. "I know, but it's not as wild as you think. It's about unity, bringing people together to worship the same God."

Jerad had no idea what else to say. "Still interesting."

"Good. I'll have seats reserved for you and...?"

"Nichole."

"For you and Nichole. After the event, come to the backstage area, and we can decide whether or not to proceed."

Jerad placed the postcard on the table, dead center. "Okay, now that we have your conditions, I'd like to list mine."

Stone seemed taken aback at first, but his smile flashed back in place. "Of course."

"One, I'll decide if Nikki—Nichole comes with me."

A curt nod. "Okay."

"Two, I can't proceed without knowing who told you I was sick."

The hum of the restaurant filled the gaping silence spanning between them.

Eyes diverted, Stone ran a hand over his mouth. "I'd rather not say."

Was he nervous? The man's carefully procured persona appeared to slip a notch.

"Then I guess we're at an impasse." Jerad rose. The risk outweighed the loss. The idea that Stone could 'heal' him still ran on the impossible side in his book.

"I knew your sister." He blurted out the statement, looking around as if the entire restaurant had overheard him.

Shockwaves rippled through Jerad's body like an earthquake. He gripped the back of his chair. "How did you know Leah?"

"From Stanford. I worked there at the time."

"Then you know Leah committed suicide." He slipped back into his chair. Dredging up the past still sapped his energy.

"Yes. I was very saddened to hear of her death." Stoned dropped his gaze as if he were truly affected by her death.

Jerad flipped through his memory catalog, recalling Leah's friends and those at the funeral. None of the faces matched Stone's. "And we never met?"

Stone dropped his gaze to the table. "No. I was an intern pastor at the time. Leah came into the campus church quite a bit to talk to me."

Like a Geiger counter gone wild, Jerad's 'rat' radar shot to full alert. "How did you know I was sick?"

"After Leah's death, I felt *compelled* to keep tabs on her twin. You two seemed really close according to what she shared with me."

Jerad regarded Stone through narrowed eyes. "Funny, she never mentioned you."

"She always talked about you." Stone stared at him, his gaze softened with his compassion.

Every inch of Jerad's body tensed. Memories of his last conversations with Leah sped through his mind with lightning speed, specifically her mentioning someone she had growing feelings for. Could Stone have been that person? "Always? Sounds like you two were close."

Stone glanced down again. "I guess you could say we became friends."

He leaned forward. "You know, I never understood why Leah took her own life. She always sounded hopeful on the phone, even right before her death. The last time we talked, she mentioned that she'd met someone. I could tell, as you can imagine as her twin, that she was falling in love. Any chance that was you?"

"I don't think so." The man's smile returned but seemed forced.

"I see." Something didn't ring true. Stone was holding something back. Maybe Jerad had more than one reason to stay connected to the man. He pushed on a smile for Stone's benefit as he picked up the conference postcard. "Well, if Leah considered you a friend, I guess I can too. Nikki and I will be there."

SAN FRANCISCO

Nichole stared out her office window, unable to do anything else. She'd given up finding peace in the tepid waters of her apartment swimming pool and decided to give work a try. Her attempts to throw herself into the growing pile of documents on her desk hadn't succeeded either. Nowhere could she outrun—or out-swim—her thoughts and worries.

First the death of her father. Then Jerad's illness. Every time he had a mini-seizure, she had to ask God for help to forgive a dead man.

The routine was getting old. Soren may be gone, but his poison had left its mark. The antidote had come too late to prevent the damage done to Jerad's brain and put an expiration date on their future.

And now the Strauss Foundation seemed to be crumbling around her. Without her father's charisma to enthuse their financial supporters, the Foundation's future had turned a bleak corner. They'd lost more partnerships over the last month than they'd acquired during the last two years.

If she didn't know better, she'd blame her own lacking sense of diplomacy, but this...no, this had more to do with reputation and something, or someone, targeting the Foundation—her father's only legacy.

The Collective.

She still couldn't figure out who exactly they were, but she did know giving in to their demands to expose the *Natsar* would be the same as making a deal with the devil. She didn't buy into their 'noble effort' to protect precious artifacts and share them with the world. They tried entirely too hard to present themselves as selfless in their efforts. She could smell their agenda without even knowing who they were.

A knock on the door broke her inner tirade. "Come in."

Robin swaggered in, a plate holding a sandwich in one hand and a file folder in the other. "I bring good news and bad news."

"Start with the good. I'm falling fast here."

Robin stuck the plate in front of Nichole. "I made my world-famous chicken salad, just so I could have the pleasure of seeing you eat for once."

"Thanks, but I'm really not hungry."

"I don't care. Eat." Robin pointed at the food.

Nichole grabbed half the sandwich and took a small bite.

"Keep chewing." Robin waved a file in the air. "I got the final approvals from customs in South Africa, but now we don't have the funding we need for the Clean Water & Farm Project in Zimbabwe."

Though small, the bite went down like an oversized bite of dry rice. Nichole pushed the plate away. "So the really, really bad news is Jaensen Investment pulled their support."

Robin dropped into the chair in front of Nichole's desk. "You're good. They called last night just before I left. I didn't have the heart to tell you then."

Nichole put her elbows on her desk and held her head. Jaensen Investment Group was just the latest of many. "Dad would have been so upset."

"And so are you." Robin's voice reflected her concern.

Nichole parted her fingers enough to see her friend, secretary, mentor, and the only person in the world who seemed to care anymore. Besides Jerad, of course. "I thought I'd kept it hidden well."

"You've got everyone fooled, except for me and Jerad. And I've known you a lot longer than he has." Robin rose from her seat and nudged the sandwich back to front and center. "But if you don't eat, I will have to hurt you." She flounced out the door, all attitude as usual.

Nichole took another bite, flipping open the folder Robin left on her desk. They'd waited months for approvals, and now it didn't matter. She balled her fists, wishing she could let her anger loose and pound the desk like a raving maniac. Nothing seemed to work anymore. Every effort they made seemed to hit a brick wall.

Her cell phone chirped from beneath the papers covering her desk. She wanted to ignore the interruption and wallow in her anger, but what if Jerad had suffered a major seizure? She scrambled through the paper clutter. Jerad's name showed on the touch screen but as a missed call. She swiped the screen to call him back.

"Jerad, are you okay?"

"Yeah, just fine. Are you?" A soft chuckle followed his question.

Nichole took a deep breath. "I thought maybe something had happened." Her voice dropped. She tried to show a brave front but enough had happened today to sap what little strength she had left.

"I'm fine. But now I'm worried about you. Are you sure you're okay?"

Suck it up, Strauss. "Yeah, I'm good. Just tired." She rubbed her forehead.

"How are our plans for CWFP? Did you get the approvals yet?"

She fingered the file folder sitting on top of the mess on her desk, weighing the pros and cons of telling him the truth. "Yeah, we did."

"That's great. So when do we leave?"

"We're still working on scheduling, but I'll keep you posted." Not a complete lie. "How did your meeting go?" Not the smoothest segue, but she really did want to know. Maybe he had good news. For a change.

"Interesting. Did the funding—"

"Does he think he can help you?" *Come on Jerad, take the hint and leave it be.*

"Sort of."

She sat back against the high back of her desk chair. "What does that mean? Either he can or he can't, right?" Even she could hear the irritation hedging her voice. Jerad didn't deserve her anger.

"It's more complicated than that, and I really don't want to explain over the phone. I'll give a full report when I get back. Right now I have a plane to catch, which is why I called. I'm taking a detour to LA first so I can see Tom. He's gonna shuttle me back and forth."

She rubbed her forehead. "Why?"

"Just thought I'd take a little detour, see an old friend in his new digs. And I want to grab something from my storage unit there. I still fly in tonight though. You up for a late dinner?"

"Definitely." That would at least give her several hours to practice her happy face.

He chuckled. "Good. Then it's a date. I'll call you when I land." He paused. "Stop worrying, Nikki. Everything's going to work out fine. Trust me, okay?"

She let out a sigh. How did he do that? "Okay. I'll see you later."

Nichole let her cell phone slide from her fingers to the desk. The tightness in her throat had nestled into a band across her chest. How much longer could she pretend she had everything under control?

Even though she had no proof, she knew the Collective had to be the one causing their benefactors to withdraw funding. She spun her chair around and stared at the pictures covering the wall like a crossword puzzle. Each block embodied a unique event in her life and the sum represented many lives saved. She noticed that every shot of her had a common element—children.

How many would perish thanks to the Collective's unreasonable demands and influence? How many lives would end prematurely due to polluted water—water they could have replaced with wells to provide a continuous flow of fresh, clean drinking water. Or starvation? The only thing stronger than the pain ripping her heart was her mounting anger at the deeds of selfish, self-glorifying people.

Her thoughts leaped in a new direction. Just because the Strauss Foundation couldn't be a part of the equation didn't mean the wells couldn't be drilled. She still had some connections of her own and a warehouse full of equipment. What better way to prove to those Collective goons that their manipulations were ineffective?

She grabbed her phone and pulled up the address book on her laptop. One way or another the wells would get dug. Those children deserved a chance to live.

Each one threw down his staff and it became a snake. But Aaron's staff swallowed up their staffs. — Exodus 7:12

DECEPTION

"Did you make contact?" He held his breath as he waited for an answer. All his planning, all these years...now the final culmination waited, ready for the plucking like a ripe plum ready to burst in the blazing sun. He could taste the sweetness, luxuriated in the way it tickled his senses in pure pleasure, yet understood nothing of the blackness growing in his soul.

"Yes, at the airport."

"And?"

"As you predicted, Mizrahi's name grabbed his attention."

"Good. You did well, Artemis. Jerad Nebal is Nichole's weak point. Through him, we can get what we want."

"For a man dying, he didn't appear that...*weak*."

"Trust me, the man is dying. And his fate will ultimately rest in our hands."

Or so he believed. Perhaps pride deceived him, like an enemy posing as a friend. But he didn't have time to wait and find out.

A knock came from his hotel door. "Inform the rest of the committee it's time to put the final stage of our plans into motion."

"Consider it taken care of."

The man tossed his phone onto the bed and opened the door.

A young man stood at the threshold, toting a large box. "This just arrived for you, sir."

He craned his neck just enough to see the young man's name tag shoved to one side of the carton, pulling and twisting the pale blue of his hotel uniform. "Thank you, Ricky. Set it down over there." He pointed toward the window.

Dim light cascaded a nebulous stream across a generic beige carpet.

The box slipped in the youth's precarious grip and bumped the long case lying on the bed, causing it to drop to the floor with a thud.

"Watch what you're doing!" He leaped to the case and gingerly placed it back on the center of the down comforter.

A blush rose up the young man's cheeks. "Sorry, sir." He paused, waited. "Did you need anything else?"

The man stroked the black case with his gaze like a lover. "Yes, yes, please just leave now." He dug a five-dollar bill out of his pocket and shoved it into the young man's hand.

Once the door closed, he returned to his beloved. He hadn't planned to open the case yet, but he needed to know the contents remained unharmed. With trembling fingers, he flipped up the clasps and lifted the lid. The silk-lined cushion had protected his treasure well.

The staff lay still, as inert as the dead branch it once resembled. Only now it lived and grew in strength. Patches of green had replaced the near-black decay on its surface. How could he resist such beauty? His longing gave way. He lifted the staff from the case, supporting the weight of the rod across both palms. So perfectly balanced.

Energy vibrated and swirled up his arms like a dance of ecstasy. His shoulders tensed at first, then relaxed, allowing the power to continue its upward course. His confidence grew each time he handled the staff and maintained control.

He closed his eyes, willing the staff to obey him. He would master this instrument and prove to God he was worthy to command such force. Then and only then could he claim his destiny.

The staff began to vibrate in his hands. His mind said to let go, but his soul refused.

More...just a little more.

With his permission, the staff's power increased, surging through every fiber of his being. He relished the sensation until it threatened to consume him. He had to let go or die.

With a guttural roar, he let the staff go, releasing the force of its energy like a silent explosion. The staff fell onto the bed. Drenched in sweat, the man gulped for air.

Sounds came from the hallway. The clatter of a tray, then a scream.

Death had come once again.

CHAPTER FIVE

LOS ANGELAS

"Hey, man!" Tom slapped Jerad on the back. "Glad you could come my way, even for a few hours." He took Jerad's pack and stowed it in the back of the SUV.

After admiring Tom's latest all-terrain-family-sized vehicle, Jerad noticed the extra weight brimming his friend's midsection. "I see Allison's treating you well."

Tom patted his gut and laughed hyena-style. "Yeah, well, you'll be a married man soon enough."

"Let's hope so."

His friend opened his mouth before busying himself with securing Jerad's pack—again.

"Don't get all clammed up on me, buddy. One way or another, I'll figure something out." Jerad slid into the passenger seat. His words echoed back to him like a hollow promise. He'd done what he thought God wanted him to—forgiven himself and Nikki for his sister's suicide, risked his life and nearly lost it for the woman he loved, and shifted his life and career geographically to be with her. So why did the future still look so bleak?

The whoosh of the back door slamming shut muffled the

thrum of plane engines and a car alarm blasting nearby. Tom climbed onto the driver's seat and turned sideways, one arm propped on the steering wheel. The leather seat creaked under his weight. "Can't the doctors do anything?"

"Not the ones we've talked to so far." Should he tell Tom about Stone Abrams? And his suspicions? Jerad wasn't sure how he'd react, considering what he and his wife had gone through two years ago.

Tom steered the vehicle toward the exit. "What about that guy, the doctor, I told you about in New York?"

"Nikki and I are going to see him next month."

"I hope he can help you."

Jerad stared out the window. "Me too."

"You know, Allison told me to tell you she's praying for you to be..." Tom glanced at Jerad and toggled his hand toward him. "You know—healed."

If she only knew... Did his face look as red as it felt? "Tell her I said thanks."

Tom's tone went serious. "She's been pushing me to go back to church since Tye's birth."

A pang shot through Jerad's gut. Allison's first pregnancy and miscarriage during the fifth month had brought Tom's church attendance and his faith to a screeching halt. Maybe the recent birth of a healthy son had started the reconciliation process.

"Sounds like a good idea."

"Yeah, I guess. I still can't figure it all out though, you know?"

"Figure out what?"

"Why it all happened. I thought we did everything right."

"You did." Jerad rubbed his brow. Why did he get the feeling God was trying to tell him something? "But I know what you mean. Sometimes things just happen."

He didn't pay attention to the clock on the dash or begrudge the continuing silence. Made the ride more comfortable. The closer they came to the storage center, the more familiar the landmarks.

Finally, Tom stopped at the entrance. Jerad gave him the code to punch in. The security gate opened. They wove through a maze of corrugated orange steel doors and gray concrete to a building in the back that housed smaller units.

Jerad got out of the car, then leaned in. "Shouldn't take me long. I know what I'm looking for."

He inserted his key card into the slot at the main door. A long hallway shrouded in near darkness loomed in front of him. Overhead lights flickered for a moment before dousing the walkway in a feeble glow.

Keys jingling from his fingertip, Jerad approached the unit holding what remained of his past. The fluorescent bulbs buzzed. Dust floated in the air. An odor akin to chalk or stale mothballs pressed his nostrils shut. He lifted the lock, his key ready to open the door but paused.

Memories flooded in. His sister's funeral. Nikki crying. Leaving San Francisco and vowing never to return. Then here in LA, trying to build a new life. Storing the few things he'd kept of Leah's with his parent's possessions had made sense when he was offered a job in Chicago. More history locked away with her death, left behind for a new city.

Kept the grief away. Kept the pain away. Kept him away.

He snapped open the lock and thrust the door upward. The slats rattled on the track and disappeared into the ceiling. Stacks of dusty boxes lined the right side. His father's burgundy leather chair sat to the left in front of his mother's china cabinet. He searched his memory and the room for the one box he sought. There, on the footstool, waiting as if its contents knew he'd return one day.

Jerad pocketed his keys and sighed. The stale air no longer teased his nose. He pulled the cardboard flaps free and pushed them down. Leah's diaries lay on top. He took one out and let the pages fall open. Her delicate handwriting filled both sides. He lifted the book to his face and inhaled, yet the pages held no residue of her flowery perfume. Just the smell of old paper and the dim essence of a once vibrant young woman.

What would life be like if she were still alive? As twins, they'd been close, but not like some. He never had any strong twin vibes about Leah, although he'd wished he did. Maybe he could have helped her more. Kept her from spiraling down to the point that she thought suicide was a solution. He'd never battled depression like she did and never knew how to relate to that side of his twin. Perhaps that was why he stayed away at times. He seemed to only fail her.

Just like he had Nikki too.

Weariness weighted his limbs. He slid into his father's chair. A tingling sensation ran through the inside of his mouth, leaving an odd taste like rank medicine. He knew the signs. Nothing he could do but let the seizure come. Tom would look for him if it lasted too long. He tipped his head back against the soft leather and closed his eyes. Leah's journal slipped from his hand and slid down between the chair and his thigh.

What seemed only a moment later, he felt himself being shaken into consciousness. Tom stood over him. The corners of his mouth dipped down into his pudgy cheeks. "Hey man, you okay?"

Jerad inhaled and lifted his head. His neck ached as well as his head this time. "How long was I out?"

Tom glanced at his watch. "You've been in here over fifteen minutes." He stuffed his hands into his pockets and slumped his shoulders. "Is this just fatigue or did you have a seizure?"

"Both." Leaning forward in the seat, he rubbed his hands up and down his face. The foul taste still lingered. "I'll be fine. Just give me a minute."

"Maybe I should call Nikki."

Jerad pushed to his feet. "No. I'm fine." The thudding in his head threatened to force him back down, but he clenched his jaw and stiffened his stance. He didn't want to lie to Tom, but he also didn't want to worry Nikki anymore than he already did.

"You don't look fine."

"Trust me, this is the norm these days."

"How often do these things hit you?"

"Without the medication, just about every day. With medication, once a week, maybe." Except lately the seizures hit him two times a week, but he'd deal with that later.

"You sure you don't want to call Nikki?"

Jerad scooped up the stack of Leah's journals and tucked them under his arm. "Get the door for me, will ya?" His head ached and his vision tunneled out. Another symptom the doctor warned him was a possibility. He blinked rapidly and rubbed his neck. His sight expanded back to normal, though the edges still blurred.

"Yeah, sure." Tom pulled down the cranky door and snapped the lock shut. "You know, you could've just told me what you needed and sent me a key. I could have shipped it to you."

The throbbing eased to a dull ache. Jerad mustered a smile. "What, and miss seeing your ugly mug?"

Tom did his hyena imitation again. "Look who's talking."

One of the books slipped out of Jerad's hold and hit the floor. Before he could react, Tom lifted it from the gray concrete.

His smile fell when he noticed the cover. "I thought you were done with the past."

"Yeah, I did too. Something came up." Who would have thought his condition would bring the past to meet the present? Coincidence?

"You sure you want to do that?" Tom studied him, concern weighing his bushy brows down lower than normal. "You and Nikki seem like you're in a really good place now."

Jerad took the journal and secured it with the rest of the stack. "I met with someone in Denver who knew Leah. He might know more about what happened before she died."

Tom tugged open the main door to the storage building and held it for him. "Be careful, Jerad." Tom only used his name when he was serious—dead serious.

Jerad stepped outside and stopped. "I need answers."

"Some questions aren't meant to be asked." Tom headed for the truck.

The door slammed behind him. Jerad glanced over his shoulder and caught movement from the corner of his eye. Or was that just his peripheral vision returning? "Trust me, this time they do."

A breeze tousled the hair at his neck. He searched the fence near the back of the property. Nothing. The trees rustled louder as the wind kicked up. He chalked it up to a leaf-laden branch hanging over the chain-link fence. He'd taken to glancing over his shoulder more often lately. Like an expectation of death.

Jerad climbed into the passenger seat.

A puzzled expression tightened Tom's face, making him look like a pug dog. He started the engine. "Sounds like an invitation to trouble."

Jerad stared out the window, his gaze fixed on the dusky horizon. Night encroached like an ominous plague. "Trouble doesn't need an invitation."

SAN FRANCISCO

After maneuvering the maze of San Francisco International Airport, Nikki pulled up to the curb where Jerad stood waiting. He tossed his duffel bag into the back seat before sliding into the front. He looked more haggard than usual, which could only mean one thing.

"You had a seizure, didn't you? A big one by the looks of it."

He tilted one side of his mouth up into a tired grin. "And don't you look ravishing as well, my love."

She smiled back. "You better mean it."

"Don't I always?" He leaned over to kiss her but the car behind them honked their horn.

After checking her side mirror, she hit the gas to pull them into the flow of exiting airport traffic headed toward the freeway.

"Anything major happen while I was gone?"

Nikki shot him a quick glance and sighed. No point in waiting to tell him. He'd figure out she held something back with that radar of his. "Jaensen pulled out."

Jerad nodded. "I was afraid of that."

"Seems to be our new norm these days. We're losing investors faster than Chester sheds."

His chuckle warmed her through and through. "How is that ol' beastie doing?"

"He's fine. Sends his love."

"Yeah, I bet he does. That cat still doesn't like me." Jerad leaned forward and turned the radio on. Jazz music drifted out of the speakers. He switched to the news.

"That's just because you're not Henry."

"Don't plan to be either."

She shot him a glance. "You mean as in dead?"

He shrugged.

"That's not funny." She didn't like it when his sense of humor turned dark.

"I'm sorry my joke fell flat. I'm just tired."

"Would you rather skip dinner? I can just take you home."

Jerad grabbed her hand and pulled it to his lips. "No, I'm starving. For food and for your company. Let's start over, okay?"

She nodded as she squeezed his hand. Silence settled between them except for the newscaster's rhythmic voice.

And in Denver today, a one-block radius surrounding one of the city's major conference hotels remains quarantined indefinitely after a mysterious plague outbreak yesterday that left twenty-three dead and fourteen fighting for their lives. All guests on the top floor, officials are saying.

"Turn it up." She took the next exit, pulled into the parking lot of a Backyard Burger, and cut the engine.

Others there during the strange occurrence have been taken to a special

facility for observation. As of yet, the CDC has made no official announcements as to the nature or severity of this outbreak. No statements have been made concerning airport and ground travel shutdowns. For now, the situation is being treated as isolated.
In other news...

Jerad turned off the radio. "Any chance that's just a coincidence?"

Nichole shook her head. "Not likely."

He ducked his head, looking at the brightly lit fast food joint. "Is this our stop for dinner tonight?"

"Works for me." She got out of the car and joined him on the sidewalk.

He pulled her against him, slipping his hand behind her head and kissed her deeply.

She held onto the loops of his jeans, aware of the spectacle they made but not caring. Every moment counted.

When he pulled away, she brushed back the lock of hair that fell onto his forehead. He needed a shave and a haircut.

His eyes showed his tiredness. "Think we'll be hearing from Achem and Liran soon?"

She sighed. "No doubt about it."

CHAPTER SIX

JERUSALEM

At the sound of distant footsteps, Achem removed his reading glasses. Any moment Liran would walk through the ornately carved Persian doors to the small library that housed a full array of research books, some ancient religious texts, and a few historical trinkets. But only a select few knew of a hidden chamber directly below in the catacombs that contained the most precious and protected objects like the history of the *Natsar*, the Ark of the Covenant, and the gold manna jar.

And now that it had revealed itself, the staff of Aaron would soon be restored to its proper place in the Ark. That would leave only the stone tablets. He sensed deep in his spirit that Liran would be the one to see that through.

Achem stared past the opened texts and newspapers piled around him and rubbed his eyes. Rows of shelves surrounded a mosaic tiled floor containing a long cherry-wood table and several high-backed chairs. Twin arched windows filled the wall, giving a clear view into the garden courtyard and filled the room with natural light. Unlike the secret passage below where no natural light penetrated the catacombs. Nor its secrets.

Liran entered the room, and, judging by the downward turn of his mouth, he'd read the itinerary for their impending trip. "Why are we going to the US? I thought we were pursuing the staff."

"We are." Achem tossed yesterday's edition of the New York times in front of Liran. The thick newspaper smacked the table with a soft thud. Bold letters filled the masthead.

Plague Kills All but One at Denver Hotel

Liran glanced at the paper. "I was on site all day and didn't have a chance to read any news. You think this is connected to the staff?"

"Read the article."

With a skeptical grin, Liran opened the paper to read below the fold. Seconds passed, as did his smile. His gaze locked with Achem's. "One young woman lived."

"Yes. She was in Denver to receive a transplant. Now she doesn't need it. Sound familiar?"

Liran dropped the paper onto the desk. "How is this possible?"

"The staff is now in the US. Denver to be exact. Obviously, the stranger Umi told us about is trying to control its power and wanted more freedom and new ground to experiment. I've already reached out to our contacts in Denver to let them know we're coming. From there we'll go to San Francisco."

"San Francisco? Why?"

Achem attempted to read a text on his phone without his reading glasses. "Because I want to see Jerad and Nichole."

"Wouldn't it be better to leave them out of this? Their involvement in Malta to reclaim the manna jar turned into a complicated mess."

He recognized Liran's attempt to corner him. "Only because Nichole didn't fully understand what she held."

"But even when she did, she chose to hold onto it."

"Because she thought it could be used for good. Her heart was in the right place."

"Yes, I understand that, but I don't understand why they should be involved this time. I still think it's too risky."

"Nichole had a vision about the staff. I need to ask her more questions about what she saw and if she's had any more revelation connected to that, especially now that we know the staff is in the US."

"And this has nothing to do with the staff's ability to heal?"

Achem looked up. "Why would you ask such a question?"

"That should be obvious." Liran crossed his arms. "You could simply just call her from Denver after we're done investigating."

Liran's sabbatical had improved his discernment and his confidence. Achem could appreciate that, but he wanted—no, needed his protégé to understand that he didn't have to know all the details in order to trust the order of what God was calling them to do. Liran tended to question before listening to what God was saying. He hoped...prayed...the young man would learn soon. The majority of the leader of the Keepers' time was spent listening—to Yahweh and the people He connected them to. Action came only when the heart and vision of God became known.

"Yes, but I sense that God has something for us to do in San Francisco as well. I suggest you seek His heart in this so you can plan our trip accordingly. Notify our contacts there. I'm putting that part of this mission under your control."

Surprise blanketed Liran's expression. He slowly unfolded his arms. "Thank you, Achem. I won't disappoint you. But I would like to state for the record that I believe you're wrong to involve them."

"I have every confidence you'll handle the mission well, Liran, and your position on the matter is noted. However, our course of action remains unchanged. If there's a chance Jerad could benefit from the staff, I see no conflict of interest."

"And this has nothing to do with your friendship with Nichole's father?"

Achem pushed back his chair and stood. "Explain your meaning, please."

Liran drew closer, gesturing as he spoke in earnest. "I mean no disrespect, Achem. But Nichole's mother died because of the Ark.

Then her father was murdered for the manna jar. This cause has taken her family away and now threatens to take away the man she loves. Perhaps healing Jerad would relieve some of the guilt you may be feeling."

Liran's degree in psychology must have kicked in. Even Achem had to admit the young man's words rang of truth and revealed things at play that he may have been unwilling to consider. "I will bear in mind your words, but in the meantime, I suggest you leave my guilty conscience to me."

He nodded and turned to leave but paused at the door without turning around. "I did not wish to offend. Only to point out the possibility that your feelings for Nichole may be clouding your judgment."

"I understand your concern, but have you ever known me to make critical decisions based upon feelings?" Achem lifted his brow in question as Liran looked over his shoulder.

"No."

"Then trust this situation is no different."

Once certain Liran had left, Achem shut the library doors—a clear signal that he didn't want to be disturbed. He'd be arrogant not to consider Liran's question. Perhaps he did feel obligated to help Nichole reclaim some form of happiness. She was the closest he'd ever come to having a daughter of his own.

He checked his watch and did the math. Nichole would be asleep so he sent her a generic text:

> Have you kept current with the news in Denver, my dear? Will be making a trip to the States soon. See you soon. —A

As he prayed for wisdom, his thoughts strayed to her father and Achem's vow to protect Nichole. "Gabriel, I won't break my promise."

Liran ended the connection—his last call on the list to arrange their private flight to San Francisco, thanks to a benefactor, and a private flat arranged by another. He had to admit, he looked forward to being in the United States again. The schedule he created for their time in Denver allowed for some exploration of the city's fine cuisine he'd heard so much about.

A text message popped up on his phone.

Can you meet me at the garden? Usual spot.

Mira.

In light of how his brother broke off their engagement a year ago, he was amazed that she continued to stay in touch with him. Perhaps because she wasn't the only one Eben had left. His brother had cut ties with everyone and left the country without any real explanation. Although, Liran suspected Eben had been restless for much longer before that.

Yes. About to leave work. Be there in ten.

He left the estate grounds through a back gate behind the courtyard that opened to a path leading to the garden of Gethsemane. He sat on a stone wall near a gnarled tree that was wider than he was tall—his favorite place to sit in the famous garden and reflect. And at nearly dusk, most of the tourists had left.

The drop in temperature brought a rush of goose bumps to his skin. He closed his eyes, inhaling the cool air, and exhaled the tension of the day, even though one of their contacts had yet to send a text, confirming a meeting. He moved his hand to rest on the side pocket of his cargo pants housing his phone in case it vibrated.

"You look like you need another sabbatical."

Liran opened his eyes to see her standing in front of him. "Do I look that tired?"

Her long, black hair draped over one shoulder in a thick braid.

The corners of her full lips turned upward, matching the mischievous glint in her gray eyes. Yet she remained silent as she held out a small brown bakery box.

Liran held the package near his nose. The faint smell of cinnamon and almonds made his mouth water. He lifted the lid. "Babka. My favorite."

She sat down next to him. "I know."

He stared at her, unsure of why she'd reached out to him. The last time they spoke was nearly two months ago, right before his sabbatical.

"Go on." She gestured to the box.

Liran lifted the piece and took a bite. Cinnamon hit his taste buds first, then the almonds as he chewed the bread. Knowing Mira expected some form of reaction, he expressed his pleasure with a small *hmmm* before swallowing. "It's delicious. Thank you."

She folded her hands in her lap, appearing suddenly shy. "How *was* your sabbatical?"

He lowered the box. He hadn't been forthright with Achem about seeing his brother, but he had mentioned it to Mira right before he left out of his concern for her. "It was good."

The usual sparkle that lit her eyes when she smiled didn't make an appearance. It never did when the subject of Eben came up. "Did he ask about home?"

He knew what she really wanted—to know if Eben has asked about her. Losing his desire for the Babka, Liran closed the box. "Eben wasn't interested in hearing about things here."

Though silent, she nodded. "Did you mention me?"

He reached over and squeezed her hand. The softness of her skin struck a sharp contrast to his calloused fingers from working at the digs in recent days. He swallowed again, mustering the courage to speak the truth. The cinnamon in his mouth turned almost sour. "Mira, it's long past time to let go."

She shifted to look him straight in the face. "I have, Liran." She pulled her hand from his and cupped his cheek. "I'd hoped that you had." She gave him a tremulous smile before she launched to her feet and strode away.

As he jumped up to go after her, his phone buzzed. The call he was expecting...he'd have to reach out to Mira tomorrow. He checked the screen.

Not a text from their contact but from Eben.

> I hear you're coming back to the US. Perhaps I will see you in Denver...

A knot formed in his gut that had nothing to do with the Babka. How could Eben know about the trip so quickly? He replayed their last conversation in his mind, but at that point, he didn't know about the trip because he'd yet to speak to Achem.

Somehow his brother knew of their plans. Was one of their contacts giving him updates about their plans?

And why was his brother in the US?

CHAPTER SEVEN

SAN FRANCISCO

From his slumped position on her office sofa, Jerad admired Nikki with gritty eyes. She sat at her desk, like a vision of articulated beauty too real to comprehend, yet too painful not to try. He inhaled deeply. The subtle scent of her flowery perfume filled his nose and tickled his senses with something familiar...like the fresh scent of jasmine after a rainfall. Memories of his mother's back porch and garden flooded his mind. Along with snapshots of playing with Leah in the backyard.

He'd spent too much time rereading his sister's diaries and contemplating his own uncertain future. Too many questions remained unanswered about her death. And her life the weeks before her suicide. Part of him still refused to believe she would take her own life. And the more he read her journals, the more he had reason to be suspicious.

He pushed the memories aside. A rough night, filled with fitful dreams had woken him just as a seizure hit. Besides, he and Nikki had bigger fish to fry. The packet from the Collective sat on the coffee table in front of him, untouched. First things first. His delightful distraction with Nikki and memories of his sister fizzled into a puff of misgiving.

"Jerad, what do you think?"

His attention snapped front and center, bereft of any clue as to what Nikki had asked. Did he fake it or fess up? He rubbed his eyebrow. "I'm sorry. I guess I zoned out there."

A smirk tilted her lips. "I just asked if you wanted to drive to Las Vegas and get married."

Jerad swallowed then coughed. "You did?" His voice betrayed his shock, making him sound like an adolescent. As off the wall as the suggestion sounded, the idea appealed to him. Why wait if time had condemned them to so little?

"No, just wanted to see your face turn that nice shade of green." She shuffled the papers on her desk. "Don't forget we have Clown Day at the hospital this week. Robin already picked up the supplies and gifts for the kids. And I think I may have found a way to make the Zimbabwe trip work, but it's going to take some real negotiating. We may have to fund some of it from our own bank accounts."

"We could, you know."

She glanced up and dropped the folder she'd finished organizing into the outbox on the corner of her desk. "Could what? Pay for the trip ourselves? I wish we could, but that's too—"

"No, elope." He jumped to his feet, his exhaustion forgotten. "Why not?"

Nikki swiveled in her chair to face him and leaned back. "You've got to be kidding, because I know I was. I thought we wanted to do the ceremony thing, remember? Maybe on that hillside that overlooks Golden Gate Bridge."

Jerad closed the distance between them and crouched in front of her. The sooner he told her the full details of his meeting with Stone the better. If only he had some notion what her reaction might be to Stone Abrams and his proclaimed healing abilities. Instead of gazing at the spectacular San Francisco Bridge, she may tell him to take a flying leap from it.

But more pressing, she needed to know about the documents from this dweeb-man, Artemis Tombs. How did he broach that sticky ball of conglomerated subterfuge called the Collective? Even Tom's stellar investigative skills had led to very little information about the group.

He rested his hands on her knees. "Listen, there's something I need to tell you first."

She leaned forward and laid her hands over his. Her sun-kissed hair swung forward, brushing the top of her shoulders and cupped her cheeks. Her hazel eyes held the wealth of her love and the trials of a lifetime. Yet the contents of a manila envelope would only add to the weight still lingering from her father's death. And his impending...

He prayed he was doing the right thing in telling her. "At the airport in New York, a man approached me with knowledge about Achem and the *Natsar*. He gave me a packet of very incriminating evidence."

She sighed. "Let me guess. Artemis Tombs."

He jerked back in surprise and nearly lost his balance. How in the world did she know? And why hadn't she said anything? "When did you find out?"

"Tombs contacted me last month. I told him I wasn't interested in his antics and to go away. Except I was a lot ruder." She leaned back in her seat. The circles under her eyes had turned a shade darker.

He stood and ran his hands over his face before dropping them to his hips. "What are we going to do about it?"

"I don't play games with men determined to control history under the guise of doing it for the good of all." She made air quotes to bracket the 'for the good of all,' but the sneer on her face lingered to effect.

"So do nothing? You sure that's a good idea?"

"I didn't say I wasn't going to do anything." She fiddled with her phone a moment before sliding it across her desk to show him something. "I got this text from Achem last night. I'm sure he can help us deal with Tombs while he's here."

Jerad read the message. "Yeah, we called that right. You really think he can help us with Tombs?"

Nikki snorted. "Achem has his sources." She opened a folder on her desk and started reading.

"Then what about the affidavit? I mean, your dad's signature—"

Her head shot up. "Dad's signature? What are you talking about?"

What game were Tombs and his Collective clan playing? Why would he withhold that vital piece of information from Nikki and yet include it in the packet he gave Jerad? He grabbed the envelope off the table and pulled out the documents as he approached her desk. The picture of the two of them in Malta fluttered to the edge of her desk.

Nikki tugged the photo closer to get a better look. Her gaze hit his, questioning, almost accusing. "They were there?"

He nodded. What else could he say? His own stomach recoiled every time he looked at it. Were they being watched now? He handed her the affidavit and then waited for her to reach the bottom line—literally.

Suspicion and confusion flickered across her face like a flashing slide show. Then tears puddled in her eyes, reflecting the betrayal he'd anticipated. She tossed the paper aside like an intrusive insect. "Pembry? How could he be a part of this? My father trusted him. I trusted him."

"I know. I remember." Jerad picked up the photo and shoved it back into the envelope. In college, he'd almost wound up jealous of Dr. Pembry. Nikki had spent hours in the man's office, discussing rare finds and theorizing where some of the world's lost treasures might be hidden.

Like the Ark and its elements...

"I don't believe this." She crossed her arms as she sat back in her chair, moving back and forth in short swivels. She may think she hid her tears, but he felt every single one of them. "I didn't think things could get any worse."

Guilt stabbed him square in the back and froze him where he stood. Those words confirmed his worst fear—what the circles under her eyes implied. How could he add more to her burden? His illness only seemed to make matters worse. He'd swore he would never walk away from Nikki again, but now his presence seemed to just add to her burden. Could this be the one time he *should* walk away? The idea made him sick to the core.

He had to turn this around. His mind scrambled for alternatives. What if he'd called the shots all wrong? What if telling her about Stone would give her hope? He'd pursue just about anything to make things easier on her.

Including the healing abilities of one Stone Abrams.

THE WHOLE WORLD SEEMED DETERMINED TO CRUSH HER DOWN, and he just stood there. Nichole wanted him to wrap his arms around her and tell her everything would work out. She slumped back in her seat, waiting for him to do something.

She shook her head at herself. When had she become so weak?

Jerad stared at the floor with his hands shoved into his jeans pockets. He looked thinner and lost in thought. His haggard appearance hadn't gone unnoticed. Even Robin had raised an eyebrow when Jerad first arrived. She loved having him by her side, working with the Foundation, but had she asked too much of him? He needed rest, not her complaining. And certainly not the burden of another complication. Like this Artemis Tombs clown and his costume called the Collective.

What a joke.

She could handle that riffraff-in-disguise Tombs, and she'd confront Pembry as soon as her anger cooled. One thing at a time and first things first.

Nichole wrapped her arms tighter around her waist and closed her eyes. Warm hands settled on her shoulders. The comfort of Jerad's touch seeped into her tense muscles. She tried to reach out to God, but words failed her. Since her father's murder, she didn't know what to pray anymore. Why was it still so hard? Still, just focusing on God seemed to give her some comfort and bring her closer to some peace.

A soft sigh escaped her lips. "I'm sorry, Jerad. I didn't mean to whine."

"You didn't." He kissed the nape of her neck, then leaned against the edge of her desk, facing her. His gaze penetrated like a search beacon. Question marks curled around his pupils. He appeared ready to speak but something held him back.

She touched his arm. "What's on your mind?"

He shook his head.

"I promise I won't melt down again. I can handle whatever you have to say."

His gaze pierced her again. "You know, you don't have to always be the strong one."

Her turn to look away. She fidgeted with a couple of paper clips. "I know, it's just that..."

"Just what, Nikki?"

She didn't like holding back, not with Jerad. So why did she now? "This Foundation is all I have left of my father. I don't want to lose it too."

He nodded. "I understand that, but you don't have to do it alone."

"I'm not. You're helping me."

"Am I?" Determination lined his mouth and set his jaw. Like he had a bone to pick the size of one of those African buffaloes they'd seen and the attitude to match.

"Of course you are? Why do you even ask?"

His resolve seemed to falter, giving her a glimpse of some inner struggle. He walked toward the broad windows behind her overlooking the street. "I just wonder sometimes if my presence...my illness just adds more chaos to the mix."

Always protecting her. He still didn't get it. "I can handle this, Jerad. Like I said, I want it all, good and bad."

He retraced his steps back to her desk. "I'm trying, but I see the strain it's putting on you."

She didn't like the way he picked her apart with that gaze of his. Yes, at times she wanted to crawl under the covers and hide, but that didn't mean she wanted him out of her life. Nichole blinked back a fresh press of tears. Was that what Jerad kept holding back? Was he considering walking away again, like before? Her mental walls threatened to rebuild. "We'll figure something out."

Again, he studied her like he had the blueprints for the wells, analyzing every detail. What did he want, a signed confession of doubt?

"What if I told you I'm considering another possibility?"

"You mean the staff? We have no idea if Achem is right—"

"No, something else."

Her fear surged higher. More bricks of protection fell in place. If he wanted to leave again, she'd let him go and deal with it. She sucked up her courage and shoved the panic down. "Then spill it. Lord knows we could use more options here."

He hesitated. "It's regarding my meeting with Stone Abrams."

At yet another pause, Nikki lifted her eyebrows. She almost breathed a sigh of relief. No plan to disengage and run away. God must have read her mind. "You said you thought he could help, so what's his angle?"

He inhaled, then let the breath out in a noisy gust. "I wasn't completely up-front with you about him. He's actually a healing evangelist."

"A what?" She crossed her arms. "I thought you went to see him about a new treatment for your seizures."

"I did, but it's not exactly a treatment, per se. Stone Abrams is a healer."

"A healer?" Before she could stop it, a giggle erupted from her chest, more out of relief than humor. She covered her mouth. "I'm sorry. I believe people can be miraculously healed, but to hear you say it...just never thought I'd hear something like that come out of your mouth."

Jerad slanted a grin and scratched his head. "I know. It sounds a little off-the-wall, but this guy contacted me."

Any humor she found in the situation disappeared. "He contacted you? What, is he some kind of nut-job? What if he's a con artist, or worse," she picked up the affidavit, "what if he's part of this scheme to tear down my father's foundation."

"Nikki, don't you think I checked this guy out? He's legitimate. I did my research. Besides, he contacted me because he knew Leah."

She felt her mind get sucked into the past like falling off a cliff. Scattered details rushed to the forefront of her memory. Snatches of Leah flashed in succession until the final image—her lifeless face. The dread Nichole had fought back surged forward and took shape. "You can't do this."

"What?"

She should win points for the shocked expression on his face. Truly classic. "It's too dangerous."

"Hold on a minute. You think talking to a guy who claims to be a healer is dangerous, yet you have no qualms blowing off a guy like Tombs?" Jerad pinched his brow. "Forgive me if I'm missing something here."

Something about the whole scenario just seemed too familiar. Yet how could she explain the source of her fear if she was too afraid to even look at it herself. "Please, just trust me on this one."

He dropped his hand. "Then give me a reason. I can't just drop this."

"Why not?" She rose to stand in front of him.

His voice dropped to a desperate whisper. "What if he's the real deal?"

She rested her palms on his chest. His warmth seeped into her hands, calming her fears, yet heightening her agitation to some degree. "And what if he's not? What if he hurts you? We have that appointment with the doctor in New York. I'm sure—"

"Nikki, every doctor we've seen has said the same thing. They don't know how to counteract the damage Umberger's poison did to my brain. I want to at least check this guy out. He's organizing a faith conference next weekend in Sacramento. I've decided to go and see for myself. And I want you to go with me."

His words came out in a tumble. He only did that when it was something very important to him. How could she say no?

He wrapped his hands around hers against his chest. She let her head drop to her favorite resting place just below his chin. His heart thrummed steadily beneath her ear. Weariness surged over her in a fierce wave.

"All right. I'll go." She owed him that much at least. Maybe these feelings had more to do with exhaustion. Things always seemed worse when she was tired.

She closed her eyes, but the memory of Leah's unseeing eyes stared back at her.

CHAPTER EIGHT

SAN FRANCISCO

Nichole studied the affidavit again. Maybe she thought she'd find something there that would explain or help her understand the reasons behind it. Or better yet, something that would prove it was a forgery. She hated the thought that someone she loved and trusted could betray her. There had to be some other explanation.

Jerad had left after lunch to run his own errands, and Robin had cleared out shortly before six. She had the place to herself, a little peace and quiet to collect her thoughts and think. Yet the silence of the office seemed to make the heaviness in her heart much louder than she could stand.

Nichole pulled up Dr. Pembry's contact information on her phone. She hadn't really spoken to him since her father's funeral. And now, she didn't know if she wanted to ever again. But she had to know—had to know why he would betray the memory of her father like this.

If he had...just didn't seem like something Doc would knowingly do.

She trusted him almost as much as she had trusted her father.

How could she not? He'd been a constant fixture in her life as far back as she could remember. So why had he never told her about the affidavit? Why would he give it to the Collective? Didn't he realize what that would do to the Foundation? And to her?

Time to end the circular torment of her thoughts. She tapped his number.

After two rings, his voice boomed in her ear. "Nichole! How wonderful to hear from you."

"Hi, Doc. Have I caught you at a bad time?"

"No, no, not at all. How have you been? Are you well?"

She sighed. This would be harder than she thought. "I need to talk to you about something."

"All right...I'm all ears." Concern blanketed his voice.

She remembered how he used to say that to her when she was a child. At one point when she was a child, he almost had her convinced he had a head full of ears hidden beneath his hair. "Have you heard of a group called the Collective."

"Yes, actually I have. Why do you ask?"

"How do you know them?"

"Well, they asked me to consult on a project a couple years ago and just recently funded my current research, specifically to do with historical relics from the Holy Land."

"Just recently?"

"Yes, why?"

Her body began to tremble. Struggling to keep control of her voice, Nichole rose from her desk chair and stood by the window. The scurry of people on the sidewalks and in cars trying to make their way home mirrored her racing heart. "They're trying to take apart Dad's foundation."

"What? Why?" The timbre of his voice deepened with his fervor.

"I know about the *Natsar* and the Ark. I know about all of it."

Silence came over the line.

'Doc?"

"Then you remember that day?"

"Yes. Everything."

He expelled a deep breath. "I wanted to ask at the funeral, but it just didn't seem the right time."

"I know. But now we have a bigger problem. The Collective is after the Ark and the relics. And they're willing to expose Achem and my connection to the *Natsar*. They have an affidavit you and Daddy signed."

"Nichole, do not get involved with any of this. Your father paid a very high price for his involvement with them." His voice turned emphatic. Almost angry.

"The Collective?"

"No, the *Natsar*."

"Is that why you signed that affidavit? Did you force Daddy to sign it?"

"Of course not. Your father was devastated by what happened. I suggested he draw up a sworn statement to protect himself and you from any repercussions that may come from that horrible incident. We weren't sure what level the US government would investigate if it became public knowledge. Gabriel wanted to be sure you didn't lose the only parent you had left."

"And it didn't strike you as odd that they came to you specifically for your research on the Ark and the artifacts?"

Doc cleared his throat. "At the time, no."

He wasn't telling her something. What could he be hiding? He'd been nothing but supportive and caring to her all her life. She grabbed a tissue from her desk drawer to wipe her cheeks. "How did the Collective get the affidavit, Doc?"

Something between a sigh and a grunt came over their connection. "Nichole, I'm so sorry. I didn't mean for you to get hurt. That was never my intention. I didn't think it would have that much importance now that your father is gone."

A sob slipped out before she could control it. She closed her eyes and covered her mouth."The Foundation is all I have left of him. Of both of them. I can't lose it too."

"Then Achem and his *Natsar* are the ones you should be questioning. They're the ones responsible for your mother's death. Erica would be here today if were not for them." His voice had grown cold yet impassioned with an anger she'd never heard before.

The way he reacted...the way he said her mother's name. Something she'd sensed long ago settled into her gut and clarified. "You loved her, didn't you? You were in love with my mother."

He didn't reply right away. "Yes, I did, but I resolved to never act upon it. But when I learned the circumstances of her death, I could never forgive Achem."

"Doc, Achem is the one who saved my life."

"Had he not involved your parents, you would never have been put in harm's way."

Nichole didn't know what to else to say. She hated what he did but could understand why. Hadn't she nearly killed Soren for almost killing Jerad?

"Nichole, please forgive me. I just couldn't stand by any longer. The past needs to be rectified."

And the price would be everything she held dear. Hadn't she lost enough? How could he do this to her? "Not like this, Doc. Not like this. You *have* to stop them."

"I'm sorry, Nichole. It's too late." His voice sounded cold, distant, and disconnected. "What's done is done."

The connection ended.

"Doc!" She yelled at her phone, then threw it against the wall. Something shattered. One of the pictures of her with her father fell from the wall, its glass in shards.

Just like her heart.

STANFORD UNIVERSITY, PALO ALTO, CALIFORNIA

Memories of his days on campus flooded back in rush. Especially as he walked past the chapel. Happened every time he dropped in to visit Dr. Pembry. A good reminder of what he did wrong and what he did right.

Like a soldier about to enter combat, Stone mentally prepared himself for the inevitable debate to come. Dr. Pembry had a way of cutting right to the heart of Stone's faith, which only forced him to examine his own beliefs in the end. No hedging around the noble doctor. No, that just led to more scrutiny, and he'd dealt with plenty of that in his lifetime.

Yet he always came back for more. Some would call him a glutton for punishment. He chose to view it as opportunity to grow stronger. Training for the opposition he knew would be inevitable.

Dr. Pembry's office door stood partly open. Stone slowed his steps because once he crossed the threshold, he had to commit to the battle. His pulse quickened, releasing a rush of adrenaline through his body and *whooshed* in his ears.

Let the debate begin.

He knocked on the door. And waited. No answer. He checked his watch. Unless he had the wrong day, he was right on time. He knocked again. Still silence. He pushed the door open.

Dr. Pembry still hadn't organized the wall of bookshelves concealing his desk from the door. Hundreds of books cluttered the shelves, stacked upright and at odd angles. Some toted shiny new spines, others wore years of use like tattered burlap. The smell of paper, ink, and dust saturated the air, entombing the doctor's office against worldly contamination.

Artifacts of various types and sizes speckled a table whose heyday passed with the 50s and cluttered a bench windowsill spanning the full length of the office. A few had even landed on the bookshelves as makeshift bookends. Pembry's office was like a time capsule in the middle of modern civilization.

Stone rounded the ended of what he called the wall-o-books. Pembry sat at his desk, his head clutched in liver-spotted hands. A reminder of the doctor's heart condition sent warning alarms through Stone's limbs and sped his approach. "Dr. Pembry, are you all right?"

Dr. Pembry lifted his head, blinked. "What? Oh...Stone, I didn't hear you come in..." He turned in his chair, slow and lethargic. The doctor seemed confused...or distressed.

"I think I'd better call for help." Stone pulled out his cell phone.

"No, I'm fine. Really." He waved his hand as if swatting away a fly.

Stone scrutinized him again. "You don't look well at all."

Dr. Pembry smiled. The color returned to his face, but his eyes remained troubled. "Please, put your phone away. You simply caught me at the tail end of a difficult situation. Ever have one of those days where the past seems determined to haunt you?"

The question made Stone pause. If the man only knew... "I can honestly say yes."

"Then just give me a moment to adjust."

He pocketed his phone. "Why don't I come back another day."

"No, no, please. Our conversations always invigorate. It's just the remedy I need." The doctor took a deep breath and smiled at Stone. "How long will you be in California this time?"

"Possibly several weeks. My work has me busier than usual."

"Good, then perhaps we'll get to have more than just one discussion this trip. And I hope you plan to speak at the campus church at some point. You know how they love to have alumni return to their roots."

Stone quirked a half-felt grin. The darkest shadow of his past still loomed, but that would soon be rectified if Jerad would allow him to help. Seeing Jerad healed would make up for missing the mark with his sister, Leah.

Pembry rose to his feet and pulled out a book from the shelf behind his desk. "I found that book I told you about last time. I think you'll find some rather good arguments about religion simply amounting to rituals based upon delusions. Let me know what you think."

Still unconvinced of the doctor's condition, he accepted the book but kept alert for any signs that the doctor needed medical attention. "So you're not going to tell me about this past that's come to haunt you today?"

Dr. Pembry brushed past him to the worktable on the other side of the room. "I wouldn't dream of wasting your time with the details of my life. Besides, I'd rather share some good news."

Stone followed and stood across the table from Dr. Pembry. Papers and books covered most of the surface except for the center.

The doctor unrolled a large document resembling a blueprint diagram overlaying a map and spread it on the table. He moved several books to hold down the corners. "Take a look at this."

"Is this part of your research?"

"Yes. Something I've waited years to pursue." Pembry's hands shook slightly as he ran them over a diagram of locations and notes centering mostly over Ethiopia and partially into Egypt. "My funding finally came through. A group called the Collective. Ever heard of them?"

Stone continued to study the map. "No, I can't say I have."

"Hmm, interesting. I thought you might know more about them. They seem most interested in biblical artifacts at the moment."

"What exactly are you searching for?"

The doctor looked up from the map, studied Stone for a good minute. A smile broke his face into a series of wrinkles resembling the diagram on the table. "You will find this most amusing. I'm about to embark into your territory."

"Now I'm intrigued. Have you crossed to the side of belief?"

Dr. Pembry waved his hand again. "No, nothing like that. I have a theory as to where the Ark of the Covenant and its elements may be."

Stone set the book the doctor had given him down on the table. What could he possibly say to that? Since when did Dr. Pembry believe anything from the Bible?

The doctor's shoulders shook slightly with his chuckle. "Yes, I had a feeling that would get your attention."

"For a man who doesn't believe there is a God and that the Bible was written by deluded men, you certainly seem to be looking for Him."

"Not for God, but for these artifacts. You know, the manna jar, the staff of Aaron, and the stone tablets."

"Yes, I remember. But I thought you didn't believe in any of it."

"No, I never said that. I do believe the Bible to be quite accurate historically. Enough evidence exists to support the elements and rituals of the temple, but I still believe them to be the creation of man, not some all-powerful creator."

"Ah, I see. And what do you hope to accomplish by finding these artifacts? Some would argue that their discovery would be proof of God's existence. Especially the stone tablets."

"Why, because they were supposedly written by the finger of God?" Dr. Pembry made a scoffing noise.

Stone nodded. "Exactly."

The doctor's knowledge of the Bible was staggering, yet he still refuted God's existence. The more the man learned, the more entrenched he seemed in his unbelief. Stone hadn't met anyone else, in all his years of ministry, as baffling as the doctor.

"I believe it will do quite the opposite. Once we have the artifacts, we can dispel the myths surrounding them with solid scientific facts."

"I don't see how that's possible, since God created science as well. I don't believe they're mutually exclusive."

"And thus we return to our usual impasse. It always comes down to that, doesn't it?"

"Yes, it does."

"Yet you continue to return, determined to change this old man's mind." Dr. Pembry stared pointedly at him, glassy brown eyes raised above his glasses, the corners of his mouth upturned in a mischievous smile.

"Doctor, you're not the only one who finds our discussions

invigorating. I believe God uses you to keep me on top of my game."

Dr. Pembry frowned. "Now there's a topic I don't think we've covered. Can your God truly work through an unbeliever? Why would He want to? I find no logic in that."

"No, I imagine you wouldn't." Stone glance down and retrieved the book. "Never-the-less, I can list several instances just from the Scriptures, let alone what I've witnessed."

Dr. Pembry gazed out the window, appearing lost in thought.

Stone had never seen the man so unsettled and unfocused. "Dr. Pembry?"

He brought his gaze to Stone. "Yes?"

A sadness had replaced the glint of intellectual excitement in his eyes again.

Stone pulled a chair over near the desk and sat down. "What happened, Doc?"

The man's eyes fluttered as he cleared his throat. "Nothing. Nothing at all. Now, where were we?"

CHAPTER NINE

JERUSALEM

Only a heart in turmoil would think of doing such a thing.

Mira Kohen had stepped many a time inside the doors of Achem's firm while engaged to Eben. She knew the place well but not at all. Not really. She'd read enough between the lines of what Eben had off-handedly shared at times to conclude much more went on at the Archeology Consultants Group than met the eye. And since Eben's departure, she'd continued to keep in touch with Achem.

Unbeknownst to Liran.

Which weighed heavily on her heart now. She wanted him to understand that she did this not out of a need to stay connected to Eben. Not at all. Something quite different and unexpected.

Something she never saw coming until she realized it had hit her a long time ago.

But coming here today bordered more on the official side of her growing connection to what she now knew to be the *Natsar*, the Keepers of the ancient relics. Today she would step into this place in a more serious capacity. To help Achem. And Liran.

Because she had no choice in light of what she'd discovered.

She paused on the step in front of the door, considering what she'd say if she saw Liran first. She'd almost told him at the garden that day. That had been her intent, but when he told her she had to move on from Eben, she'd nearly lost her patience with him.

The man must be truly bull-headed to not see the truth. She held onto the past? He should take a deep and lingering look into that mirror. And she almost told him that too. She'd barely managed to hold her tongue as she stalked off. If she hadn't left when she did, she might not be here today—

Mira took a deep breath to calm herself. The worst thing she could do was go in guns blazing. But maybe...maybe now she could be bluntly honest with him once he saw her part in this is not about getting over Eben but about following her heart.

She pushed open the door and stepped into the main entry area. The smell of old wood and parchment calmed her nerves quicker than a cup of tea. That smell would always take her back to her days at the Institute of Archeology, where she first met Eben and then Liran.

The door to her left stood open and revealed Achem's gray head bent over his desk. The door to Liran's office on the opposite side remained closed, which could mean he was busy or at a dig site.

She strode to Achem's door and knocked. "May I come in?"

Achem tugged his readers off and rose. "Mira, yes, please. Come in." He gestured to the chair in front of his desk.

She sat down, crossing her ankles, and closed her hands in her lap. Her back never touched the chair. Her nerves kept her spine straight and her heart thumping in her chest as she kept the door to Liran's office in her periphery.

"I hope you don't mind me dropping in." She shot a glance at Liran's door.

Achem smiled. "Not at all. I am surprised though." He tilted his head, using his glasses to point in the same direction. "He's not here at the moment. Would you prefer I shut the door?"

She smiled and glanced at her hands. Somehow having someone else understand her worry lifted the burden. She sat back in her seat. "No, he'll find out sooner or later, right?"

"Yes..." He leaned forward. "But don't you think sooner would be better, Mira? You asked me to let you be the one to tell him about your growing involvement with the *Natsar*, which goes a hair against my better judgment, but in light of your situation, I agreed."

"I know, and I did plan to tell him, but he said something that made me angry." She covered her mouth after the words toppled out.

Achem chuckled. "I can only imagine. You and Liran are very much alike."

She felt her mouth drop open as she blinked. "But—"

He held his hand up. "What I mean is, you are both passionate people who sometimes speak before thinking. This requires giving each other grace, my dear."

Tilting her head, she snorted, more at herself than anything. "No kidding."

Achem folded his hands on the desk. "So what brings you here today?"

"I came across a name that struck me not as odd in and of itself, but also in the way some had attempted to conceal it."

"Oh?"

She scooted to the edge of her seat. "Artemis Tombs. I came across his name in a back channel yesterday while doing research for the project they gave me. I think he may be using Cantor Business Solutions as a funnel for some of his acquisitions. Not entirely sure what those are though. Not yet at least."

Achem's facial expression turned more serious than she could ever recall seeing. "Mira, be very careful. If Artemis Tombs is in any way involved, you can be sure the Collective is as well. I am concerned that your discovery might not be a coincidence."

"How do you mean?"

"Considering the historical significance of the area in which we live, archeology is a small community here that integrates in many ways. Entrepreneurially speaking especially. I'm sure your manager is aware of your connections to me."

"Yes, but I'm almost positive he knows nothing about the *Natsar*."

"Almost..." He sat forward again. "Mira, you could have just shared this over the phone, but I'm guessing you felt that was a risk."

She hesitated before nodding. "I've noticed my manager is keeping a closer eye on the interns lately, but sometimes me more so than others. I didn't want to take the chance."

He frowned. "Please be careful, my dear. Do not put your safety at risk. It may be time to cut your ties there."

"I think you may be right. And that brings me to my next question. May I officially accept your offer to come work for Archeological Consultants Group?"

Achem's brows shot up with his surprise. "My dear, I haven't drafted the offer yet."

Smiling so hard her cheeks hurt, she jumped forward in her seat. "Yet!"

He laughed. "You are a very clever and discerning young woman, Mira. And a fine addition to our team...both teams." He gave his last words an air of mystery. "Shall we unofficially shake on it until I can make it official?"

As they both stood, she put her hand in his for their handshake. "I accept. Thank you, Achem. I'm excited to be a part of this place." She swept her gaze up and over in appreciation of the building's architecture, everything it held, and everyone it represented.

"You do realize much of what we do most of the time is research?"

"Yes, and I'm going to brag for a moment and say that's one of my strengths. Thus how I dug up Artemis Tombs."

Achem chuckled at her pun. "Then you will enjoy our library."

As she stood to leave, he came from behind his desk to see her out.

She paused short of the doorway as her heart pushed a question of its own into the mix. "Achem, can I ask you a personal question?"

"Yes, by all means, but my answer may be limited, depending upon how personal this question might be." He laughed.

She felt her cheeks grow warm. "No, nothing too personal, just more of an opinion..." She shut the door to the office, which made Achem raise his brows in question. "When I was with Eben, it was...nice...comfortable, you could say. So when he left, I felt more like I lost a..."

"A friend as opposed to a fiancé?"

"Yes." She dropped her chin for a moment. "Is it wrong that I find myself thinking of Liran all the time?"

"Since Eben's departure?"

His question hit a deep place that required a confession. Tears burned her eyes. "No, even before."

His smile warmed his eyes and relieved her heart with his silent compassion. "No, my dear. Perhaps that's just your heart telling your mind who you really want."

Again, her cheeks felt warm but in a good way. "I think you're right."

The sound of the outer door opening alerted them to someone's entry, followed by a knock on the office door.

"Achem, may I come in?" Liran's voice filtered through the transom window above the door.

Achem raised his brows to her in question again.

She smiled and opened the door. "Hello, Liran."

He tucked his hand back with his confused expression. "Mira? I didn't expect to see you here."

She smiled. Maybe she could ease him into this new arrangement. "I know, but you should get used to seeing more of me." She dared a glance over her shoulder. Achem appeared entirely too pleased at the moment. Perhaps a good sign. "I'll be a regular fixture here from now on."

"Oh? I had no idea?" He sent a questioning look to Achem, who nodded. "Well, isn't that nice." His troubled expression did little to ease her concern, but what did she expect? Liran carried a similar stubbornness like his brother. And she'd learned to deal with that.

"Yes, it is." She turned to face Achem. "I will give my notice and let you know if I discover anything else."

Achem's concerned expression returned. "Be very careful, my dear."

As she left the office she patted Liran on the shoulder, noting his dumbfounded expression. "Good to see you, Liran."

Life had taught her to always leave a room with an advantage.

Score one for Mira.

LIRAN LOADED THE FILES THEY WOULD NEED FOR THEIR TRIP into his satchel before shutting down and loading his laptop as well. He preferred to have duplicates of everything they could possibly need—paper and digital. He would pack his personal items tonight at his apartment. He slung the strap over his shoulder and grabbed the copy of their itinerary for Achem.

But yet again, his thoughts drifted to Mira's face as she left the day before. The woman had looked positively pleased with herself as she dropped the bomb of her new involvement here in his proverbial lap. He didn't know what to make of it then and still didn't. And he hadn't had the words to even discuss it with Achem, who seemed quite content to stay on the topic of their impending trip.

Why hadn't Achem discussed this with him? Liran would have shared his concerns about the two of them working together. He had his reservations about that working well in light of her past involvement with Eben.

And what exactly had Mira discovered that would cause Achem to caution her like that? That concern alone would not leave him alone and had stolen most of his sleep during the night. He didn't like the thought of her being in a compromising situation and would make that clear to Achem. He felt a responsibility to look out for Mira. He owed her that much at least, especially after the way Eben walked out on her. On all of them.

His frustration seemed to threaten a conversion to anger and thrust him across the hallway to Achem's office. He gave the closed door a brisk knock.

"Come." Achem's voice filtered through from the open transom window above.

Liran entered the room, noting the usual arrangement of Achem's workspace and tables. Yet something seemed different. He stopped in front of the desk and held out the paper. "Our updated itinerary."

"Thank you."

"I'd like to talk to you about something."

"About the trip?" Achem studied the document.

Liran found himself distracted by the arrangement of the room. "Something is different."

Achem smiled at him. "Good observation. Now tell me what it is."

He glanced at his watch. Unless he left in the next few minutes, he'd miss his bus. "Are you testing me?"

"Perhaps. Observation skills are crucial to what we do, Liran. We must fine-tune them constantly."

With a sigh, Liran lowered his satchel to a chair and resolved to catch a later bus. He went back to the doorway before turning around to scan the entire room. "You've shifted your desk approximately twenty degrees, the books on the shelf behind you are in a different order, and you've added a new plant to your entourage in the corner by the window. The one with the yellow pot."

"What kind of plant is it?"

"Seriously? Now I have to know the names of plants?"

Achem smiled. "You'd be surprised what could come in handy at times."

"I will keep that in mind. How did I do otherwise? Did I pass the test?"

"For the most part." Achem stood and pulled on his suit jacket. Even when not on a mission, the man maintained a semblance of uniformity.

"What did I miss?"

He pointed to the shelf. "The books are actually now alphabetized, my desk is actually turned twenty-five degrees west, and the plant is a peace lily."

Liran rolled his eyes. "Unbelievable."

"Yet true." Achem's shoulders bounced with his laughter.

He tilted his head slightly. "You're in a good mood tonight."

Achem gathered papers and items into a satchel similar to Liran's and grabbed his keys from the desk. "I'm always happy to roam this world and leave the confines of my office." He swept his hand across the room. "Come, I'll give you a ride home since I made you miss your bus."

"I didn't say anything about the bus."

Achem came from behind his desk. "You didn't have to. I was aware of the time and *observed* how you looked at your watch. Normally you walk home on the days you leave early so you must be eager to get home, which means you haven't packed yet. Am I right?"

Liran followed him out into the hallway. "Embarrassingly so."

Achem patted him on the back. "See? There is much you can deduce from observation."

Once in the car, Achem turned on the news in his ancient BMW and headed toward Liran's apartment complex. The headlines did little to distract his thoughts from filling with concerns regarding Mira. He ran a hand over his mouth.

"What's on your mind, Liran?"

"Just our trip."

"Are you sure that's all it is?"

Liran studied his profile as he drove. "Why do you ask?"

Achem stopped at a traffic light and looked at him. "You haven't said a word about Mira working with us."

He nodded as he folded his lips inward with his thoughts. "Yes, actually, that's been on my mind a lot since yesterday."

"And you have concerns."

Liran directed his attention out the passenger side window as the car moved forward with the light changed. "Yes, I do. I don't want to see Mira put in any compromising situations. She's been through enough."

"Meaning your brother."

"Yes."

"She's the one who approached me, Liran. She believes the work that we do is important."

Liran spun his attention back to Achem. "And how does she know about the *Natsar*?"

"Again, your brother."

Head back, he closed his eyes for a moment. "I should have known."

"Known what?"

"That Eben would have shared information with her."

"It's inevitable, Liran. How could Eben not share his life with the person he intended to marry?"

"Now you defend him?"

"Not at all. Just telling you it's human nature. And your brother had good taste, by the way. Mira is highly intelligent and clever. I've no doubts about her ability to help us."

"I do wish you had discussed it with me before you offered her a position."

"I had intended to, but she deduced I was heading that direction and came today to accept my offer."

"But you hadn't given her one yet."

"I know." He laughed. "She's a very clever girl, that one. And very discerning it seems."

Liran groaned. "And we know how you prize that."

Achem laughed again.

"But you won't put her in dangerous situations?" Though he worded it as a question, he meant it as a directive.

"I think you should have a chat with Mira and listen to what she wants for herself."Achem pulled to the curb in front of his building.

Mira stood outside near the entrance.

"Looks like providential timing to me." Achem lifted his brows at him.

Liran pulled his gaze from Achem to look at Mira. For some reason he still couldn't fathom, he hadn't told Achem about his visit with Eben during his sabbatical. "She's stayed in touch with me over the last year. I think she's still hoping Eben will return and renew his promise to her."

"Are you sure about that?"

He returned his attention to Achem. "What do you mean?"

"Observe carefully, Liran. Perhaps there's more here than you're seeing." He nodded his head in Mira's direction.

Liran got out of the car and then shut the door. Achem drove off as he turned around. "Mira, I didn't expect to see you here."

She clasped her hands together as she shrugged. "I know. I hope you don't mind. I wanted to apologize."

"For what?" He stepped onto the sidewalk.

She wore her hair loose, cascading over one shoulder. The waning sun made her dark hair look glossy. She took a couple steps toward him. "For not telling you sooner. I told Achem I wanted to be the one to tell you, but I didn't know how, to be honest."

In all the time he'd known, Mira, he'd never seen her so unsure of herself. "I wish you had. Been honest. I don't want you stepping into the *Natsar* for the wrong reasons."

"I'm not, Liran." She frowned, causing a cute indention between her brows.

He found himself wanting to smooth the crease away, along with whatever else troubled her. "This won't bring Eben back."

The uncertainty he saw earlier vanished as she narrowed her

eyes and pulled her chin back. “Eben has nothing to do with my decision. Never mind. I should go.” She turned to leave.

The thought of her walking away made him keenly aware of how much he wanted her to stay. Liran lunged forward and caught her arm. “Please don’t.”

Before he could say anything more, she was suddenly against him, her lips pressed to his. His shock immobilized him at first, but when she started to pull away, he tugged her closer. He brought his right hand up to her head, cupping her cheek. Her hair felt like silk under his fingertips.

His brother’s face flashed in his mind. Liran lifted his head, breaking the kiss, but he didn’t want to let her go. Everything about her felt right, but was it? He couldn’t be a fill-in for his brother. That would hurt both of them in the long run.

He searched her eyes. “I don’t know if this is a good idea.”

Face upturned, her gray eyes darted back and forth as she searched his face. “Why not?”

“Are you sure I’m the one you want?” He pushed her hair back just so he could feel its softness again.

She frowned. “You think I would kiss you if I was still in love with Eben?”

“I don’t want to be his replacement.” He played that role already in the *Natsar*. He’d not play second choice in any woman’s heart.

She pushed away. “For a man who’s so knowledgeable about the past, you seem to have little understanding of the present.” She turned to walk away.

“Wait! Mira, please.”

She stopped and turned around, silent yet resolute.

“I’m leaving for the States in the morning. Can we talk about this?”

She shook her head. “No, you need to think about what you want. Maybe when you get back, we can talk.” She spun around to leave again.

“What about Eben?”

She whipped around, tossing her hands out. "What about him?" Frustration filled her voice as she shook her head. "Liran, he's not the man I want."

With that, she turned around again and strode off.

CHAPTER TEN

SAN FRANCISCO

Nichole slid the last container of art supplies into the back of the van and then stepped back to assess their inventory. Hands on her hips, she stared at the array of supplies, goodies, and gifts filling Robin's oversized SUV—the one she claimed necessary for future grandchildren— from the floorboards to the top of the seats. Any higher and they wouldn't be able to see out the rear window. The kids at Lucille-Packard Children's Hospital were in for a huge treat today.

She sighed. Her father would have loved this.

Robin came up next to her and tossed in another bag of small stuffed animals. "Your father would have loved this."

Nichole pushed the bag to the left side in the one remaining gap in her Tetris arrangement. "I was thinking the exact same thing."

As she faced Robin, she didn't bother to hide the tears burning her eyes. Over the years, she'd grown even closer to the woman who had worked as closely with her father as she had. "I miss him every...single...day."

Robin pushed the auto-close button to close the door. "Me too, doll. Me too." She pulled Nichole into a quick hug. "But you got this. And if anyone tells you otherwise, you know what I would say?"

"Yes, ma'am. The famous Robin chompers quote." She giggled. "Dad used to love that too."

This time, Robin's eyes glassed a bit with moisture. She cleared her throat as she checked her watch. "We better get moving if we want to get there in time. The clowns get there mid-afternoon. We need to set up and be ready by then so the kids can have a good time."

"Roger that." Nichole climbed into the passenger seat and checked her phone to see if Jerad had tried to reach her in the last hour or so.

Robin settled into the driver's seat, buckled in, and started the engine. "Is Jerad coming?"

"He's meeting us there. When his doctor found out he'd started having seizures at night, he ordered him to come in for some blood work."

"Ordered?"

"Yeah, you know how stubborn that man can be."

Robin adjusted her glasses and pursed her lips. "Yeah, and I know how far I can throw the man if he doesn't behave."

Nichole broke into a full laugh. "He knows it too. I think you're the only thing in this world that truly scares him."

"I'm sure I'm not the only thing." Robin held her gaze.

She sighed and looked away. "Yeah, that too. But he won't talk to me about it."

Robin pulled away from the curb and onto the street. "I noticed."

Nichole checked her phone again for any updates from Jerad but her screen remained blank. No news should be good news except when it concerned Jerad.

"Nothing yet?"

"No." She grunted and shoved her phone into the small satchel she'd brought with her.

Robin turned the radio on. "How about some music."

Closing her eyes, Nichole settled back in her seat. Weariness from her fitful night weighed her eyes down. The upbeat song had transitioned into something slower, lulling her into a doze.

The moment it started, she recognized the dream...

As she felt the vibration of the drums, the same man strode onto the stage—tall and dark-haired, but when she tried to see his face, a bright light shrouded his features. Jerad stood next to her, transfixed. But when she turned to ask him if he saw it too, he wasn't there.

The crowd broke into a frenzy, pushing her closer to the stage. She pushed to her right, fighting to weave her way out of the throng. When she broke free, she stumbled onto the floor. Darkness surrounded her. Light seeped around a door ten feet in front of her. As she stood, the door seemed to open slightly, as if inviting her to enter.

She nudged the door open and recognized the room. Leah's apartment. Everything looked the same, just like she remembered from that awful day. She rushed to the bathroom door. A watery red puddle had formed at the base of the tub.

"Leah!"

She didn't want to look but some part of her thought she could save Leah this time. Nichole pushed back the curtain. But it wasn't Leah's lifeless eyes she saw. It was Jerad's.

She screamed.

"Nichole!"

The seatbelt snapped against her chest as she jerked forward and her surroundings became familiar again. She pushed her hair away from her face. "Sorry. I guess fell asleep."

"You okay?" Robin gave a nervous laugh.

"Yes, I'm sorry." She grabbed her phone from her satchel. Still no texts or messages from Jerad.

Robin turned off the radio. "I thought I was going to have to pull over and shake you."

She sat back in her seat. "It's that same stupid nightmare." Memories of it flooded back. "Except different. This time, I...this time it was different."

"Care to fill me in."

The image of Jerad's lifeless form threatened to send her over the edge. "Not really. Are we almost there?"

"Just about." Robin sent a concerned glance at her before focusing on the road again. She took the exit for Palo Alto. "You sure you're up for this today? I'm sure I can enlist one of those clown volunteers to help me while you go have some downtime."

"Thanks, but I'm fine." She recognized her curt tone right away. "Sorry."

"No worries, chick-a-dee. I've had worse bites." Soft laughter accompanied her words.

Robin turned into the hospital entrance. After retrieving a ticket from the parking gate, she drove to the front entrance to unload.

One of the security guards approached with two hospital carts. Robin hopped out and opened the back hatch.

Nichole tucked her phone into her back pocket as she climbed out and took one of the carts. She glanced at this name badge. "Hi, Harry. How's it going?"

He nodded. "Good. Clown day is always a good day, right?"

Nichole giggled. "Are they already here?"

"Not yet, though one clown came early. He's already upstairs with the kids."

They loaded the one cart with as many containers as it could hold. Harry held onto the top of the stack with one hand and held the handle with the other. "I'll take this one up there while you load the other."

"Thanks." Nichole gave him her biggest smile. "Appreciate it."

He pushed the cart through the sliding glass doors and turned right toward the elevators.

Robin rolled the other cart closer to the vehicle. "Not sure we can fit the rest."

"Is that a challenge?" Nichole loaded a container onto the cart.

"No, just a statement of reality."

"I bet we can do it. I can carry the bags of stuffed animals."

Once the cart was filled, Nichole held out her hand. "Give me your keys. I'll go park and carry up the rest."

Robin handed her the keychain. "You go it, Boss."

After she found a spot in the lower level of the garage, Nichole headed back to the entrance, carrying a large bag of stuffed animals in each hand. As she approached the doors, Several people ran out. One older man collapsed on the sidewalk.

A woman about his age knelt down next to him. "Sam? Honey?" She shook him when he didn't respond. "Sam!"

Nichole dropped the bags. "I'll go in and get help."

The woman focused on her, shaking her head. "Call 9-1-1."

She took a step toward the doors. "I'm sure they can get him over to the main hospital."

"No, don't go in there! There's something wrong. People are dropping everywhere."

Nichole froze. "Which floor?"

"Third. Something's...wrong." The woman collapsed on her husband.

Nichole yanked her phone out of her back pocket just as another group of people stumbled out the doors.

She tapped 9-1-1 on her phone.

A man's voice came over the line. "9-1-1, what's your emergency?"

"I'm at the children's hospital, Lucille-Packard. Something happened inside and people are collapsing. Please send help!"

JERAD LEFT THE FREEWAY AND HEADED TOWARD THE HOSPITAL. He mulled over the irony of his day. Left his doctor's office with a dim prognosis that seemed to be chasing him down faster than they expected and now he would be helping children laugh and forget about their prognoses.

Yet something in it felt orchestrated. Only God would do something like that, right? Put him in a place to face the threat of death with laughter? The thought did trippy things to his head.

He turned down the street where the hospital was located. He noticed the news vans first. Had Clown Day made the news this year? That kind of publicity could really work to the Foundation's advantage. They needed some good PR to show their investors they were truly an entrepreneurial entity. He turned into the entrance. Nichole and Robin would be thrilled to—

Multiple police cars lined the entryway to the hospital. Two police vehicles blocked the barrier gates to the parking garage and main entrance. Fire trucks and ambulances created a flashing cluster of red and yellow lights beyond.

A police officer waved him to a stop. Jerad opened his window. "I'm with the Strauss Foundation, here to help with Clown Day. What's going on?"

"No one's allowed in. Best if you turn around."

Jerad leaned out his window, trying to see more. "Was there a fire or something?"

"Can't give you any details. Just move on, please."

Jerad's heart kicked into high speed. "But the people I work with are probably in there. My fiancée—Nichole Strauss—do you know if she's okay? She's here with another woman."

The man shook his head. "I'm sorry, sir. I don't have any information. And we can't let anyone in until we know what's going on."

Jerad turned the vehicle around and headed back to the main road as a van turned into the entry area. Large white letters on a blue background read 'CDC.' Jerad pulled onto the road, passing two more like it.

He drove into a parking area in front of one of the medical buildings on the opposite side of the street from the hospital. Two more ambulances screamed down the road. He picked up his phone and called Nikki. After multiple rings, her voice message played. He hung up, waited a few seconds and tried again.

"Jerad, where are you?"

His eyes closed as he leaned his head back. Never had her voice sounded so good. "I'm out by the street. They won't let me in. Where are you?"

"I'm in front of the hospital."

"What's going on?"

"I don't know. They won't let me inside. They won't let me leave either." She let out a soft whimper. "People are dying, Jerad. I don't know what's happening."

"CDC vehicles are pulling in."

A voice in the background filtered over the line. "Ma'am, please hang up the phone and come with us."

Nikki's voice boomed over the connection. "Not until you tell me what's going on."

"We've set up a decontamination examination area. We just want to make sure you're not contaminated."

"With what?"

"That's what we're trying to find out. Please come with us."

Nikki cried into the phone. "Oh God, Jerad, they're bringing Robin out. She's so pale."

"Ma'am, hang up the phone."

"Wait, that's my friend. Is she okay?"

"No, you can't go near her! Come with us now!"

A loud *clatter* came over the line. Nikki's voice shouted from a distance. "Jerad, call Achem. It's just like Denver!"

CHAPTER ELEVEN

JERUSALEM

Excitement fueled her steps to the double glass door entry of Cantor Business Solutions. Along with a small amount of jitters and a plan. Before she went to her station to start the day's work assigned to her, she would explain to her manager that she had another offer and give her notice. Maybe in the time she had left at CBS, she could dig up a little more information on one Artemis Tombs too.

The name had to be made up. She couldn't imagine a woman in her right mind who would give her child a name like that. Although, she had met some characters during her stint at the Hebrew University. Come to think of it, she could totally see one of the archeology majors that Eben had associated with adopting the name somehow.

The idea took root and gave her a lead. Perhaps there could be a connection to the college that she hadn't thought about. She pulled out her phone, opened her notes app, and entered a reminder for herself to explore that possibility, adding it to her to-do list.

As she closed the app, a text popped up from Liran.

I'm sorry. Please be careful.

She smiled, bringing up the emoji panel to send a heart back, but then thought a thumbs up would be more appropriate. She refused to push Liran into something he wasn't sure he wanted yet. But she wouldn't wait around forever either. The man would either wake up or not.

Once she reached her floor, she stepped out of the elevator and headed to her manager's office.

After dropping her purse off at her desk, she stood at the threshold of his open door. "Mr. Belitz? May I speak to you a moment?"

He diverted his gaze from his monitor. "Yes, come in, Mira. I was actually hoping to get a chance to speak to you today."

"You did?" She made her way to the seat in front of his desk.

"Yes, I spoke with the owner and we agreed that you're really a star player here. I know we started you out as an intern, but we'd like to make your position more official. Several of our clients have expressed their pleasure in working with you, so we'd like you to take a key point on a few of those. What do you think?"

His question left her speechless for a moment. She hadn't expected anything like this at all. For the briefest of moments, she considered what it would be like to step into that level of managing the investment accounts. But then her heart reminded her of what she really wanted. To help Achem and Liran, to be a part of the *Natsar*, to be part of something bigger than herself. If she left CBS now, she'd lose the chance to feed Achem and Liran with additional and much-needed information.

"Thank you, Mr. Belitz, I'm stunned."

"You'll receive a twenty percent pay increase and an official signing bonus."

She smiled. "I'm flattered that several clients think highly of me. That means I did my job right."

"Yes, you did. Beyond expectation, in fact. This is why we'll be putting you over some of our international client's accounts.

They're smaller but need more hands-on attention." He came from behind his desk and sat on the side edge to her left. "And to be clear, this means you may need to be available beyond regular hours to handle one or two international accounts. Will that be a problem?"

"No, not at all."

"Does that mean you accept?"

She nodded. "Yes, very much so."

As he stood, he tapped his thighs with his palms. "Great. HR already has the paperwork ready that you need to sign."

"Wow, you were pretty certain I'd accept."

"Of course. CBS is a great company. And you're a rising star, Mira. We'd be crazy to lose you to some other organization."

Was he implying something? Her gut squirmed. And that usually only happened when something was off in a situation. Maybe Achem and Liran were right to be concerned. Or maybe she was just being paranoid now that she was the one with an ulterior motive for staying.

She smiled and let out a short laugh. "No danger there."

Belitz nodded as he lifted the handset of his desk phone. "I'll let them know you're on your way down."

"Great. Thank you. I just need to grab my purse."

As she left the office, she glanced over her shoulder. Belitz was still on the phone. She made her way quickly to her desk, plucked the jump drive she kept in her purse and inserted it into a port on her computer.

Two client folders had caught her eyes last time she logged on but she'd run out of time to dig further. Once HR made the changes and assigned her new clients and passwords, she'd lose access, and she knew there was something fishy about these two accounts.

She dragged the folders to the drive icon. Then she stuck her phone down in her chair and pretended to be searching in her bag for it. Once the files finished, she right-clicked 'eject' just as Belitz came out of his office and headed her direction.

As she stood, she swiped the drive into her hand as part of reaching for her phone. "There it is."

Belitz paused in front of her desk. Was that impatience or suspicion in his expression? "HR is waiting for you."

"Sorry about that. I wanted to take my phone in case they needed any additional information from me." She held up her phone. "I keep everything on this thing."

He nodded. "Great. Go on down now."

Careful to keep her smile in place, she tucked her phone into her purse, dropped the jump drive in as well. "I'm on my way."

While Belitz strode back to his office, she headed toward the elevators and pushed the button. Once inside, she turned around, catching a brief glance of Belitz back at his desk and on the phone.

Her gut squirmed again. She'd listen to it this time. A little paranoia would keep her on guard.

DENVER, COLORADO

When he had made their reservations at the hotel, the manager had been obliged to tell them part of the building was under 'construction.' Achem was certain that meant they were still decontaminating parts of the hotel due to the outbreak, but dutifully informed the man they represented the Antiquities Robbery Prevention Unit—Special Investigation Task Force.

Sent by the Israeli Antiquities Authority, they needed to investigate one of the guests staying at the hotel at the time of the incident—a suspect under suspicion of smuggling a rare artifact into the US. Past commissions with the IAA and his connections to the Institute of Archeology gave Achem some authority, which came in quite handy at times for the *Natsar*.

He had to admit, being in the place had an eerie feel. The few staff members he'd seen as they made their way to their rooms the first night still appeared a bit shell-shocked. He wondered if they'd even be there if they didn't need the money, and he didn't blame them for being afraid one bit.

From what they'd found out from back channels in Israel, the plague seemed to have a very short shelf life. Egyptian news channels had broadcast the same reassurance to the general population, and with no recent indigents there, the region seemed to breathe a sigh of relief as they returned to business as usual.

Their local inquires and subtle investigations since they arrived seemed to confirm the same information, which seemed evident from his window view of the city's transition from day to night. Yet he could imagine the world stood watching, waiting to hear if the plague outbreak here in Denver was in any way related to those in Egypt. And if so, wondering when and where the next outbreak would occur. He prayed that wouldn't be the case, but the mystery man wielding the staff seemed determined to control its power.

A knock came from his hotel door. He waved Liran in and shut the door.

Liran sat in the single chair in the room. "The manager said the young man who brought up a delivery for this guest will be on duty shortly. He'll send him up when he arrives."

"Good. He may be the only one to truly get a good look at this man, whoever he is. Hopefully, he has a better memory than the manager."

Liran nodded. He seemed somewhat agitated.

"Liran, is everything all right?"

"Yes, why do you ask?"

Achem shrugged. "You seem unsettled." He tilted his head. "Did something happen with Mira?"

"No, nothing happened."

He laughed. "Perhaps that's the problem."

Liran stood and turned his back to him to look out the window. "As you predicted, the mystery man's name turned out to be fictitious."

"Of course it did. I expected nothing less. He has an agenda and won't let anything stop him."

Liran turned around again. "What's his agenda? To wreak havoc?"

"No, that's just the consequence of his attempts to figure out how to control the staff."

"Then we can expect more incidents?"

"Most likely."

A soft tap sounded from the entry.

Achem opened the door. A young man stood there, nearly Liran's height but lanky in build. "Please, come in."

The young man glanced past him to Liran and hesitated. "My manager said you had some questions?"

Achem smiled, bowed his head at him, and spoke an octave higher than his norm. The persona of a gentle professor always seemed to put people at ease. "Yes, please come in. I promise we'll be brief. We just need some information about the chap you delivered a package to."

"Sure." He visibly relaxed and walked in.

Achem raised a brow at Liran.

He smiled and clasped his hands in front of him. "Thank you. We appreciate your help. Ricky, isn't it?"

"Yeah." He looked over his shoulder at Achem. "I wasn't in his room long, but the guy was definitely memorable."

Achem tilted his head. "And why was that?"

"He was intense. Real intense."

Liran sat on the edge of the bed. "The manager said you delivered a box. Do you remember any details about it?"

"Yeah, my manager said you were looking for some kind of ancient relic or something, right?" His eyes lit up, as if he were suddenly part of some conspiracy.

Achem forced a chuckle. "I'm sure it sounds very mysterious, but we're just trying to reclaim and restore this historical piece to its rightful place in Israel."

Ricky nodded. "Well, I don't think the box I delivered had anything valuable in it."

"Oh?" Liran crossed his legs. "What makes you say that?"

"The box came from Amazon. And it was light. About two-foot square."

Achem nodded. The young man appeared more observant than expected. "How about the man's appearance?"

"He was tall, dark brown, almost black hair. He looked foreign but didn't have an accent. At least I don't think so. He didn't say a whole lot. He was too obsessed with the case on the bed."

Liran uncrossed his legs and leaned forward. "What kind of case?"

Ricky held his hands about five and a half feet apart. "About this long and black. Looked like an instrument case actually. Custom made. Hard on the outside, like to protect the contents. When I went to set the box down, it slipped and bumped the case. He got really upset and held it like it was alive or something." He rolled his eyes. "Like I said, intense."

Achem crossed his arms. Alive or something? The words left him a tad unsettled. "Did he say anything else?"

Ricky shook his head. "No, just gave me a tip and asked me to leave. Which I did, but I don't even think he noticed. He wouldn't stop stroking his case. Really weird, if you ask me."

Liran stood. "Thank you, Ricky. You've been most helpful."

Achem pulled a twenty from his jacket pocket and held it out to Ricky. "Yes, most helpful indeed."

Ricky smiled. "Thanks. Glad to help."

Liran showed Ricky out before sitting down again in the chair. "Somewhat disturbing, to say the least."

Achem took off his jacket and laid it on the bed. "But not surprising. We already witnessed the effect the manna jar had on those who tried to claim its power. The Ark was even worse."

"That was before my time."

"You were still a baby, but your brother probably remembers."

Liran frowned. "Why would he remember?"

"Your father almost died that day. He was shot during our efforts to rescue Nichole's mother. You both had lost your mother just six months earlier. I think Eben was terrified that your father was going to die as well."

Liran ran his hands over his face before he stood. "I didn't realize the same incident that took Nichole's mother also took my father's legs."

"I'm sorry, Liran, I thought you knew." Achem studied Liran. He seemed inordinately agitated.

He shook his head. "Father refused to talk about it. Eben said he didn't remember anything."

"That may be the case. He was very young—maybe three. Four at the most. He never left your father's side. Perhaps he blocked it out." He paused, waited for Liran to say something. He appeared lost in his own thoughts. "Is there anything else you'd like to know?"

Liran cleared his throat. "No. I think I'll turn in for the night."

Liran's sudden change of direction baffled Achem. "I thought you wanted to try that restaurant you mentioned."

"I'll just get room service. Our flight leaves early so I better get packed." Liran strode to the door before Achem could say anything more and left.

Achem sat on the bed. For someone who prided himself with keen observation skills, he'd missed something in that exchange. What had upset Liran? What he shared with Liran was common knowledge. For the most part...

Again, he discerned a peculiar shift in Liran. With all that was at stake for the *Natsar* and retrieving the staff, Achem sensed an urgency to find out what.

Their enemy may very well loom closer than he realized.

The LORD said to Moses, "Put back Aaron's staff in front of the ark of the covenant law, to be kept as a sign to the rebellious. This will put an end to their grumbling against me, so that they will not die." — *Numbers 17:10*

DEFIANCE

Even concealed, the power of the staff beckoned to him.

To be held. To be revealed. To be wielded.

Small nodules covered the upper portion, pushing into his fingers as if to push him away like an angry lover. Yet its call sucked him in like a drug. And each time he tried to control the power that surged through him, he became more addicted.

But he determined to control it, even knowing that fools lied mostly to themselves.

A sick boy had been healed in Kneph. More needed what the staff carried. What better place than a children's hospital to test its ability. Science advanced through experimentation. This was no different. A cure was a cure.

That's what he told himself as he strode across the parking lot to the main entrance. Broad daylight would serve his needs. Seen by everyone yet noticed by no one.

He clutched the staff closer to his torso. An artificial sunflower blossom the size of a basketball adorned the top above a red horn. He left the white lab coat he wore open to reveal the rainbow suspenders holding up his baggy trousers. Clown makeup made his skin itch and sweat beads formed between the bulbous red nose and the oversized plastic glasses he wore.

More smiles greeted him as he waited for the elevator. The staff had long since grown used to such 'unusuals' traipsing in and out. Once a month, professional clowns from all over the state volunteered here, which gave him the perfect cover.

He rode in privacy to the top floor, the cancer ward. He closed his eyes but found the image of the young boy in Kneph starring back at him, terrified.

Accusing as his mother's life ebbed away.

He forced the image away and watched the lights move across the lighted panel above the doors; as if counting down his arrival to hell.

Or to heaven. God would see. God would finally accept him. This time he would get it right and make amends for the others.

A bell dinged and the doors slid open. Strong antiseptic grabbed him by the throat and yanked him out of the elevator. Giggles came from his left. A small girl, slight and lost in the folds of her hospital gown covered her mouth with a frail hand. Face pale. Dark circles ringed her faded eyes.

He grinned and honked the horn. Giggles again, and a smile from the nurse behind the girl's wheelchair. He crouched, holding the staff in front of him. The girl focused on the flower. Her pupils dilated.

He watched in fascination, his own life force captured as well. The power of the staff pulsed through his hand as he squeezed the horn again. A hum reverberated up from his chest and rattled his teeth. He struggled to hold it back, to just let a little through.

Sweat ran down his back. Eyes closed, he held his breath and clutched the staff to keep from falling over.

And then it ended. He rose on shaky legs. The nurse stared at him, her face as pale as the white shirt she wore under her turquoise scrubs. The little girl laughed, eyes bright and cheeks pink. The dark circles had fled with her disease. He smiled at her before continuing down a hallway lined with doors.

The rest of the children waited.

CHAPTER TWELVE

Liran paced his hotel room like a caged, wild animal.

The more he thought about past conversations with his brother, the more he realized what he had subconsciously observed or sensed but didn't acknowledge—every time they spoke of their father, Eben would change the subject.

Liran attributed it to his grief over their father's untimely death due to complications related to his past injuries. But in light of what Achem had told him, he suspected it was much more. After their father died, Eben began to change. He grew angry and challenged Achem more.

A year later he took a sabbatical and never came back.

And if what Achem said was true about Eben never leaving their father's side after the incident, then Liran didn't believe for a second that Eben didn't remember what happened.

Every muscle in his body felt like a wound spring. He picked up the hotel menu but after a brief glance, tossed it back on the desk.

Why had his brother lied to him?

He grabbed his duffel bag and started packing, but once he realized he'd shoved everything in, including what he needed for tomorrow, he threw the duffel onto the floor and dropped down on the bed, holding his head in his hands.

Was what happened to their father the catalyst behind Eben leaving the *Natsar*? He pulled out his phone and dialed his brother. After the fourth ring, he started to hang up but heard his brother's sleepy voice come over the line.

"Brother, to what or who do I owe this pleasure?"

"Did I wake you?"

"No, just resting from a strenuous day."

Liran remained quiet as he collected his thoughts. He should have thought this through before rashly calling.

"Liran, just spit it out."

"Why did you lie to me about father?"

Eben grunted and let out a long breath. "So, you learned the truth?"

He didn't even deny it. Liran shot off the bed. "What happened that day?"

"You should be asking Achem that."

"I did."

"And what did the great *Natsar* leader tell you?"

Liran ignored the barb. "That he was shot from behind while trying to rescue a woman."

"Yes, he was. Did he tell you who shot him?"

"I assumed it was one of the men they were fighting." With his free hand, he held the back of his head as he paced.

"Assumptions are dangerous, *achi*. I suggest you ask Achem for a full account of what happened that day. And watch your back when you do."

The line went silent. Liran lowered his phone to confirm Eben had ended the call. He fell back on the bed and stared at the ceiling as he directed his thoughts to the past and re-examined his conversations with Achem. If Eben's implication was true, why would he want Liran—or even Eben for that matter—to be his successor?

Another reason presented itself, launching him into a sitting position. Hadn't he suggested to Achem that his actions to involve Nichole and Jerad in the search for the staff could be guilt-related? To make up for the loss of her parents and possibly help Jerad?

Could Achem's choice for the next Natsar leader have been driven by that very same guilt to make up for their father's death?

Suddenly the room seemed to be closing in on him. He grabbed his jacket and pocketed his room key. Sleep would elude him tonight but the time awake would allow him to pray and think about what to do next.

He paused in the hallway, second-guessing his decision to go out without telling Achem. But only for a moment. He was tired of feeling like he had to account for every decision he made. A walk would help him clear his head and would have no effect on their plans.

The sun had just started to set when he stepped outside. Traffic still filled the streets as people made their way home. Much like Jerusalem. Liran headed toward the sun to watch the sky change colors.

Several blocks later, he noticed a police station. They would have been first on the scene during the hotel incident. And if memory served him right, certain records were available to public inquiry. Maybe they had a few more stones left to turn over for clues.

He pulled open the door and walked in. Chatter reached him from all directions of the station. An unusual character dressed in an array of fashions glared at him as he headed toward the main counter.

The officer stationed there glanced up from her paperwork. "May I help you?"

Liran leaned over the counter. "Yes, I would like to see the police report regarding the recent hotel incident."

She looked up as she tucked papers into a folder. "Were you present the day of the event?"

"No."

"Were you an eyewitness to anything you feel might be significant to the event?"

"No."

She stared at him a moment. "Are you just being nosy?"

Liran started to laugh but stopped when he realized she was dead serious. "No. Not at all. Just doing my own investigation." Perhaps this was a big mistake. He stepped back from the counter. "Never mind. I'll just be on my way."

"Could you wait a moment please? I'll check with my sergeant."

"Sure."

Liran kept an eye on her as she headed to a glass-enclosed office behind the scattered desks in the front area. Within moments she headed toward him, with her sergeant close behind. She stopped at her previous position, but he, however, came out to where Liran stood.

"Come this way please." The sergeant held his hand out toward a door.

"Where are we going?"

"You have some questions. We may have some too." He accepted a folder from the officer Liran had spoken to first.

"Questions for me?"

"Yes. It will only take a moment."

"All right." Liran followed the man through the door.

"Right this way." The sergeant stood in front of a second door, which he opened as Liran approached. Inside stood a small table with a chair on each side.

Liran held his hands up. "I don't think I made myself clear. I'm only looking for information."

"As are we." He held up the folder. "And my lieutenant seems to think you bear a resemblance to the man we're looking for. But if what you're saying is true, I'm sure we can clear this up quickly."

Resembled the man with the staff? Liran tried to keep his breathing steady while his mind raced through past conversations with his brother. Was it possible? Could Eben—?

"Please go in and sit." The sergeant's tone had turned firm.

Liran didn't see any choice but to cooperate without making the situation worse. He feared his future—maybe even his life—

could very well depend upon how he answered this man's questions.

❧

THE STREETLIGHTS TWINKLED THROUGH THE WINDOW TO HIS left. A light rain added to the effect, giving this part of the city an enchanted feel. Achem pushed his plate away and then wiped his mouth with the cloth napkin. Soft chatter surrounded him from the other diners. A young couple walked past him. The older couple seated nearby ate their meal in silence, each staring at their smartphones instead of each other.

He nodded at the waiter who whisked his plate away.

His waitress arrived with his check. "Can I get you anything else before I give you this? A glass of cognac perhaps?"

Achem smiled. "No, thank you. Just the check."

She smiled as she lay the folio on the white tablecloth. The restaurant's logo filled the front in gold. "Have a great night."

He slipped his credit card inside. Liran would have enjoyed his choice of restaurant tonight. Again, Achem checked his phone to see if Liran had replied to his text about joining him. Achem didn't have a problem eating alone—he'd grown used to his own company over the years—but he sensed Liran teetered on the edge of something...critical.

What, he couldn't quite fathom, which only added to his confusion over their earlier conversation. Somehow he had to find a way to get the young man to open up and share whatever he was struggling with. Achem suspected Liran's brother might be a key factor, but until Liran gave him some indicators of what he—

A text from Jerad interrupted his train of thought.

Nichole is in trouble. Can you help?

Jerad used Nichole's full name—that couldn't be good. The waitress returned with his check folio. He finished the receipt before getting up from the table.

Once outside, he paused to reply back to Jerad.

What happened?

Same as in Denver.

Where's Nichole?

Right in the middle of it.

Achem dialed Jerad's number.

Jerad's voice broke over the line after one ring. "Achem?"

"Yes. Fill me in."

"She had a gig today at a children's hospital. The whole place is blockaded. Police won't let me in."

"Were you able to reach her on her cell?" Achem started walking back toward the hotel, his mind ticking on various strategies to get to San Francisco sooner than planned.

"Briefly. They were dragging her off to decontamination."

"That's good. Then she may not have been affected. Did she see anything?"

"I didn't get a chance to ask her. We were disconnected."

Achem paused outside the hotel entrance. "We're scheduled to get there tomorrow afternoon, but I may know a way to get there sooner."

"Thanks. In the meantime, I will keep trying to find a way to her."

"Be careful, Jerad. We've no idea what we're dealing with here. You're already compromised."

"I know. But I have to know what's happening to her. I'll see you tomorrow."

The line went silent, signaling the end of the connection. Achem slipped the phone into the breast pocket of his jacket and pushed into the hotel. He headed straight for Liran's room once he left the elevator.

When his first knock yielded no answer, he did so again, only louder. Still no answer. Achem let himself into his room and called

Liran's number. Where had the boy gone off to? He had said he was tired. Clearly, he had other plans in mind.

The phone went to voicemail. Achem hung up and tried again. Still no answer.

He'd try again after he reached out to a contact he hoped would be helpful. A private plane is what they needed and an old friend just might be the ticket. As he scrolled through his contacts, his phone began to vibrate. Denver Police Department showed on his screen. His momentary shock at the name delayed his response for a moment. He tapped the green accept button.

"Achem, I—"

"Liran, where are you?"

A sigh came over the line. "I'm at the police station."

"You're what? What happened?"

"It's a long story. But I'm not being arrested." He sounded like a petulant schoolboy.

"Are you being released?"

"Not yet."

"Then when?"

"As soon as I can convince this kind police officer that I had nothing to do with what happened at the hotel."

"With the outbreak?"

"Like I said, a long story."

"I'm on my way."

A sigh came over the line. "The station is just a few blocks from the hotel."

Following the map locator on his smartphone, Achem kept a fast pace to the station. As he walked in, he spotted Liran sitting in the front area.

When he headed toward him, an officer came from behind the main desk. "Are you Achem Mizrahi?"

"Yes."

"I told your friend here to be more careful."

"He told me he wasn't being charged. Is that correct?"

"Yes."

"Then what exactly did he do?"

The office raised his brows as he shot a glance at Liran. "Nosiness."

Achem stared at Liran, who shook his head. "I'm sure it won't happen again."

"Good. He's free to go."

Liran stood, then strode past them both and out the door.

Achem nodded at the police officer. "Thank you very much."

He found Liran standing out front, waiting for him.

Liran remained silent as they headed back to the hotel.

Before making any assumptions, Achem wanted details. "Care to fill me in?"

He dropped his chin to his chest. "I had to know more."

"About what?"

"What happened at the hotel."

"We interviewed everyone."

"Yes, I know. But I had more questions."

"And?"

"I couldn't sleep so I went for a walk. When I saw the police station, I went inside to ask some questions. My understanding is that it's public knowledge so I asked to see the report. My inquiry seemed to cause a stir."

"Why?"

"I seem to resemble descriptions of our mystery man with the staff. They wanted to confirm I wasn't in the city when it happened."

Achem laughed. "Half the men in this country fit that description."

Liran stopped. Something haunted him.

"Whatever it is, Liran, just say it. We'll work through it together." He patted Liran's arm.

His shoulders dropped with the breath he released. "Eben called me before we left Jerusalem and gave me a warning."

"A warning? Why didn't you tell me?"

He shook his head. "I'm sorry. I just didn't think it mattered. But then he somehow knew we were going to be in Denver."

Achem ran a hand over his mouth. "Again, why didn't you tell me?"

Liran remained silent.

The revelation of the truth hit Achem square in the chest. "You were with him during your sabbatical, weren't you?"

"Yes, I was."

"And this you kept a secret as well?"

"I didn't think you'd approve."

Achem turned his back to Liran for a moment to collect his composure.

"I'm sorry. I didn't mean to betray your trust."

Achem turned around. "No, I'm the one who's sorry, Liran. Eben is your brother. I never expected you to cut contact with him. I only cautioned you to be careful. Whatever lie has twisted his thinking...I didn't want that to influence you or your future."

Liran swallowed. His eyes turned glossy with his emotions. He spoke through clenched teeth. "Eben said things were about to change and that I should be prepared. He didn't want me to be on the wrong side."

Achem searched Liran's face for more clues as to where this was headed but found none."Your brother never agreed with our stand to keep the Ark and its elements a secret."

"He still believes they should benefit the world."

"Yes, but at what cost? Did you share with him what almost happened with the manna jar?" Achem would prefer no one knew the details of that near catastrophic event but could understand Liran sharing some of it in order to convince his brother otherwise.

"Yes, but as little as possible."

"And he was still unconvinced?"

"Yes. He's determined as ever."

They started walking again toward the hotel. Achem went over in his mind the things Liran shared, trying to make sense of the picture presented. But something didn't fit...

At the hotel entrance, he held his arm out to stop Liran. "You still didn't tell me why you went to the police station. What were you looking for?"

"I needed to know more about this man. Discover more details so I can figure out..."

"Figure out what, Liran?"

He turned away from Achem, but then spun back around to face him. "If Eben is the one wielding the staff."

CHAPTER THIRTEEN

"Nikki!" Jerad checked his screen. His home screen confirmed the call had disconnected. He shoved his phone into his pocket and jogged to the sidewalk. He'd find a way to get to Nikki, one way or another. More police cars had arrived, blocking traffic on the road. He crossed over and headed toward the side of the campus.

As he made his way around to the back of the complex, he noted that most of the uniforms roamed the front area of the main entry points. And upon reaching the back side of the property, he stumbled upon a narrow sidewalk running between two buildings that seemed to head in the general direction of the main hospital.

He paused, first checking for patrols before continuing. Two policemen lingered near a patio with tables and chairs behind the cafeteria. To the left, on the other side of a narrow courtyard, he spotted the corner of a white tent. A good place to start looking for Nikki.

A woman in a hazmat suit with her headgear pushed back approached the uniforms, which meant their backs would be to him. He took off, full speed, toward the tent. Jerad dared a glance over his shoulder. The woman in the suit gestured frantically at him. The two policemen took off in a run, shouting at him to stop.

He pumped his legs as hard as he could, but he could feel the lag in his body. Thanks to Soren's little poisonous gift that just kept on giving. His heart pounded so hard his head felt like bursting and his vision grew strangely brighter.

Just as he reached the tent, he caught a glimpse of Nikki inside. Right before one of the cops tackled him to the ground. He landed with a loud *oomph.* At least they face-planted him in full view of the woman he loved. If she ever doubted his commitment to her, he'd remind her of this very moment.

Nikki ran toward the tent opening. "Jerad!"

The other officer helped lift him off the ground and cuffed him. He gulped in air and exhaled his words. "Thank God I found you."

She glared at him. "You idiot!"

Okay, so not a great reminder moment after all. "I had to make sure you were okay."

"I'm fine. I would have called you, but my phone died." She studied his face. "You, on the other hand, don't look okay at all. Jerad? Jerad!"

He kept trying to form words to answer her, but his entire body felt paralyzed. His heart pounded louder in his ears. His mouth felt dryer than sandpaper. He couldn't get enough air into his lungs. The edges of his vision began to close in until everything went black.

"His vitals are improving. That's a good sign. O-2 levels are going back up."

Nikki glanced at the masked nurse for only a moment. He watched Jerad like a hawk, waiting for him to regain consciousness. The man frustrated her beyond reason sometimes. How dare he put his life in danger like that?

His eyelids fluttered a few times before he finally came to. "Nikki?" He tried to sit up.

The nurse pushed down on his shoulders. "She's right here, Mr. Nebal. Sit back for me, okay?"

"I'm right here, Jerad." Nichole crouched by the side of the medical cot. She didn't know whether to kiss or smack the man.

He looked right at her as he reached out but didn't seem to actually see her. "Are you okay?"

"I'm fine. Can't you see me?"

"Not really. It's pretty dark in here. Can you turn on the lights?"

She glanced at the nurse. "Can you get a doctor in here ASAP?"

The nurse nodded before jogging out of the tent.

Nichole swallowed down the lump of panic in her throat as best as she could. "It's not dark in here, Jerad. Can you see me at all?"

He cupped her face. "Just barely." He lifted his head and kissed her.

She held on tighter, pressing her lips to his, trying to keep from sobbing. He was getting worse.

He spoke against her lips. "Ouch."

She leaned back and did a rapid search of his face and body with her gaze. "What's wrong?"

Jerad rubbed his arm where she'd held on to him. "Guess I have some bruises from being tackled."

"You'd have even more if those police officers hadn't caught you when you passed out with your hands cuffed behind you."

He moaned and fell back on the cot. "I'll be okay, Nikki. Just give me a minute."

She held onto his hand. "Why did you risk yourself like this, Jerad?"

He lifted his head, looking at her as if she were crazy to not understand his why. "I didn't know what was happening to you. How could I not, Nikki?"

She felt like the Grinch at Christmas, whose heart doubled in size. "Well, it was a pretty stupid thing to do." She kissed the back of his hand to lighten the sting of her words. The man took too many risks.

He dropped his head and pressed his thumb and forefinger against his eyes. "I'm sorry. I just needed to know you were all right."

"If you could see me, you'd see how livid I really am, but also how much I adore you for it." She let go of his hand and went to the tent opening. Where was the nurse with that doctor?

He dropped his hand and blinked. "My vision is clearing." He pushed up on his elbows. "See? I'm okay."

Nichole crossed her arms. "You could have exposed yourself to whatever this is, Jerad. You didn't see Robin. She looked horrible. And no one will tell me if she's okay or what's going on."

He swung his legs to the ground and sat on the cot. "That's why I had to get to you, Nikki."

His eyes pleaded with her. How could she stay mad at him? She sat down next to him and leaned her head against his shoulder. "I know. I just can't lose you again."

She didn't intend to say the words. They just slipped out.

Jerad shifted to sit across from her on the next cot as he cupped her face. "You're not going to lose me again. I promise. I'm not going anywhere."

Tears pricked her eyes as she nodded.

Thankfully, Jerad saved her from having to say anything by kissing her. She held onto his shoulders as if she were holding on for her life. And he kissed her like his life depended upon it.

The sounds of a throat clearing broke the moment. "I see the patient has improved."

Nichole glanced up. A man in a hazmat suit with the headgear pushed back and a stethoscope around his neck stood just inside the tent. "Sorry. I was just scolding him for putting himself in danger."

The doctor slipped his stethoscope into his ears and leaned over to listen to Jerad's heart. "Sounds like her scolding worked."

He straightened with a chuckle before looking at the nurse. "Blood work?"

"Just on her and it's clear so far." Her eyes took on a deer-in-the-headlights look as she glanced at Jerad.

The doctor pulled off his headgear, revealing a mess of salt and pepper hair. "He wouldn't be improving if he'd been infected. He'd be dead."

Nichole gasped. "Is everyone dead?"

Jerad held her hand.

The nurse had handed the doctor a chart. He looked at them from under his brows. "Just about. A few are in isolation at the main hospital. Looking for someone else?"

"Yes, a dear friend. She was already on the cancer floor. We came to help with Clown Day."

The doctor's face lit up as he lowered the clipboard he held. "Oh, the Strauss Foundation."

"Yes, Nichole Strauss. At your service. Any chance you can find out how she is?"

He shot a grim look at the nurse. "I'll see what I can find out. In the meantime, I'm going to have the nurse draw blood from your friend there to see what might be causing his issues."

Jerad held out his hand. "Uh, no need. We already know the cause."

The doctor crossed his arms as if he were about to hear something he'd heard before. "Do you now?"

"He was poisoned," Nichole said it at the same time Jerad did.

The doctor did a double-take. "Aren't you two a lively pair?"

Jerad quirked a half-smile. "It's a long story and my doctor is fully aware. About our friend?"

"I'll call over now, but..." He shook his head. "Whatever this is, it's almost one hundred percent lethal."

CHAPTER FOURTEEN

DENVER, COLORADO

A private plane waited on the tarmac, courtesy of one of their US benefactors. Achem approached the plane, checking his phone again to see if Jerad had replied to his text. Nothing yet. He'd even tried calling Nichole's number, but after one ring it went to voicemail. With only the high-pitched whine of jet engines filling his ears at the moment, the lack of news made him a bit anxious.

No telling what may have happened. Or what he and Liran may be walking into in San Francisco. Their contacts there still hadn't received any updates from their sources. The CDC was holding this one close, they said. First Denver, now Pablo Alto. Despite the lethality of the plague variant, it seemed completely contained. But they weren't sure...

The pilot descended the few steps and approached Achem. "Mr. Mizrahi?"

Achem shook his hand. "Yes."

"Mr. Onk sends his regards and regrets that he could not come as well." The man spoke fluent English with a British accent and looked to be of Indian descent.

"Please convey our deepest gratitude to Mr. Onk." Achem glanced at Liran, who stood a few feet away, finishing a conversation with their people in Jerusalem to keep them updated. Hopefully, nothing eventful had happened there during their absence.

The man nodded as he smiled. "We are scheduled to depart in twenty minutes." He glanced at Liran. "I assume you and your counterpart will be ready?"

"Yes, of course. We'll board immediately."

The man nodded again before returning to the plane.

The Collective had been surprisingly quiet the last several days. And Nichole and Jerad hadn't mentioned any more contact from the infamous Mr. Tombs. But Achem knew it would only be a matter of time before the group inserted themselves again. That's what concerned him most. Along with the devastation unleashed by the mystery man wielding the staff.

Liran walked over to where he stood. "Our people in Jerusalem have heard no reports at all, but they're on alert."

"Interesting. Guess we can consider that good news."

Liran pocketed his phone. "For now at least."

"The pilot is ready for us to board."

Liran fell into step next to him. "Any news from Jerad?"

Achem shook his head. "Not yet."

As they approached the small plane, Liran's cell buzzed from the side pocket of his pants. "Could be important." He pulled his phone out, glanced at the screen, and gave Achem a furtive glance.

Achem paused; one foot on the first step. "What is it?"

Liran hesitated. A wall seemed to go up between them. "A text from Eben."

"What does he want?"

"I don't know. He just says it's urgent."

Achem studied him a moment. "Call him quickly. We have little time to spare."

As he called his brother, Liran stepped further away from the jet with his free hand against his ear to block the noise.

Telling Liran to call his brother went against his better judgment at the moment, but after what happened earlier, Achem had to make sure Liran didn't feel the need to conceal anything. Yet a dozen scenarios raced through Achem's mind. And none of them were good. With Eben, it could be almost anything. The lad always had a penchant for the dramatic.

Achem leaned into the plane to check the cockpit. The pilot glanced over his shoulder at him, his smile not quite as big as before. Achem would have to tell Liran to wrap it up. He called out but couldn't hear his own voice over the 747 that had started its taxi down the runway.

Sensing a growing urgency, he stepped back down to the tarmac.

FROM HIS VANTAGE POINT OF THE HANGAR, HE CAUGHT SIGHT OF Achem waving to him. The pilot must be ready to taxi. He pressed his hand harder against his other ear as he moved behind a small Cessna he hoped would help block some noise. "Eben, I can't hear you. You're cutting out."

"Don't...plane..." Crackling came over the line.

Plane? How did Eben know...

A surge of adrenaline spiked through him at the exact moment the thought came of danger.

He took off toward Achem, waving his arms and yelling. Achem had started to walk toward him. A fireball rose behind him just as the sound of the explosion reached Liran, sending him backward to the ground.

His next awareness was of the ringing in his ears, so loud he could only feel himself groan. Liran opened his eyes. A night sky lit by a fiery glow arched over him. He lifted his head, then regretted it. His head pounded louder. The last thing he remembered was running toward the plane.

Achem!

Liran pushed up on one arm. The world spun for a moment before settling into a smoky haze. Flames engulfed the private jet they were about to board. The faint whine of sirens pierced his muffled ears.

Achem lay on the ground nearby, unmoving.

Liran crawled over to him. "Achem." No response. He felt for a pulse...steady. "Achem, can you hear me?"

Achem started to stir. His eyes cracked open.

Liran waited for Achem to come to full consciousness.

Achem's gaze finally connected to his. His lips moved. "Liran..."

"Are you hurt?" Liran shifted into a crouching position. His body felt like a punching bag but nothing worse. And he was hearing things more.

"Are you?" Achem's sardonic tone relieved Liran's immediate concerns. Achem had taken more of the brunt of the explosion than he had.

"Nothing serious."

Achem rolled to his side toward the blazing wreckage. He propped himself up on his elbow. "The pilot...did he...?" He glanced over his shoulder at Liran.

"I don't think so." When Achem shook his head and pointed to his ears, Liran shook his head.

Rescue vehicles exploded on the scene in flashes of red and yellow. A fire crew began dousing the remaining flames with foam. EMTs ran toward them.

Liran hardly noticed the one examining him. He kept a keen eye on Achem to see if they discovered anything serious.

Once checked out, they let Liran get up on his own but insisted Achem needed to be taken to the hospital for further tests.

Liran followed the wheeled stretcher carrying Achem to an ambulance. As they passed the smoking wreckage, he overheard one of the firefighters yell out that they found one body—the pilot.

He lagged back a bit to see if he could pick up on anything more while keeping Achem in his peripheral vision. The fire truck captain approached the police officer in charge, holding the charred remains of something in his hand, but Liran couldn't make out what they were saying.

His brother's call must have been to warn them. But how did he know? Liran picked up his steps to climb into the back of the ambulance. He sat near Achem's feet as the paramedic rechecked his vitals. "Still stable. You're a lucky man." She glanced at Liran. "You too."

Achem gave her a weary smile. "I wouldn't call it luck."

She smiled back before moving forward to speak to the driver.

Liran moved closer to Achem so they could hear each other better. "This wasn't an accident."

"I know. I suspect we have the Collective to thank for this." Achem leaned back on the stretcher and was silent a moment. "Your phone call? What did Eben want?"

"I couldn't get a strong enough connection. He kept cutting out."

Achem lifted his head and frowned. "Did you hear anything he said?"

Liran hesitated to answer. "Just the words 'don't' and 'plane.' I think he was trying to warn us not to get on the plane."

Achem frowned. "But how would he know about our change of plans?"

Liran swallowed the knot of apprehension forming in his throat. "I don't know. I'm just grateful he got wind of it in time to warn us."

Achem rested his hand on Liran's shoulder. "We may have to consider the possibility that Eben's involved with them."

"Do you really think he would—" Liran returned to his previous perch when the paramedic returned.

Once at the hospital, he remained in the waiting area while they took Achem up for scans. He checked his phone for further messages from his brother.

Nothing. His finger hovered over the call button.

One way to find out.

But did he really want to know?

CHAPTER FIFTEEN

SAN FRANCISCO

Jerad settled into a cozy chair in his living room and laid his head back against the chair. Nikki had finally agreed to go home once she knew he was doing okay. Besides, Robin was the bigger concern at the moment, and Jerad was almost ashamed to admit he was glad it wasn't him for once.

Even though he promised her he would follow up with his doctor, he knew he wouldn't. What was the point? The doctor would just tell him what he already knew. The longer his condition progressed, the more he would suffer. And lose.

Right now he wished he could turn off his brain completely and be in ignorant bliss. He lifted his head and looked around the room. Television didn't interest him much at the moment. Then he spotted his sister's journals on the coffee table. Maybe he could make sense of her life since he was having no luck with his own.

He flipped open her last journal and allowed himself to delve into a mind he never fully understood. The guilt still rode him hard. Despite being twins, they hadn't developed the bond he'd heard a lot of twins had. And as they'd gotten older, the gap of minutes between them had grown to eons.

Maybe if he'd been a better brother—been around more—Leah would still be alive.

With a heavy sigh, he scanned the first page. Then another until he was transported back in time through his sister's words. Old sensations of college took him back to stuffy classrooms, arguing environmental issues with friends determined to change the world, and trips to Santa Cruz to walk the beach while holding Nikki's hand.

Several entries later, Jerad came to a page with the corner turned down—the first entry where she spoke of her faith in her new 'friend' to help her. He clearly remembered doing that to mark where he sensed her world took a nosedive when he first read them after her funeral.

His fingers shook slightly as he flipped to the next entry dated a mere two weeks before her death. Leah's handwriting appeared hurried and difficult to read. Her words made no sense, yet her growing pain riddled the page as if written in her own blood.

Over and over, she continued to mention *him*. Her words intimated friendship, but what existed between the lines implied borderline delusion. A complete and utter belief in this mystery man's ability to save her. From what, she didn't say. Her depression? What else could she mean?

His guilt gave birth to anger and frustration.

Why hadn't he tried to find out who this man was when he read this six years ago? No, instead he'd just walked away from it all. His grief and Nikki. But he'd made things right with Nikki. He could still do right by Leah and find out who this man was. Maybe he had tried to help Leah. Jerad had learned the hard way that a person's perspective didn't necessarily encompass complete truth.

As he closed the journal, he noticed a page stuck to the one he just finished. He separated the slightly puckered pages and found a final entry. A lump formed in his throat only surpassed by the knot in his gut.

Two lines: *No hope now. E failed me.*

Who was "E"? Had Leah meant to say "he"? Why hadn't he

noticed this before? But would it have made a difference if he had? He'd gone over her suicide a hundred times but never came up with anything different. What could he have done to save her?

Nothing. Absolutely nothing. But it had taken him several years to finally accept that reality. And to quit blaming Nikki for not being there that night.

Jerad forced himself to close the journal and replace it on the stack. Stone Abrams's business card sat next to them. He picked up the card.

He had two reasons to follow up with Stone. One, to see if the man could really heal him. And two, find out if he knew who Leah's mystery man was.

Two birds with one Stone. He laughed out loud as he reached for his phone.

STONE'S PHONE CHIRPED, BREAKING HIS PRAYER MEDITATION. The interruption sent a surge through his body and tensed his muscles. He growled, annoyed at himself for forgetting to silence his phone.

The screen revealed a text from Jerad Nebal.

Ready to move forward. What's next?

His pulse sped. This was a welcome interruption. He started to text back but checked the time. Why not keep it personal? He hit the call icon to dial Jerad directly.

"Well, that was unexpected." Jerad's chuckle came over the line.

Stone laughed as well. Best to keep things easy and comfortable. He'd learned that early on in his dealings with people. Worked to his advantage in the long run too. "I hope I'm not disturbing you. I'm glad to hear you want to move forward. Is Nichole on board?"

He found remembering names also seemed to establish a deeper trust too. Remembering Jerad's fiancée's name would help put them both at ease and move things along more smoothly.

"Yes, she is."

Stone detected a slight hesitancy there. If he had to work around Nichole, he could but preferred she be part of the process. They'd end up with a more believable testimony that way. "Are you sure about that?"

Jerad laughed again. "Yes, she'll be there. She's a little wary, but I reassured her I did my homework."

"You did?"

"Yes, I did a fair bit of research on you before we even met that day."

"Good, I'm really glad to hear that, Jerad. That means we have a much better chance at succeeding."

"It does?"

"Yes, trust is key for this process to work. I need to know you're willing to trust me, to trust me to heal you."

"I thought this was about trusting God." Jerad's voice had dropped in tone.

"It most certainly is. And that means trusting that God had given me the power to heal you. Is there anything else I can explain to help alleviate any doubts you may have?"

"Just help me understand how this will work. What's the procedure to all this?"

"No procedure really. Like I said when we met, come to the conference, and then we'll talk some more."

"More talk? Why not just pray?" Jerad chuckled.

Stone kept his tone light. "I think you seeing how I work in person will allow you to step onto a stage without doubts."

A stage? "Excuse me?"

"That's a key part of my success, Jerad. If you did your research then you saw the videos. This isn't just about my belief, it's also about pulling upon the belief of everyone in attendance."

"I didn't realize I would have to do that too."

"You don't have to, but I find that's part of the success in the healings I perform."

Jerad's pause lasted long enough to make Stone think he may have hung up. But this was his only way of making sure Jerad was fully vested. If he was willing to be uncomfortable on the front end, before even stepping into anything, then that meant he was dead serious about letting Stone help him.

"Jerad?"

"Yes, I'm here. Just thinking this over a bit. I wasn't expecting to be up front and center. I thought you'd just take us into a room and pray."

"I am. Just think of it as a big room with a lot of prayer warriors standing by. I know you want to be healed, Jerad. I know Nichole wants that too. Sometimes we have to be really uncomfortable to go after what we want. But that's why I want you two to come and observe first. Then you can make your final decision."

Risky, risky, risky...he knew he was pushing hard, but he had to know Jerad was invested. Too much was at stake now. This could be the breakthrough he'd been waiting for—his premier in a way. To bring a man sentenced to death back to life? He could see the audience's reaction now.

The risk was even higher for him. But making it would mean taking his plan and purpose to a whole new level of success and visibility on a more global scale.

Jerad's long exhale traveled over the connection. "Okay, then. We'll be there. I don't see any other brilliant options coming my way and my doctor isn't getting anywhere either."

Just where Stone needed him to be—out of options. "Then I'm your guy, Jerad, your last hope, it seems. I won't let you down."

CHAPTER SIXTEEN

NEVADA

By the time they left the hospital, it was nearly dawn. They headed back to the hotel to retrieve their bags and arrange a rental car, which the concierge was happy to help them with when Liran explained they'd been 'innocent bystanders' at the airport explosion everyone was talking about. Naturally, the man understood their desire to avoid flight travel after witnessing such a thing.

But the truth of the matter was they no longer knew who they could trust. Their benefactor, Mr. Onk, had become unavailable, giving them both pause for thought. And the pilot...a somberness had settled on Achem especially as they both grieved the loss of an innocent life. Had the explosion been a setup on the highest level of their network? Someone who knew of their plans had leaked the information. Eben's call alone confirmed that.

What else it might confirm, Liran couldn't fathom and he wasn't ready to travel down that train of thought. Instead, he suggested they take complete control of their own arrangements moving forward. For their sake and others. And they agreed to hold things tight for the remainder of their trip until they could investigate further who the source of the leak might be. The only ones they updated were Nichole, Jerad, and Mira.

Despite being cleared for travel, Liran wondered if they should have stayed in Denver one more night. Achem seemed wearier from a day of travel, despite Liran doing all the driving. They'd stopped just inside Nevada for the night, where Achem fell into a deep sleep almost immediately after dinner, while Liran booked a flat in San Francisco through an app that private individuals used to rent their residences. Another way for them to stay in anonymity.

Now, day two of their road trip, he could tell Achem was in a fair bit of discomfort from what the doctor had called minor injuries. No concussions, stitches, or broken bones. Just aches and bruises. Even Liran felt sore through most of his body, and he hadn't experienced as much of the explosion as Achem had. Plus he was twenty-nine years younger.

Liran crossed his arms, waiting for the gas pump to pop, signaling a full tank. His phone vibrated in his pocket. A burst of excitement went through him when he noted Mira's name on the screen. Had she forgiven him for being such a lug head? She'd never replied to his text.

He accepted the call. "Mira, it's good to hear from you."

"Are you surprised?" Her voice sounded throaty over the connection.

He checked the time on his watch. Nighttime in Jerusalem but not too late. "Maybe. You never replied to my text. I'd begun to think you didn't want to talk to me again."

"Why in the world would you think that, Liran Dakarai? Have we not been friends for a long time?"

"Yes, but I wasn't exactly friendly last time we, uh, chatted."

"You mean kissed."

"Yes...and I'm very sorry for that."

"For what? The kiss or your attitude?"

She really didn't pull any punches where he was concerned. And oddly, he kind of liked it. "The attitude of course."

Her soft laughter tickled his ears. "Then we're making progress."

What exactly were they progressing to though? Doubts still pestered him about what or who he could be to Mira after her involvement with his brother. So part of him wanted an answer to that question before moving forward. Yet part of him didn't, because he wanted to rush in for once and not worry about the potential meaning or consequences.

"Stop overthinking it, Liran."

He laughed. "How do you do that?"

"Do what?"

"Read my mind."

"I'm a woman." She laughed. "No, actually, I know you. I know how you think and operate. So trust me when I say I have no intention of using you to fill the space Eben vacated." She paused. "After he left, it didn't take me long to realize he never really occupied that space in my heart, Liran. I'd developed an...attachment to someone else."

"Are you implying that's me?"

"Yes, you blockhead."

"Why didn't you say anything sooner?"

Her time to let loose a lengthy sigh. "If I had said anything to you after Eben left, would you have believed me?"

"Probably not."

"Exactly. Even after a year I knew you might think I was on the rebound, but I hoped you would believe me."

He leaned over to check on Achem through the driver's side window. He sat in the passenger seat with his head back and eyes closed. "How about I believe you from this point forward?"

"Deal."

He lowered his voice. "Then I can say I will look forward to getting home even more than usual."

"I'm glad, Liran. Just be careful, okay?"

He felt himself frown. "Are you worried about me?"

"Of course I am, but I have to confess I had another reason for calling."

"Oh?"

"Something interesting happened. I'd intended to give my notice at work but before I could say anything, my boss offered me my own accounts and a raise."

"I assume you turned his down." Silence met his statement. "Mira, please tell me you told him no."

"How could I? This might give me more access to whatever Artemis Tombs is doing with the Collective. This brings me to my real reason for calling. I truly hate to be the bearer of bad news, but..."

She sounded downright pained. "What is it, Mira?"

"You two were right about Mr. Onk, Liran. I swiped some files from my old workstation before they moved me and I can confirm his involvement with the Collective. There's more, I just haven't had a chance to finish digging."

"Mira, are you sure you're safe?"

"Yes, I'm fine. I was careful. My boss thinks I'm eager to please. For the most part anyway."

"What aren't you saying?" His entire body tensed with the mental image of her in danger. And he could do nothing to help her since he was thousands of miles away. He found the thought intolerable.

"I don't know if I'm being paranoid, but something he said made me wonder if this was all a play to gain my loyalty somehow."

"Mira, please be careful. I'd feel much better if you'd just resign. Something sounds off."

"I promise I'll be careful, but don't you see? This gives me a way in. I can do more to help you and Achem."

"Yes, of course." A silent pause on both ends gave him a moment to think. "I'm just concerned about the risks you're taking."

"I know, but right now you and Achem are the ones in danger. And that's why I need to do this."

He'd become so engrossed in what she was saying that he didn't notice Achem had gotten out of the car and stood next to him, pointing at the phone with raised brows. "Mira, Achem is here now. I'm putting you on speakerphone so you can fill us both in."

Her voice went up an octave with her concern. "Achem, how are you doing?"

"On the mend, my dear. I hear you have some information for us."

"Not a lot but enough to confirm Mr. Onk's involvement with the Collective. I told Liran I got a promotion at CBS, so I'm going to stay a little longer and see what else I can dig up for you."

Achem shot a concerned look at Liran. "You're what?"

"Liran will fill you in. There's more data here that I need to go through, so be careful. Their network is bigger than I realized. You can't trust anyone at the moment."

SAN FRANCISCO

Once they dropped their bags at their rental flat, Achem called Nichole's cell. It went straight to voicemail again. He dropped the phone in his lap and stared out the passenger window of their car as Liran navigated onto the freeway.

"Still no answer?"

"No." He propped his elbow on the door, holding his fist to his mouth. All day yesterday, neither Nichole nor Jerad had been reachable. Something was wrong. He could sense it in his gut. But he didn't need discernment to know that.

Nichole had sounded cryptic when they'd explained what happened in Denver, and he'd urged her and Jerad to stay alert. The Collective had upped their plan to dangerous levels and felt they couldn't trust anyone in their own network, which Mira confirmed for them. He thanked Yahweh for her aid and prayed for her protection.

"We'll be there within thirty minutes. I'm sure we'll find out more once we get there."

Achem moved his fist away from his mouth. "If they're even there. I'm concerned something has happened with Jerad. The man can be a wild cannon at times."

Liran chuckled.

Achem shifted in his seat to see him better. "Are you seriously laughing at me?"

Liran's smile dropped faster than a boulder from a cliff. "Sorry. It's just that...I've never seen you this unsettled."

"And that amuses you?" Achem tried to contain his own laughter, yet failed.

"I rest my case." Liran glanced at him, smile back in place.

Achem shook his head. When had things spun so out of his control? That alone should make him laugh like a hyena. In reality, he knew he controlled very little. He trusted Yahweh with his prayers and His power to work in all situations, but fully understood that never meant controlling the free will of another person.

Traffic allowed them to get to the Strauss Foundation in record time—something working in their favor for once. Liran parked on the back side of the building and shut the car down. Achem gingerly worked his way out of the passenger side. Even the short ride had allowed his sore muscles to grow stiff.

Once inside the building, Achem approached the security desk. "I'm here to see Nichole Strauss."

"I'll call up and see if she's here." The uniformed man looked to be in his forties. Former military or ex-cop. Nichole must have felt the need to beef things up since they were there last. Or had the Collective exerted more pressure of late?

Achem leaned against the high-top counter.

The security guard replaced the phone handset on the base. "She'll be right down."

They strolled to the elevator area to wait for her. A bell dinged announcing the arrival of people. The doors slid open. Nichole and

Jerad stood inside, waiting only long enough for the doors to fully open.

Nichole strode to stand in front of Achem. A wildfire blazed in her hazel eyes. "I'm done."

Liran started to move forward, but Achem held his arm out. He glanced at Jerad for some clue as to what Nichole meant, but he tucked his hands in the top of his jeans pockets and nodded her direction, as if to say 'listen first.'

"Done with what, my dear? Please tell me what's happened." He reached for her hand but she stepped out of his reach.

"With you and your whole *Natsar* regime. I've lost too much, Achem. Too much!" Her bottom lipped quivered and tears pooled in her eyes.

The disdain in her gaze was like a dagger to his heart, but he saw more there. Deep grief. He ached to make things better. But he had to know what happened first. "What can I do to help?"

Her tears reached the limit of containment and slipped down her cheeks. "You can't fix this, Achem." As her shoulders shook with her sobs, Jerad came up behind her and tried to pull her into his embrace.

She shrugged him off. "No! He needs to know." Now she faced him. "Robin is dead. Whatever that staff thing is, it's killing anyone who comes near it. So you and Liran can go chase it on your own." She grabbed Jerad's hand. "He's all I have left now, and I will not let you take him from me too."

CHAPTER SEVENTEEN

Part of her still wanted to slap him across the face. The other part of her wanted to collapse in his arms like she used to do with her father when she was a little girl. She knew her anger was running fierce at the moment. But did she really want Achem out of her life for good?

Robin had always been like family to her. Reminded her of family. Treated her like family. Every time she thought of Robin and seeing her whisked away, her resolve stood firm. She's lost too much. Her mother, her father, and now Robin. Achem and his *Natsar* agendas only seemed to bring death in their wake.

But he was also like a father to her. Could she walk away from that? She buried her face in Jerad's shoulder and wrapped her arms around his waist.

"Nichole, I am so sorry." Achem's voice sounded rough, thick with emotion.

She refused to look at him because she didn't want to cave in her resolve. She had to be firm this time. She clenched the back of Jerad's shirt in her fists. Enough was enough.

Jerad stroked her hair. His voice rumbled in his chest against her ear. "We just got the call about Robin right before you arrived. We're still processing."

Nichole lifted her head. She wiped at the wet marks left by her tears on Jerad's shirt before turning to face Achem again. She bounced her hand back and forth between them. "I'm sorry too, but I just can't do this anymore." Then she stopped and stared at him. She shifted her gaze to Liran and studied him too. Both of them had scrapes and bruises on their faces. She could very well have lost Achem too. Too much death.

"You two look awful." Another sob choked her voice. She pressed her fingers against her mouth until she regained control. "I just can't be involved in this anymore."

As she started to turn away, Achem dared a step toward her. "I'm sorry to say you have no choice, my dear."

She stopped and let her shoulders and head slump. Would she ever get away from the death and destruction that had dominated her family? She spun around. "What now?"

Liran had moved to stand next to Achem. "We know for certain now that the Collective was behind the bomb."

Jerad had stepped forward and inserted himself between her and Achem. His tone inflected disbelief. "To what gain?"

Achem shrugged. "I assume they thought it would make things easier to get what they want if I was out of the way." He sent a telling glance at Liran.

What exactly was he not saying? Didn't matter. She'd heard enough. She stepped out from behind Jerad. "This is what I mean. I don't want any part of it anymore."

Achem nodded again. "I understand, Nichole, and as much as it would break my heart to give you what you want, I would be more than willing to do so, except for one thing."

"And what's that?"

"I made a promise to your father to protect you. And as long as the Collective is at work, we're all in danger. That means my job is not done."

Jerad had somehow managed to get everyone upstairs and out of earshot of prying ears. Quitting time had come for several of the other businesses in the building, and people were moving about the building more. Bad enough that the security guard had overheard everything, but at least Jerad knew the guy would keep what he heard to himself.

Benny had signed a confidentiality contract with the job and, as ex-military, Jerad knew he'd honor it. And in light of this recent event with Achem and Liran, he was glad he hadn't argued harder to talk Nichole out of hiring him after the Collective had become more intrusive.

Now they sat in the conference room in the Strauss Foundation offices. Alone. When they got the news about Robin, Nikki had sent everyone home. An eerie silence filled the room making the air feel stale and close.

Nikki pushed out of her seat. "I'll grab some water for us."

Even from behind, Jerad could tell she was bone-weary. He shifted his attention across the table to Achem and Liran. "I'm glad you two are okay."

Achem clasped his hands on the table. "As are we, that you and Nichole escaped the effects of the staff."

Something in Jerad's gut twisted. He leaned forward, surprised by the sudden intensity of his own emotion. "Only because she told Robin to go ahead while she moved the SUV out of the main entrance area. Do you realize how close we came to losing her too?"

Hands splayed on the table, Liran kept his eyes diverted. "We are fully aware of the ramifications."

"Are you?!" Jerad came part way out of his seat with his words. "Who else has to die to make this stop?"

Nikki stood in the doorway, two bottles of water in each hand.

As he sat back, he met her gaze. No words were needed to see her appreciation for standing with her. She rounded the table and sat back down as she placed the water on the table.

Another band of silence wrapped the room until finally Nichole leaned forward. "What do we need to do to end this?"

Achem glanced at Liran before continuing. "The Collective is after the Ark and its elements. They've made that clear. What better way to force the issue than by attaining the staff. We need to find it before they do."

Jerad tilted his head. "What's their end game?"

Achem raised his brows. "To wreak international havoc and chaos."

Nichole took a drink from her water bottle. "But then the Ark, the manna jar, *and* the staff would be revealed to the world."

"I dare say that's been their plan all along." Achem sat back in his chair with a grimace.

The thought didn't bring much comfort to Jerad. "To what end?"

"Become the power in control of the objects of the Ark. A savior of the world, you could say."

Jerad shook his head. "Do you have any leads on who has the staff?"

"We have a theory." Achem turned in his chair to face Liran. He tilted his head at the young man, prodding him to speak up.

Liran licked his full lips and balled his hands into one fist on the table. "We...I think it's my brother."

LIRAN MENTALLY FORMULATED HIS WORDS. HE'D HAD ONLY A little time to figure out how to explain his suspicions so he touched lightly on details to explain his brother's disassociation with the *Natsar* and his most recent contacts with Liran.

Leaning forward, Jerad rested his arms on the conference table. "Did Eben share anything with you during your sabbatical to clue you in that he could be involved with the Collective?"

Liran shook his head. "Nothing that set off alarms. Just what he'd shared in the past..." He cautioned a glance at Achem, who gave a quick nod to go ahead. "That he disagreed with the *Natsar's* stance to keep the Ark and its elements a secret."

"Even after hearing what happened with the manna jar?" Nichole's expression turned to surprise when he nodded. "Wow. He sounds intense."

"That's an understatement." Liran blurted the words before he realized what he was saying. But Achem nodded his agreement with his words.

Nichole sighed. "I still don't understand what it all really has to do with Jerad and me."

Achem cleared his throat. "One, my hope had been that discovering and attaining the staff would lead to restoring Jerad's health and—"

"Oh, no, that's not happening." Nichole shot up from her chair. "You're not bringing that thing anywhere near Jerad. Everyone who's come in contact with it has died."

"Except for those who were sick. Like the little boy in Egypt." Achem's tone was gentle but even Liran could tell that was not going to have much impact on Nichole's decision. And he couldn't say he disagreed.

Jerad held out his hand. "That's what they're saying about the children at the hospital here. Several were cured."

Nichole shot him a frown. "You're not a child."

He quirked a grin at her. "You sure about that?"

Achem held a finger up. "And the woman in Denver in need of a heart transplant."

She growled in her throat.

Jerad reached out and clasped her hand.

"As I was saying, and two, the Collective has already involved the Strauss Foundation. Just because you decide to cut connection with the *Natsar* won't let you off the hook with them. They clearly know about the long association we've had and plan to use your father's legacy to manipulate you to get to us. As they already are doing." Achem swept his hand as if gesturing toward a descriptive picture of the entries into the scenario.

Nichole dropped back into her seat. "I hate this."

The weight of the implications hit Liran in the chest and tightened like a vice. If his brother was the one behind the staff and its destruction, Liran would have to somehow make him see the consequences of his actions. Eben was never good at that though. He plowed through life without a care for how it affected others. Would he see things any differently this time?

His brother had never mastered humility. Liran would have to somehow convince Eben the power of the staff was warping his mind. Perhaps then he would be more willing to turn it over and realize the necessity for the Ark and its element to remain a secret.

Maybe...

"Liran, you seem lost in thought." Achem had leaned forward to stare at him. "Hatching a plan for our next move, I hope."

He shifted his gaze from Achem to Jerad, then to Nichole. A resolve formed in his mind as he spoke. "We need to find Eben. I know he's in the States. He's intimated this twice now. If he has the staff, we take it and make sure it's safely with the Ark. The Collective won't be able to touch it then. Or you."

Nichole pinned him with a fierce stare. "I hope you're right, Liran. Everything seems to ride on you and your brother right now."

Liran swallowed the weight of her words and nodded. He hoped he was right too.

CHAPTER EIGHTEEN

HEALING CONFERENCE, SACRAMENTO

They approached the conference center's main entrance. Nichole scanned the scene, noting the steady flow of people streaming into the doors, the excitement of some who congregated in small groups just inside the entrance, and the steady beat of instrumental music playing in the background of the concert hall.

"It's a free event, so where did Stone tell you to check-in?" Nichole studied Jerad's face to gauge where he was at in all this. She'd agree to come mostly because she understood it mattered to Jerad. More than she expected. But in light of the threat of the staff and the unsuccessful attempts to treat his condition medically, she held a tiny hope that this Stone Abrams was the real deal.

Her concern lay in the fear that she was grasping onto something crazy in the hopes it could work. Had all the death and loss in recent events made her that desperate? Her emotions still felt too raw to makes sense of anything.

"He said to look for his assistant. She's wearing a pink hat. She's keeping an eye out for us too." His voice was quieter than normal and his expression stern. She sensed he was on edge to some degree too.

Nichole slipped her hand in his. "Should I have worn a hat too? A big floppy purple one?"

His eyes closed with his laugh, crinkling the corners and softening his expression. "Do you still have that hat?"

"Actually, I do. One of the things I kept from our first date."

His green eyes caught hers. Surprise mixed with a hint of delight registered there as he held her gaze. And gratitude. "Thank you for not giving up on me."

She felt her cheeks warm with a sudden and unexpected shyness. "I'm kind of tenacious that way. Even when I think otherwise."

He gave her a quick kiss. "I know."

"Mr. Nebal?"

They turned toward the female voice to find it attached to a petite woman with a bright pink hat. More like a skull cap actually. A purple flower adorned the front with edges that looked hand-stitched as part of the design. Her T-shirt had the conference logo splashed across the front and her jeans had patches to match her hat. She held a yellow clipboard and couldn't have been more than twenty years old.

"Jerad, please." He held out his hand. "You must be Rachel."

The young woman nodded. "Yes." She shifted her attention to Nichole. "And you must be Nichole, right?"

"That's me," Nichole answered with an enthusiasm she didn't feel. But for Jerad's sake...

"Great. I have special seats reserved for you. Just follow me."

Rachel headed toward the stage, then turned left at the end of the aisle. The entire front row on that side had sheets of paper on the seats with 'reserved' in capital letters. Rachel led them to the first two. She grabbed the signs off the seats.

"Front and center I see." Jerad flashed a nervous smile before craning his neck to look around and take in more of the room.

"I hope that's okay. Stone said he wanted you to feel welcome."

Jerad tucked his hands into the top of his jeans pockets. "Certainly feeling some of that. Did he want to talk before things get started?"

Rachel clutched the clipboard to her chest. "He said to tell you that during the break after this first session, he'd meet with you and the others backstage."

"Others?" Nichole's own unease presented itself in twinge in her stomach.

Rachel's smile expanded. "Yes, there are usually several people at each conference that have sought out Stone. But no worries. He makes time for everyone." With that, she turned and sprinted back the way they came, clearly on another mission to find more of Stone's intended guests for the other reserved seats.

Nichole settled into the aisle seat, tugging Jerad down next to her. "Guess we sit and watch for now."

Jerad didn't say anything. Just sat and stared up at the stage as various people wearing the same type of T-shirt Rachel wore, scurry about doing their assigned jobs. More people filed in. While Rachel continued to seat people in the front row, a team of musicians began to position themselves on the stage.

Sitting forward in his chair, Jerad rubbed his hands back and forth across his jeans.

Nichole clasped his left hand. She hadn't seen him this worked up in a while. Would his heightened nerves set off a seizure? "Would you rather leave?"

He squeezed her hand and sat back. "No, sorry. I guess I'm nervous."

She squeezed back. "You think?"

"I'll be okay once it gets started." He ran his other hand over his mouth.

She continued to study Jerad a moment before allowing herself to take in the rest of the auditorium. The whole thing felt...strange.

The lights dimmed and the musicians began to play their instruments. The vocalists stood silent, moving their bodies to the beat of the music. With a sudden burst of moving lights, the singers burst into movement, moving to the front of the stage, and broke into song.

The drums kept a steady yet growing rhythm with action, building in intensity with the song. Nichole felt the pull of the rhythm and the beat, as did many others who now moved to the open area between the front seats and the stage. Many had their hands up in worship.

The drums seemed to intensify, coaxing more emotion and reaction from the crowd. Nichole felt it pull on her soul and her spirit. She glanced at Jerad. He seemed cautiously engaged, but did he feel it too?

The voices stopped, as did the other instruments. Only the drums continued to play and build in intensity. Anticipation grew in the room, as did excitement. Nichole could only focus on the stage as her own anticipation grew to meet the crowd's.

The bass drum exploded when a man strode from stage right and stopped, engaging the crowd on that side. More lights flashed. A low fog moved across the stage. Quite the show, which seemed such an odd thing to do for a healing conference yet Nichole felt herself being swept up into the force of the event.

She leaned her head toward Jerad. "Is that Stone?"

"Yes." Jerad stared at the man too, seeming as enrapt as those around them.

Nichole waited for Stone to move to the center to get a better look at his face. As he strode to the center microphone waiting for him, a wave of déjà vu swept over Nichole. The man's face, the stage, the drums. Suddenly she was thrust back into the vision she'd had that day in the presence of the manna jar and had dreamed—and dreaded—ever since.

She tried to say Jerad's name but her voice caught in her throat. And when she turned to look at him, he wasn't next to her anymore. He stood closer to the stage, mesmerized by the man front and center.

Dread rose in a wave of nausea that pushed Nichole back into her seat.

What on earth was happening?

❧

WHEN THE DRUMS STOPPED, JARED FELT A SNAP BACK TO reality. He glanced at his watch, shocked to see that nearly thirty minutes had passed. The people around them seem to be rousing from a daze similar to his as they returned to their seats. He looked to his side, expecting to see Nikki, but instead found her sitting with her head in her hands.

He rushed over and sat next to her. "Nikki, are you okay?"

Nikki lifted her head and stared at him. "Yeah. Just feeling a little dizzy."

He reached out for her hand. "Do you want to leave?"

"No, I'll be fine." She gave him a weak smile. "Let's hear what else Stone has to say."

He settled in his chair as the stage crew removed various pieces of equipment and set up an acrylic podium and a high-top stool. For the next thirty minutes Stone spoke about the healing movement and what his part in it was about. He rarely used the stool and podium, instead, moving back and forth across the stage as he engaged each side of the room.

Most of it sounded very similar to what Stone had already shared with him at their lunch meeting, but seeing the man in action gave Jared a whole new perspective of who Stone Abrams was.

And a glimmer of hope that he could actually be a conduit of healing for Jerad. Once the session ended, Stone's assistant Rachel came whipping to the front to address the entire row of reserved seating guests. "Mr. Abrams would love for you to join them in the back room for a brief Q&A. Please follow me."

As the chairs emptied, Jerad tugged on Nicole's hand to hold her back. "What did you think of what he had to say?"

"It's interesting, I can say that." Confusion shuttered her eyes as she searched his face. Or was it concern? "Let's go see what else he has to say."

The room mirrored a smaller version of the main hall. About thirty seats had been set up in rows with a small aisle down the middle. In front, another smaller podium in clear acrylic. Stone stood there, smiling and waving people in. "Please, come in. Sit. Make yourselves comfortable."

The majority of the crowd had already found seats. Jared and Nikki sat in the back row, which seemed to put Nikki more at ease. And he couldn't blame her. The whole thing seemed so surreal.

Stone swiveled his head from one side in a slow sweep. His smile never faltered either. The man looked almost like a kid getting his first bicycle. "I'm so glad you came today. My greatest desire is to see you all healed of whatever is ailing you."

Several raised their hands. Stone seem quite in his element as he graciously answered each one, even those that carried heavy skepticism. Which he could understand, but did that make him a skeptic? Or overly cautious?

At one point, he focused on Jerad with a small nod and then shifted his gaze to Nichole. For a brief moment, his eyes lingered on her and his smile slipped a margin. Jerad looked over at Nikki to see her reaction.

She stared back at Stone, her eyes as rigid as her back.

Jerad had been under that gaze before. Reminded him of the first day he stepped into the doorway of her office to tell her about Ranjit's death. She'd stared him down like a lioness then too.

Stone seemed to regain his composure as he focused on another question from a woman in the front row.

Leaning toward her, Jerad dropped his arm around her shoulders so he could whisper. "Care to share what's eating you, because you look like you want to tear the man to shreds."

She blinked as she looked at him. "I'll tell you later." She then gave him a smile that was less believable than her last reassurance that she was fine. He could still read the woman better than she realized. He already sensed the ride home would be anything but peaceful.

Rachel had come to the front and spoke something only for Stone to hear. Then he nodded. "All right, everyone, please enjoy the refreshments we've provided. The next session will start in twenty minutes."

As people rose and mingled, Stone headed their way. Jerad took a deep breath and mentally prepared for Nikki's reaction to Stone.

"Jerad!" Ever smiling, Stone shook Jerad's hand. "So glad you both could come." He shifted his hand and attention to Nikki. "And this must be Nichole."

To his surprise, Nichole smiled as she shook his hand. "Yes, that's me."

Jerad didn't miss the nervousness in her voice. And she didn't say anything else.

Stone sent a questioning look at Jerad. "Anything I can do to put you two at ease? You didn't ask any questions during the Q&A."

"Still processing it all, I think." Nichole kept a polite demeanor, which was not the reaction he'd expected at all.

"How about you, Jerad? Any questions?" Stone seemed to ask Jerad the question as an insertion of his presence into the situation. He could almost feel Nikki bristle next to him. She picked up on it too.

"Same, still processing. But I'd like to understand more."

Stone's smile grew as he patted Jerad on the arm. "That's great! Glad to hear that. I'd really love it if you'd give me a chance to help." His focus now settled on Nikki. And his expression seemed to be a plea for her to give him a chance.

Nikki shot a nervous glance at him before answering. "I'm here to support Jerad. Whatever he feels he needs."

Jerad could almost hear the sound of shutters closing as she clasped his hand and put on a wax smile. Something about this really didn't sit well with her. He kept searching through his own reactions to the first part of the conference and could find nothing that seemed off-kilter. Not that he could remember much detail of the beginning. The music and drum rhythm had had a mesmerizing effect on most there. Maybe Nikki's ordeal with Robin's death made this all too much for her.

A cell phone chirped nearby. Stone reached into his suit pocket. "Sorry. I don't normally even keep my phone on, but sometimes family issues require it." He frowned as he studied the screen.

Stone continued to stand there, studying his screen.

"Everything okay?"

As Stone registered Jerad's question, he appeared almost disoriented. "Yes, sorry about that." His smile returned though he seemed distracted. He shook Jerad's hand. "Nothing more powerful than a woman by your side to support and encourage." He strode toward the exit doors, waving Rachel to follow him.

Brows knitted with her own frown, Nikki watched him leave. "That was weird."

Jerad led her to the refreshment table. He handed her a bottle of cold water from the ice bucket. "Okay, what's really on your mind?"

She nabbed a cookie and took a bite. "I'm not sure you want to hear it."

"I wouldn't ask if I didn't want to know, Nikki. Come on, you know me better than that."

"Yes, but I know how much you want this too." She dropped the cookie into the trash. "Look, I want to support you in this but something isn't sitting right with me."

He held his hands out. "Then tell me what it is. Let's talk about it."

Something behind them seemed to catch her attention.

Jerad turned around. Stone stood on the opposite side of the room, watching them. He turned back around. "Okay, that's kind of...interesting."

She stared hard at him; as if assessing him.

"Just spill it."

She shifted her weight to one side. "Remember that day in the warehouse when I had that weird vision."

"Yeah, the one with the drums and the man on stage."

She arched her brows and did a pointed nod toward Stone.

"Him?"

She nodded.

He frowned. "Seriously?"

She leaned toward him, putting her hands on his chest. "That's him, Jerad. I'm sure of it. And when I had that vision, my gut said to run."

He already knew the answer but had to ask. "And now?"

Her eyes grew moist, reflecting the internal war she must be having to speak what he suspected already.

He tilted his head toward her coaxing her answer out.

She swallowed before whispering. "Run."

The next day Moses entered the tent and saw that Aaron's staff, which represented the tribe of Levi, had not only sprouted but had budded, blossomed, and produced almonds. —Numbers 17:8

DESECRATION

"We're running out of time." The man stared at the staff. The nodules had become full branches and now held delicate white blossoms with pink centers. Some of the blooms had dropped overnight and already revealed a small green promise of the almond to come.

"Why? What's happened?" Artemis Tombs asked the question like the thinker he was. Facts first. Action second. Only a fool made a move without the details, which only proved his ignorance. Delay was a sign of cowardice in his book. He'd learned that early on in life.

"Things have...developed." The players had moved into their places sooner than anticipated. But that wouldn't thwart his ultimate plan. If anything, he'd become a master at redirection.

Most attempted to adapt. He controlled.

"Then tell me what adjustments you'd like to make to our plan."

"Change the timeline. We need to move now."

"Do you think that's wise?" Even the ever-patient and calculating Tombs expressed exasperation at times, but to tell him more of the details would compromise the outcome.

"We need to show the world what this thing can do. Now."

"Have you managed to control it?"

"Yes, of course. I told you I could. It's in our blood."

Tombs cleared his throat. "Then I will make the arrangements."

"Good. I'm glad you agree."

"That's never been a question."

"That's good to hear, Artemis. Because things are going to get worse before they can get better. Much worse."

CHAPTER NINETEEN

SAN FRANCISCO

"Did he respond yet?"

Liran looked up from his phone. "No."

Achem kept his face relaxed. He didn't want Liran to see his unease over the whole situation. They'd yet to identify the leak within the *Natsar* organization, therefore could not bring in the level of help that was usually at their disposal. Not here. Not while on foreign soil. For the most part, he and Liran would have to rely on their own wits.

"Maybe he doesn't like the idea of meeting out in the open." Achem tugged back the curtain to check out the street below. San Francisco still remained a city in constant motion, much like New York but in different ways. But he still missed his city most —Jerusalem.

Liran sighed. "I dare say he's probably trying to figure out how to work the situation to his advantage."

Achem raised his brows. He hadn't expected Liran to be so forthright about his brother. "You really think so?"

"Yes, don't you?" He frowned at Achem.

"Yes, I have from the very start. I'm just surprised to hear you admit it."

Liran put his phone on the dining room table where he sat and held his head in his hands. "What's the point of trying to protect him anymore? If he has the staff, then there's not much I can do to stop him."

Satisfied that the street was clear, Achem left the window and joined Liran at the table. Should he tell him the truth now? He'd hoped for a more advantageous time to reveal such a deep secret, but perhaps this was the advantage that Liran needed now.

"That's not entirely true."

Liran lifted his head. "How so?"

Achem pulled out a chair and sat. "As I'm sure you recall there were originally twelve staffs."

"Yes, one for each tribe of Israel."

"Yes, but when they were placed before the Testimony, only one budded, blossomed, and produced almonds."

"The staff of Aaron, of course."

"That's correct. And Aaron was of the tribe of Levi, which became the priests to God from that day forward."

Liran nodded. "Yes, I know all that, but how does that help me stop Eben?"

Achem leaned forward, his hands clasped in front of him. "It was Aaron's staff, marked with the name of his tribe. I believe that only those descending from the tribe of Levi could activate the staff then and now."

At first, Liran frowned, but then as he seemed to grasp what Achem was saying, his eyes grew round. "Eben is able to wield the staff because he is a descendent of the tribe of Levi?"

Achem nodded. "As are you. It's in your blood."

FOR THE LAST HOUR LIRAN PACED BACK-AND-FORTH IN THE main living area, checking his phone each time he walked past the table. Achem had left to pick up supplies at the local grocery store a block away, citing he'd rather roam aisles than wait and watch Liran pace like a caged animal looking for an escape.

Desperate for some kind of explanation, his mind had scrambled for different explanations or scenarios to explain his brother's behavior. He'd never imagined his brother to be capable of murder.

Could the staff have that effect on a person? Like the manna jar had seemed to affect those who attempted to control its power? As boys, Eben had always looked out for him. Intervened when he needed help with a bully. Shared his life with Liran as family. Until their father died. Then he became more aloof, disappeared at times, and then finally left, disconnecting from everyone he knew and loved a little over a year ago. Could the discovery of the staff have been a precursor? That would explain his change in behavior.

Eben must be delusional.

But perhaps he didn't see the staff in that light. He'd always believed the relics were meant to be revealed for their greater purpose, but how did death serve the purposes of Yahweh?

Liran slammed his fist on the table. He could think himself in circles all day and all night but never find a solution. He needed to confront Eben and find out for sure if he truly had the staff.

And what he planned to do with it.

His phone buzzed on the table.

I will meet with you, brother. But only you. Do not bring Achem.

He studied the text. Achem would not approve, but what choice did he—they—have?

When and where?

Behind the Conservatory at Golden Gate Park. One hour.

Liran noted the time at the top of his cell screen. He'd leave Achem a note and leave right away. He knew the city well enough to know that would give him some time to scope out the area as well. Just in case his brother planned some sort of ambush.

He ran a hand over his face. Just the thought felt like a betrayal to his brother. He replied back.

I'll be there.

His thumbs hovered over the keypad, burning with the question he didn't dare ask but felt he must.

Achi, do you have the staff?

Come find out for yourself.

The implication of his brother's reply left him feeling unsteady. He slumped into a chair and began to pray. Only Yahweh would be able to help them now.

ACHEM LET HIMSELF IN THE DOOR AND SET THE GROCERY SACKS on the counter. He shrugged off his jacket and hung it over a nearby chair. The walk had more than warmed his bones.

"Liran, I'm back."

He started to unload the staples he'd purchased for them. Enough to hold them for a few days. "I noticed a grill on the back patio so I bought steaks. I haven't grilled in years."

No reply. For that matter, no sound at all came from the apartment. He put the butcher package of steaks on the counter. "Liran?"

He left the kitchenette and noticed a piece of paper on the table.

Eben insisted I meet him alone at the Conservatory in Golden Gate Park. Now that I understand what is activating the staff, I will try to get it from him and put a stop to all of it.

"No, no, no..." He grabbed his jacket and locked the door behind him. Liran could be walking into any manner of ambush, attack, subterfuge, or all of the above. How could he think he could handle this on his own? Perhaps telling him about his Levitical heritage had been a mistake. The last thing the lad needed was a false sense of confidence.

As he hit the street, he hailed a cab. Once inside he did a rough calculation of how far ahead Liran could be at this point. If his brother texted him right after Achem left, then Liran may already be at the park, meeting his brother.

Within twenty minutes they arrived at the east side of the park. The cab driver pulled over by the sidewalk leading to the conservatory. Achem handed the man twice the fare and launched out of the cab as fast as aching muscles would allow him. Yet nothing seemed fast enough in the moment.

Nor did he wish to draw a lot of attention to himself. A fair number of people roamed the outer garden areas. None of them Liran.

He headed toward the building. If he were Eben and had the staff with him, he wouldn't want a lot of eyes on him at this point.

Or would he? Could this be Eben's plan? Not about meeting his brother, but about exposing the staff to the world?

Suddenly everyone he passed looked like a potential victim of a deadly plague about to be released.

LIRAN TURNED THE CORNER AND FOUND THE BACK AREA EBEN had directed him to look for him. And there he was, his brother, looking as tall and powerful as he always did. Something in Liran steeled at that moment. Perhaps it was his resolve. Perhaps it was just his time. Or perhaps it was the long, slim black case that Eben carried —just the size he would imagine would hold the staff of Aaron.

If his gut could give off a warning siren, it would be deafening. He paused to catch his breath and his wits. He needed to be organized and prepared. As much as one could be in a moment of unimaginable and deadly power. He had no idea what Eben would do.

And as he drew closer to his brother, the look in his dark eyes confirmed that anything could happen, and he was almost one hundred percent sure it would be bad.

Eben smiled but his eyes stayed hard. "*Ach*, it's good to see you."

Liran kept his body loose and easy. No reason to let his brother know what was really going on inside of him. "And you too, brother. Though we just saw each other a few months ago."

"Yes, I know but much has happened since then." His eyes drifted to the case he carried.

As did Liran's. "So you do have it."

"I've had it in my possession for quite a while actually. I just was waiting."

"For what?" Had he known about the staff's location while he was still serving the *Natsar*?

"To see if the *Natsar*—Achem—would do the right thing."

Every muscle in his body tensed and his heart raced. He'd always considered his brother one of the most insightful people he'd ever known. How had he become so blind? "And releasing a plague that could potentially kill hundreds, thousands, or even millions of people is the right thing, Eben?"

Eben shook his head. "I'd hoped you'd be more open-minded, little brother. The staff discerns the righteous from the unrighteous. Just like our father said it would. It does not seek to release a global plague."

"Our father? He knew about the staff?"

A flash of the old Eben appeared for a moment in his facial

expression. "When he realized he was dying, he confided that he'd had an idea where it might be. We looked for it together—I was his legs. He wanted me to have it."

"Why? Why would he do that?"

Eben's almost malicious grin returned. "To prove a point. To prove Achem was wrong."

"About what?"

"Father and I agreed that the Ark and its elements were never meant to remain a secret. He also knew that because of our bloodline, we could wield the staff for good."

So Eben already knew what Achem has suspected. Because of their father. Everything he thought he knew about his father and their family began to crumble. But he'd mourn his losses later. Right now, he had to stop the monster his brother had become, thanks to his father and the staff. "But in your hands, it has killed indiscriminately."

"Only those found unworthy."

Liran took a step closer, throwing his hands out as he spoke. "Perfectly healthy people have died."

"Because they were sick morally, in their soul and spirit."

"Who are you to judge, Eben?" His question seemed to startle his brother. "Who gave you that right?"

"I'm not the judge. Yahweh is." Eben lowered the case to the ground and started to unlatch the locks.

"What are you doing?" Liran did a quick search of the area. Thankfully his brother had chosen a more secluded area. No one nearby that could be hurt. Or killed.

"I want to show you. The staff means only to heal those who are suffering." He lifted the staff up.

At first glance, it looked more like a young sapling with leaves and some blooms in need of a pot of soil. But then Liran could feel its pull on him. As if the power that pulsed through it reached out to include him in its deadly rhythm.

"It's okay, Liran. You can come closer. I know your heart. The staff won't hurt you. We could do so much good in this world together, *achi*."

Liran resisted its pull, Eben's pull. Tried to push the fog overwhelming his thoughts and reasoning, like a battle for his own will. He forced his body to move and closed the gap between them. The pulse of the staff grew stronger, beckoning. The delicate blooms intoxicated his senses with their honey-like scent. He started to reach out for it.

"That's right. Don't resist its call." His brother had lowered his voice to a soft caress.

Liran jerked his hand back. "*Ach*, you must turn it over to the *Natsar*. Can't you see the threat it poses?" He searched his brother's face for some hint of the man he once knew him to be.

Eben's expression turned hard and twisted. "No, you're the one that can't see its true purpose, to bring restoration to this world when it needs it most."

"Is that your plan, Eben? Or what you need?"

"What are you talking about?"

He'd pulled his punches long enough. Maybe his brother would respond better to the harsh truth. "Admit it, Eben. The only reason you wanted to lead the *Natsar* was to satisfy your need for power and fame. But our commitment to keep the Ark and its elements secret didn't fit that. So you decided to make your own platform and use the staff to get what you want."

His brother's face reddened with anger. He put the staff back into the case and slammed the lid, cutting off one of the branches as he did so. "You will never understand. Father said as much. That's why he never confided in you about it."

"I think he understands perfectly." Achem revealed himself from behind the corner of the building.

Liran shot him a warning look. He'd managed to only make Eben angry. Achem's presence would add fuel to the insane fire already consuming his brother.

Eben let out a derisive laugh. "Of course the *Natsar* puppet master wouldn't be far behind his puppet!" He pulled out his cell phone, unlocked the screen, and tapped something with his thumb in one fell swoop. "Always come prepared, *achi*. I thought you would have at least learned that lesson by now." He threw a sneer at Achem as if to say 'under his leadership.'

A team of men in suits emerged from places Liran hadn't even noticed, which rankled his self-perception of himself as a decently trained soldier. As they surrounded Eben, they unbuttoned their jackets to reveal concealed weapons. Illegal most likely, unless they were professionals.

Eben held the case containing the staff against his torso as another man in a finely tailored suit and rectangular spectacles moved to stand next to him.

Achem took a position next to Liran. "Artemis Tombs, I presume."

"Mr. Mizrahi, a pleasure to meet you in person." Tombs gave a respectful nod of his head. "I think Mr. Dakarai has made his point. We'll be leaving now."

Achem took a step forward, his hand out. "What exactly was that point, may I ask? A show of power?"

Tombs adjusted one side of his glasses. "Not at all. We'd hoped to give Mr. Dakarai's brother an opportunity to make a better choice and join our cause."

Liran could feel Achem bristle beside him. He clenched his jaw, along with his fists by his sides, ready to spew his retort.

Achem chuckled instead, which diffused his anger and seemed to increase Eben's. "Your cause? All I see happening is death and destruction. That seems more like terrorism in my book."

Eben jerked forward, but Tombs held him back. "Believe what you want, Mr. Mizrahi. It matters not to our *cause*." He drew out the last word for emphasis. "Though we are saddened by this stance, we will not be deterred from what we have set out to accomplish. Good day."

Then he turned and strode away with Eben. Their bodyguards followed close behind, scoping their area in a constant swivel of their heads. Within minutes they reached a row of three black

SUVs parked on the outer street running along the back side of the park. Though many heads turned their way, Liran imagined they assumed a government official or movie star had just walked in their midst.

If they only knew the truth...he was grateful his brother hadn't made that a reality. At least this time.

Achem walked forward and crouched by a branch laying on the ground. But he didn't touch it. "That was most enlightening."

Liran spotted a garbage can nearby. He tugged out a plastic grocery sack and used it to scoop up the specimen. "I'm surprised he left it behind."

Achem rose to his full stature. "I dare say that was his intent all along. To prove he had the staff and that he planned to wield it. He knew you'd never willingly join him."

He wrapped the bag around the branch, careful to encase the blooms and almond pods. "I felt the pull of its power, Achem. It would have claimed me too if I'd let it."

"What you said to your brother is completely true. But he also has an intense need to prove he's right and in control. Yet it would seem the Collective is in control of him."

Liran studied Achem, waiting for him to criticize him for meeting his brother alone.

Instead, Achem patted him on the arm. "Well done, Liran."

His voice left him as did his words but only for a moment. "I thought for sure you were going to scold me for going alone."

Achem smiled. "Well, let's just say my first reaction to your note was along those lines, but when I watched how you handled your brother, I knew you could handle yourself just fine."

"You watched?"

"Yes."

"And you don't think I made a bad decision to confront him like that?" He held up the sack. "All we have is this branch. The staff is still out there in his hands."

"True, but now we know for sure who has the staff, and better yet, we have that," he nodded at the bag, "to study and figure out how to counteract its effect."

"We're talking about the supernatural here. Do you think that's possible?"

Achem's expression grew somber. "I don't think we have a choice."

CHAPTER TWENTY

Nichole woke with a start. A new nightmare plagued her now. More like memories of the past spliced together in a haunting theme. No mystery man on a stage in this one. No, this time she knew the leading character and her demise; because it was all about Jerad's twin sister Leah.

Every time she lapsed back to sleep, the same scene repeated—finding Leah in her bathtub. But every time Nichole woke, she remembered more details surrounding Leah's death. Like the unused bottle of antidepressants in her medicine cabinet. Her claims that she was better than ever and finally free of her depression. And how Leah always seemed too busy to make plans, which Nichole realized now was Leah's way of avoiding her.

She's suspected Leah had fallen into some kind of cult but could never prove her gut feeling. And now Jerad seemed to be heading down the same path. She truly believed that God could heal people, at least she wanted to believe it, but something about Stone Abrams felt off. He came across more like a showman than a healer. More about himself than the higher power he claimed to be the true force behind his healing ability.

And the whole encounter had been so confusing too. Almost as if they had been drugged somehow...lured into some kind of mind control...

Jerad had said very little on the ride back to San Francisco. Maybe today she could gauge him better at the office and figure out what he was thinking. He didn't seem to want to share much afterward.

She grabbed her cell phone to check the time. Seven a.m. After a swim, she'd head to the office. Or, she had a better idea. She opened her text app and tapped Jerad's picture.

Want to meet me for breakfast?

THE THREE DOTS SHOWED HE WAS AWAKE AND REPLYING. THAT was a good sign. Unless he'd stayed up all night...

Sorry. Can't. Doing some follow-up blood work with the doc today.

Forgot to tell you about it yesterday. Nothing to worry about.

But she did worry. And she didn't know whether to believe him about forgetting to tell her. As Robin used to say, 'selective memory.'

Like a gut punch, it hit her how she just had that thought about Robin as if she were still alive. She flopped back on the bed, ignoring the stream of tears leaking down the sides of her face and soaking her pillowcase.

The one person she wished she could talk to the most right now was gone. And she couldn't talk to Jerad about Jerad. The thought almost made her laugh. At least that would be better than crying. She pushed herself out of bed and into her racer suit. A few laps and a lot of muscle burn would help her shake the funk and get on with her day. She still had to figure out how to undo the damage the Collective had caused to the Clean Water & Farm Project.

She threw a beach towel around her shoulders to protect herself from the morning chill and said a silent prayer of thanks again for the heated swimming pool in her apartment complex. As she walked out, she noticed a manila envelope sitting by her door.

No label. Nothing written on the outside. She opened the clasp and slid out the contents.

A single photo, showing her and Jerad with Achem and Liran. Taken while they were in Egypt. And it was attached to an article written by one of the more well-known reporters at the San Francisco Chronicle.

She scanned the copy. An exposé, to be specific, exposing the *Natsar* as the ones causing the plague outburst because of a relic discovered weeks earlier. Details included their connection to the Strauss Foundation as a way to give them access and ability to move and operate in the US.

The article went on to give supposed facts about the discovery of the staff of Aaron in Egypt by the *Natsar*, and their plan to target the United States first, thus the horrific events at the hotel in Denver and the children's hospital at Stanford. The article even relayed Nichole and Jerad's presence at the hospital when events happened.

Whatever strength she'd mustered to get moving fled her body, leaving her dizzy. Her vision started to narrow and her breathing shallowed out. She stumbled back into her apartment and to the closest seat to head off the panic attack.

Her hands shook as she dropped the article and envelope onto the table. She studied the picture as the implications settled in deeper. Someone had been tracking them from the very beginning.

Had to be the Collective.

And now they are taking things to the next level. She used her cell phone to take pictures of the article and send them to Jerad and then Achem, along with a brief message to read ASAP.

They were about to get taken down. She just didn't know

how far.

❧

JERAD SAT IN THE DOCTOR'S OFFICE. NOT AN EXAM ROOM, BUT the actual office where his doctor did his behind-the-scenes work. He drummed his fingers on the arm of the chair as he studied the room. Shelves of books, of course, along with models of various body parts to use as references.

A stack of files sat on the corner of the desk along with reference books and a closed laptop in the middle. To his right, he had a clear view of the sky overlooking the top level of the parking garage attached to the medical center. Just endless blue outside that window. No clouds. No rain. No storms.

If only life could be that peaceful and promising at the moment. He didn't expect his doctor's request to speak to him in his office meant he had good news. Jerad suspected quite the opposite.

The door opened. Dr. Truard entered, dressed in the traditional white lab coat and black slacks that matched his wavy hair. He sat down and scooted his chair up to the desk.

Jerad assumed the unopened file he set on his laptop was his. "Hi, Doc."

"Thank you for waiting, Jerad." Dr. Truard leaned on the folder.

He glanced at the file. "Any good news in there for me?"

Dr. Truard leaned back in his seat, leaving the file unopened. He sighed. "I wish there was." He rubbed a hand over his mouth.

Jerad had never seen this side of the doctor—unsure and hesitant. "Just shoot straight with me, Doc."

He nodded. "Okay. I asked you to wait so I could talk to the doctor in New York that I told you about, just to get his take."

"And?"

Truard tapped his fingers on the folder, eyes downward. "We agreed there was no point in you going to see him. There's nothing else he would do that we haven't already done."

Jerad digested his words for a moment. His hand felt sweaty on the arms of the chair. He rubbed them together as he made himself take in a deep breath. "I see. No other suggestions or thoughts? Maybe another specialist?"

Truard gave him a small smile. More like pity. "He's the best in this field, Jerad. We agreed that the poison did more damage to your brain than medical science is equipped to deal with. It's kind of like dementia and Parkinson's disease mixed with epilepsy in its effect. But the fact that the treatments for these kinds of diseases didn't work tells us there's a great factor in place that we can't identify yet. Not fast enough anyway."

"How long?"

He held his hand up. "We don't really know for sure, but based on your tests...not long."

He swallowed. Nodded. Fought the growing tightness in his chest that made him want to turn into a raving lunatic. All he could see was Nikki. All he could smell was her musky floral scent. All he wanted was a life with her.

And now the doctor was telling him that wasn't possible. Not through modern medicine anyway. He shot up and held his hand out to the doctor. "Thanks, Doc. Appreciate you trying."

Dr. Truard shook his hand from his seat, his expression holding some surprise. "Do you want to talk about making a plan?"

He noted how the doctor left out the 'end of life' part of that statement. "Can I get back to you on that?"

Truard stood as their handshake broke. "Sure. I'm here whenever you need me."

Jerad nodded and ruffed out a thanks as he started to rush out of the office. But a secondary thought stopped him. "Hey Doc, are you familiar at all with what happened at Lucille Packard?"

"You mean the plague outbreak?"

"Yeah...I was there that day. I just wondered if they'd figured anything out."

Truard looked shocked. "I'm amazed you're alive. They told us no one survived it."

"I thought the children did."

"Technically, no. They never contracted it. They figured out that the chemo still in their bodies protected them."

"I thought they were healed somehow?"

Truard shrugged. "That's still up for debate. Definitely a remission of some sort but only temporary from what I understand. They're still trying to figure it out."

"What about the woman in Denver? I thought her issue was heart-related."

He nodded. "Yes, but cancer-related as well. Seems to have put her in remission as well as kept her alive."

Jerad nodded. "Thanks, Doc. I appreciate the update."

Truard gave him a cautionary look. "Don't believe all the press, Jerad. The facts are still coming in."

He gave the doctor a quick salute and left. He didn't even stop at the check-out desk. What was the point? He wouldn't be back. The doctor couldn't do anything more for him. And now it sounds like the staff was a dead end too. He'd update Achem and thank him for trying to help.

Once he got to his car, he cranked the engine, then turned it off again. He didn't feel calm enough yet to drive. Needed to think and make sense of things first.

What did he do next?

Face the reality and start living like a dead man?

Put his life in order and start saying goodbye?

His phone buzzed in his pocket. He pulled it out and saw Nikki's name with attachments noted. He read the first screenshot, then skimmed the second and third.

Man, life sure knew how to punch him when he was down. He closed his eyes and leaned his head back. Attempted to pray but could only put together three words.

Help me. Please.

He had to find another way to make sure he was around to help Nikki through this.

Nothing else mattered.

CHAPTER TWENTY-ONE

Once they'd returned to their flat, Liran had put the branch in water for observation. Achem had kept his distance. In the morning, they'd discovered many of the blooms had dropped and already formed almost full-sized green hulls. And the hulls from yesterday had begun to split open, revealing the shell inside.

Using a pair of tweezers, Liran tapped one of the almonds into a shallow bowl. The shell looked very much like the almonds he'd seen at the orchards where he'd worked in his youth. Yet they ripened at a speed he'd never seen before. What usually took months appeared to happen in hours.

"Anything to report?" Achem hovered near the kitchen.

He glanced up from his seat at the dining room table. "Not really. They aren't much different from the ones I remember picking, but they're maturing at an amazing rate."

"No other evidence of threat?"

Liran put the tweezers down. "Not that I can tell from simple observation. If we had access to a lab, we might be able to tell more. Maybe."

"Maybe?" Achem crossed his arms as he leaned against the doorway.

"We are talking about the supernatural here, Achem. Much of that is invisible to the natural eye."

He chuckled softly. "Not always."

Smiling, Liran sat back in the chair. "Yes, of course. You're right."

"Don't agree with me just to appease an old man."

"You're not old."

"Perhaps, but I'm also right." He raised his brows at Liran as if to challenge him to a rebuttal.

"Then you've seen more than I have."

Achem pulled a chair out from the opposite side of the table and sat down. "I have and so will you."

With a long and telling sigh, Liran leaned into the back of his chair. But he kept his silence. The issues at hand needed their full attention.

"You have doubts." Not a question, just a simple statement.

Did that mean Achem understood? Liran looked at him long enough to glean the invitation to share. "Yes, at times. Not always."

Achem held his hand open on the table. "We all do, Liran. No need to feel you must keep them to yourself."

"Didn't seem important in light of what we're dealing with right now." He shot his gaze to the almond branch for emphasis.

"Matters of faith are always important, son. Especially in light of what we do."

He did it again. Achem had called him 'son' again. Nothing new, not really. But now, every time he did, Eben's implications haunted him. Did Achem really cause his father's death? He didn't know the details, but Eben seemed to think Achem was responsible. He hadn't had a chance to ask his brother about it. Once Achem showed up, there was little time to do anything else but stay in the moment and watch for Eben's next move.

His phone buzzed on the table next to him. Mira's name showed on the screen.

Achem smiled and rose. "Going for a walk." He nodded at the phone. "Don't make her wait."

Liran grabbed his phone. "Mira. It's good to hear from you."

The door to the apartment clicked, indicating Achem's departure.

"You may not think so after you hear my latest discovery." Her voice sounded serious but still held some of her usual playfulness.

"What did you find?" He switched the call to speaker.

"It's worse than I thought, Liran."

"What is? You can tell me." Liran rose from his seat and sauntered to the window. He pulled back the curtain. Achem had already reached the sidewalk below and was chatting with a jewelry vendor set up on the street below.

"It's about Eben's involvement with the Collective. I managed to follow some paper trails on my own, using the data I swiped."

"If it's to confirm his involvement, we had confirmation of that today. I saw him, Mira. He's had the staff much longer than we realized." The words tumbled out in rush and desperate need to confide in someone he could trust.

"Oh, Liran, that's awful. I'm so sorry." She paused for a moment. "But that confirms what I found. He's definitely connected to the Collective but not like we thought."

A dozen questions swirled in his mind. He wanted to know and didn't all at once. "Oh?"

"Is Achem there? I tried to reach him but he's not answering his phone. You both need to hear this. It's urgent."

"No, he stepped out. Go ahead and tell me. I'll fill him in."

"Okay," she let out a gusty sigh as she continued to speak, "Eben isn't just involved with the Collective. He *is* the Collective. The mastermind and everything behind it. I'll send a full report as soon as I can. I'm going to find a safer place to lie low until I can figure out more."

He spun away from the window, hovering over his phone. "Safer place? Mira, what's going on?"

"I think I'm being followed. Once I figure things out, I'll let you know, okay?"

"Okay, yes, but Mira, please be careful."

"I will. I promise." She started to say something then stopped.

The connection ended. Liran starred at his phone, trying to make sense of the call. He desperately wanted to understand who his brother had become. He recalled Eben's implications about Achem. In his remaining years, their father never talked about the incident. Not to him. And now he suspected why.

He'd chosen Eben to be his tool of revenge.

ACHEM ADMIRED THE DELICATE BRACELET HE'D PURCHASE FOR Nichole. A simple silver chain with a sideways cross. He hoped to give it to her as something of a peace offering. And to express his affection for her. He'd meant what he said about his promise to her father, but deep in his heart, his reasons went much deeper. He loved Nichole as if she were his own.

How could he not? He'd been a part of her life up until the death of her mother. And he never blamed Gabriel for cutting the connection after that. He understood—a father had to protect his daughter. At all costs.

Achem would make sure Gabriel's mission was finished.

And he understood Nichole's desire to cut off everything that caused her pain. She'd been through quite enough in her short life. And she was a woman of passion, just like her mother. Thus he hoped her demands that he stay out of her life were spoken in the heat of losing her close friend.

He put the bracelet back in the pouch the vendor had provided and slipped it into his pocket. As much as he wished he could protect her from any more pain, he had a sense of what was coming and could do nothing about it. Not really. Not without abandoning the call Yahweh had put on his life years ago. He'd stayed true to that call his entire life. Even at great cost to himself. Nichole wasn't the only one who lost people she loved.

His phone vibrated in his pocket. Texts from Nichole. A good sign, perhaps. Communication was still open. He tapped on the first image, then turned his phone sideways so he could read the document she sent.

The more he read, the more his intentions for that bracelet seemed useless. This would unleash a level of complication and confrontation sure to send Nichole over the edge. He had to agree, she'd dealt with enough. There had to be some way to keep this thing from going to press.

Then he noticed several missed calls from Mira.

"Achem!" Liran called from behind.

He turned around. The lad looked more serious than when he left him. "Everything okay between you and Mira?"

Liran nodded. "She was trying to reach you. Both of us."

"Yes, I just noticed that. What did she want?"

Liran appeared weary and his words converted a sense of hopelessness. "She culled through more of that data she took and followed some leads. Eben is the mastermind behind the Collective."

Though not surprised, the news sucked away his strength. And made him even more aware of how little time he had left. "Let's get back to the flat. I have some news to share from Nichole as well."

They hurried back in silence. Once inside, Achem poured himself a glass of water and sat down in a chair in the living room. "This is most disturbing."

"That's an understatement." Liran grabbed a soda from the fridge and sat on the couch. "Mira also said she thinks she's being followed. I told her to be careful."

"Good." After a long drink, Achem set his glass down. "Her family is quite connected, so I'm sure she can find a safe place while we get this figured out. Not having our usual network to rely on is making that most difficult though."

Liran rose and started pacing the floor. Something had the lad in deep thought.

Achem rose to face him when Liran paced closer. "I can only imagine this must be hard on you, my son, to know your brother is behind such darkness."

"You keep calling me son." Liran's expression contained both pain and confusion.

"Yes...I guess I think of you as a son at times. Would you rather I didn't?"

He opened his mouth to speak, then stopped and shook his head. "You said you had news from Nichole?"

Achem pulled out his phone to bring up the documents for Liran to read. "Read each one."

Once he finished he handed the cell back to Achem and flopped back on the couch like a teenager who just got grounded. "Eben is out for blood."

"Whose?"

Liran sat up and stared at him. "Yours."

"I'm gathering he wants the *Natsar* dismantled."

"No, I think it's you, Achem."

"Because I said he wasn't a suitable leader for us?"

"No, because he thinks you're the one who shot our father."

Achem sighed. He'd dreaded this moment and now here it was. "I'm sorry to say he's right, Liran. I did."

CHAPTER TWENTY-TWO

Liran took a shaky breath. He hadn't expected Achem's confession. He stood, ran a hand through his hair. He needed to think but didn't want to. He wanted to bolt but knew that would just prolong the agony.

Achem turned in his chair to face him. "I knew you'd have to know about this at some point. I've dreaded it, to be honest."

Dreaded it? He dropped his hand. "I don't understand...how could you keep that a secret?" He sounded angry, even to himself. How could he not be? Were his life and career as part of the *Natsar* just a sham to appease a man's guilt?

"Your father asked me not to tell you. Or Eben. He begged me, in fact. He didn't want you to know what he had done. He was so ashamed. Or so I thought at the time. But in light of what Eben shared, I'm beginning to wonder."

Liran spun around. "What really happened that day?"

"You know part of the story already—the day our attempt to retrieve the Ark resulted in the death of Nichole's mother."

"Yes, I remember."

"What you don't know is that your father switched sides."

"He what?"

Achem paled and appeared almost sick. "I believed it was the influence of the power of the Ark. Or the money. They bribed your father to help them."

"Who were they?" Liran sat down.

"Some sect that was intent on using it for their own gain. Much like the Collective is doing now. We never did get a full picture of who they were or where they came from."

"Eben said you shot him from behind." A wave of nausea hit him; as if just saying the words released something vile that needed to be vomited.

"No, that part's not true. They'd torched the tent where Nichole and her mother were being held. Your father tried to stop me from rescuing them. As it was, I only managed to save Nichole. And trust me when I say it was one of the hardest decisions I've ever had to make."

Nodding, Liran rubbed his hand over his mouth. Bile sat in the back of his throat. He grabbed his soda can and gulped down the rest, then slammed the can down on the table. "So my father was a murderer. Why wasn't he prosecuted?"

Achem held his hand out. "He didn't technically set the fire. And he wasn't himself." He rose from his chair and went to the window. "And as much as I don't like to admit it, to reveal those details to the authority would have exposed the *Natsar*. I had to make the choice."

Liran remained silent, absorbing what he just heard in a desperate attempt to put some order to the catastrophe. Something still didn't fit. "You really think he wasn't himself?"

Achem frowned. "I believed so at the time. His behavior seemed out of character. Why?"

"He told Eben you shot him. From behind while he wasn't looking. That you betrayed him."

"That's not true. I did shoot him, but only because I had to. He'd drawn his gun and was about to shoot me."

Clarity and realization hit him all at once. Liran's vision blurred with his tears. "Then we were both deceived. My father may have failed to shoot you that day, but he made sure he got his revenge. Through Eben."

NICHOLE MADE HER USUAL TURN TO PULL INTO THE BACK parking area of the building only to be met by a scene that confirmed her worst nightmares. A slew of news vans surrounded the back entrance. She hit the brakes, contemplating a quick reverse and working from her apartment, but no doubt they'd set up there as well.

"Might as well face the lion." She parked in her usual spot and took a moment to plan the best way to get through the mob and into the building. She picked up her phone and started to text Benny, but a tap on her window stopped her.

She expected to find a reporter but found Benny instead. She lowered her window, noticing from her periphery vision the encroaching mob about to surround them.

"I'll escort you in, Ms. Strauss."

"Thank you, Benny." After closing her window, she grabbed her keys, purse, and laptop.

As soon as she opened the door, questions peppered her like a shotgun.

"Ms. Strauss, are you aware of the article in today's paper? Would you like to make a statement about your involvement with the *Natsar*?" The reporter asking had a southern accent and pronounced the 'a' in a long drawl.

More questions fired at her.

"Do you have the staff?"

"Are you responsible for the plague?"

Benny's hulk-like stature covered her as he held her with his right arm all the while holding his left arm out like a moving barricade, pushing through the crowd. When they reached the doors,

Benny pushed her in then spun around to lock the door behind them. Outside, the reporters continued to shout their questions in an attempt to be heard through the glass doors.

Benny returned to his station at the desk. "I'll make sure the other tenants get in without issue."

"Thank you, Benny. And please convey my apologies and let them know we will be happy to make amends for any inconveniences this causes their businesses." Which would drain even more resources away from their Clean Water & Farm Project. The Collective had done their homework well. Right now, her dislike peaked into the hate category for the group. Why did they think making innocent people suffer for their agenda was acceptable?

She pushed the button for the top floor and sighed as the elevator doors closed. Her father always answered that question with, "To ask that implies you believe people like that operate on the same moral plane that you do. Sorry to tell you, Peanut. They don't."

As the elevator doors opened, she met Jerad standing there with a cup of coffee in one hand and a little brown bag in the other. He smiled as he held the coffee and bag toward her. "Sorry I couldn't meet you for breakfast, so I brought breakfast to you."

"I promise I won't hold it against you." She took the bag and followed him into her office. On the edge of her desk she noticed the additional coffee cup and bag sitting there as well. He really had brought breakfast for both of them. She put her laptop by the desk and tossed her purse onto the chair in the corner before sitting down. "I assume you met the entourage as you came in?"

"They were just setting up shop when I arrived. Benny and I came up with a plan to deal with it."

"Thank you for doing that. I have no idea how we're going to deal with this."

"It's okay, we'll figure it out."

She opened the bag. Her favorite egg sandwich. "You know me well."

"Yes, I do." He seemed distant, disconnected.

She studied him as she finished chewing her bite and wiped her hands with a napkin. "What did the doctor say?"

He busied himself with adding sugar to his coffee, something he rarely did. "Nothing major to report. My numbers are about the same."

She sat back in her chair, arms on the rests. "Are you sure?"

He looked up at her but only briefly. "Yes, why?"

The chair creaked when she leaned forward. "Because for some reason I get a sneaky feeling you're not being totally honest with me."

He put his coffee down. "I didn't want to worry you. It's no big deal."

"Yes, it is, Jerad. We're talking about your life here. And our future."

"Exactly."

"What does that mean?" She wanted to bolt out of her chair but recognized her emotions were still running high from the morning's events.

"I'm just trying to make things easier for you, Nikki. Nothing has changed so why dwell on it. We have bigger things to deal with right now."

"Did your doctor at least get things set up with the guy in New York?"

Jerad hesitated for the briefest moment but the meaning held a lifetime of impact. "He said there was no point. Truard already consulted with him and they agree he's using the best options available."

"So what does that mean?"

"It means there's nothing new to report. We just hold steady for now." He smiled, but it never reached his eyes. If anything they looked more gray than green, like a gray-green sky indicative of an impending tornado.

She started to push for more but her phone buzzed from downstairs. "Yes?"

Benny's gruff voice came over the speaker. "I just found Achem and Liran coming in through the basement and have them detained. Should I call the police?"

Basement? At least Achem had the sense to not be seen. She released the button. "Just what we need right now."

Jerad rested his hand on her wrist. "I'm sure they're just trying to help."

And detained? God love the man. Benny knew how to do his job well. "No police, Benny. Just send them up the stairs so the press can't see them. And thank you."

"No problem, Ms. Strauss."

She released the button. Ten flights of stairs might teach Achem to rethink showing up without calling first. "Remind me to tell Benny to call me Nichole."

"Don't."

"Why?"

"Because he's very regimented and strict on details. That will just throw him off his game. Don't mess the guy up."

She gave him a pointed stare as they headed to the stairway door by the elevator. "I'm not done with you yet."

Jerad's grin flashed, revealing his usual self. "I'm counting on it."

JERAD WAS GLAD FOR THE INTERRUPTION. THE LONGER HE could keep the full truth from Nikki the better. Granted, he hated himself for not being completely honest—they'd agreed to no more secrets—but he justified this one with one simple reason that overarched anything else.

He'd do whatever necessary to protect her from more pain. He may not be able to do much else for her in the time he had left, but he could do that at least. She'd probably tell him otherwise and would be angry as all get out at him. She'd have plenty of time to be mad at him after he—.

He shook off the morbid thought as Achem and Liran's steps drew closer on the stairs. Nikki joined him on the landing with her hands on her hips.

Achem stopped on the last step. Jerad made eye contact with Liran behind him. They seemed at an impasse for a moment. Jerad waited to see how Nikki would react to Achem in light of the latest development.

She dropped her arms and sighed. Then her shoulders began to shake. Achem jumped from the step to fold her into his arms. And she let him. Good sign. Jerad didn't think Nikki would maintain her grudge against Achem. She may still be madder than an agitated weasel in a well at him, but Jerad had never seen her cut someone out of her life.

As they entered the lobby, Jerad grabbed the tissue box off of Robin's desk and held it out to Nikki when she stepped back. She gave him a weak smile of thanks. Robin's desk stood as a reminder of how personal the loss had become and would remain empty until Nikki had healed enough to begin the interview process. Right now she—they—had bigger issues to contend with.

Achem appeared shaken himself. "We would have been here sooner but had some issues of our own to figure out." He sent a meaningful look to Liran, who seemed to find studying his shoes more engaging at the moment.

Jerad bounced his gaze between them. "Anything we need to know about?"

Liran's head shot up to look at Achem. His expression bordered something between panic and warning.

Achem took full notice before answering Jerad. "No. We've handled it. But we do need to fill you in about our recent discovery about the staff. Liran was correct. His brother is the one in possession of it."

They headed to the conference room. For the next twenty minutes, Achem and Liran brought them up to speed about Liran's encounter with his brother and the branch they obtained. Then they talked bout Eben and his surprising role in creating the Collective.

Eyes watery with compassion, Nikki reached out and squeezed Liran's hand. "I'm so sorry, Liran. This must be crushing for you."

Liran dropped his head as he nodded, his discomfort evident in the way he stiffened with her touch.

She sent a questioning look at Achem, then to Jerad as she let go of his hand.

Achem gave her a quick shake of his head; as if to say let it be.

Jerad shrugged. Maybe Liran took Nikki's gesture as pity and didn't want it. Jerad understood the shame that could come with the actions of a sibling. After Leah's suicide, the hardest part he had to deal with was the scrutiny he received in the guise of sympathy. Thinly disguised questions that held implications of his responsibility for her death. Or worse, because they were twins, did he suffer from the same mental instability. All part of why he left. Sometimes the questions hit too close to his own guilt of not being more aware of his twin sister's struggle.

Achem cleared his throat. "I'd hoped we had more time to prevent the story from being released, but now that it has, I think we should come up with some plans and strategies as to what we do next. Until we can figure out who the Collective has inserted or turned in our network, our resources are somewhat limited until we can establish who we can trust. In the meantime, we're trying to make new connections to help us get more information about them and what Eben's ultimate plan is."

Liran seemed to have a thought but kept it to himself.

Nikki gestured to Jerad. "With the press breathing down our necks, we're limited too."

A cell phone on silent made a telltale vibration. They all checked their phones.

"It's mine. I don't recognize the number though." She pushed the call to voicemail.

Then the phone in the middle of the conference table rang. Jerad sent a questioning look at Nikki, then grabbed the handset before she could. He'd deal with the press or whoever intended to hound them at the moment.

"Strauss Foundation." All eyes at the table were on him.

"Mr. Nebal. Artemis Tombs here. Could you be so kind as to put me on speakerphone? I have a proposition for you."

CHAPTER TWENTY-THREE

"It's Artemis Tombs." Jerad replaced the handset as Nichole pushed the speaker button.

"Good morning. I assume everyone is present?" Artemis Tombs sounded like a man in charge. Actually *the* man in charge.

Nichole clenched her fists to keep herself from slamming the phone across the room. She didn't like it. Not one bit. If Tombs thought he could take control of the situation, he should have another thought, and she would make sure of it. No way would she let him ruin her father's Foundation.

She started to reply but Achem held up his hand. "What do you want, Mr. Tombs?"

"Ah, Mr. Mizrahi. Good. That means Mr. Dakarai is with you as well. This will make my job much easier."

"Yes, I'm here. What does my brother want?"

"Unity, of course. Peace on earth."

"You mean complete control." Liran almost sneered his words.

"Perhaps that's a subject of debate left between you and your brother?"

She didn't like the way Tombs played with people's lives. "Get on with it, Tombs. I have a press mob to deal with, thanks to you. What do you want?"

"That's one of the reasons I'm calling, Ms. Strauss. The article is a small thing really. Easy to make go away. And I'd be happy to do that for you and your friends. Just say the word."

She leaned toward the phone. "And what word would that be exactly?"

"Yes."

She felt herself physically shudder. She'd not met the man in person yet but had no doubt he was a maniacal goon. "And what exactly would we be agreeing to?"

"As you now know, we already have the staff of Aaron. We want the Ark and the manna jar as well."

"That will never happen, Tombs." Achem's anger bled into his words that time.

"Mr. Mizrahi, let me point out that if the press continues to receive information about the *Natsar* and what they have hidden, every major superpower will demand they be turned over to the United Nations, *or* they will come after you. You will lose possession of the Ark and the manna jar regardless, so why not give them to us?"

"So that you can use them to wreak havoc in the world? I'd rather take my chances with the UN."

"I can assure you, that is not our plan. We see them as tools needed to help a very broken and sick world. Not artifacts to be hidden to collect dust. We have the staff. It's in everyone's best interest to give the Collective possession of the Ark and manna jar as well."

Jerad rose from his seat and leaned on the table. "You're fools if you think you can control the power these relics hold. I've seen what happens first hand."

"Yes, I'm aware of your situation, Mr. Nebal, and that is also part of this deal I'm offering—your return to health. Eben Dakarai knows how to control the staff and can heal you. I'm sure you'd like to plan that wedding."

Jerad shook his head and turned away, hands on his hips.

Heat spread up her neck to her cheeks. The Collective seemed to know every detail of their lives. "Control? You must be as crazy as Eben is. What about all the people he's killed with that thing?"

"We regret the loss of your friend, Ms. Strauss. The intent was to help save those children, which Mr. Dakarai did. Now we know the staff must be used in a limited environment."

Nikki's anger peaked as she jumped up from her chair, causing her entire body to shake. "Now you know? Couldn't you have figured that out after the first time? Then my friend and dozens of others would still be alive!"

"Remember the children that were healed, Ms. Strauss. I'm confident we can do that for your fiancé as well. We'll give you some time to think about it." A click sounded and then the dial tone blasted over the line.

Jerad picked up the handset and replaced it in the cradle.

Liran rose from his chair to grab a bottle of water from the credenza. "My brother is a mad man." He threw the comment over his shoulder.

Achem clasped his hands on the table and lowered his chin. "He's most likely being affected by the staff to some degree."

Liran spun around. "You and I both know the power is directed by the spirit of the man and his has turned to darkness."

"And he's wrong." Jerad swallowed, kept his gaze trained on her. "Turns out the only reason those children and the woman in Denver are alive is because they were undergoing chemotherapy."

Nichole couldn't look away from what she saw in Jerad's eyes. Acceptance? Admittance? Was there no other option for them? She swallowed the sob building in her throat. "But the reports said they were healed."

"Just press. My doctor explained it did cause some kind of remission. They don't know for sure."

Silence filled the room. Unmoving, Nichole stared at the phone. When Jerad tried to embrace her, she put her hand out. "Not yet."

She said it more to protect him than herself. She'd never felt rage like this before—she wanted to open a window and scream at the top of her lungs. How could they be so careless with the lives of others?

Because they are blinded by power.

Achem cleared his throat. "Very telling."

"How so?" Jerad tilted his head at him, but not before casting a concerned glance at her.

"Eben's compromised our network, even used it against us, but he's yet to figure out how to get to the Ark."

Liran nodded. "The vault is highly sophisticated, nearly impervious to destruction, and almost impossible to tamper with."

"Nearly impervious?" Jerad chuckled with his question.

"Yes. The force you'd have to use would destroy it and the contents." Liran held his hands out. "Which defeats the purpose."

"Clearly." Nichole couldn't resist a little sarcasm. "So what do we do? We can't bargain with them."

"Why not?" Achem looked at each of them, a mischievous glint in his eyes.

"You're joking, right?" Jerad's voice inflected the disbelief she felt. Could one really bargain with madness? Reasoning certainly wouldn't work.

"Not a deal exactly." Achem appeared lost in thought.

"Achem, what are you thinking?" Nichole couldn't bring her voice above a whisper, because she had a feeling whatever he was thinking would involve Jerad. She didn't want to make an assumption though until she heard him out.

He met her gaze. "Artemis Tombs is clever, as is Eben. He's also fully aware of where I stand on this. He'd never believe I'd changed my mind, even under the guise of trying to save Jerad."

She slid back into her seat. "Go on."

"But perhaps if they thought one of us was beginning to have second thoughts." He directed his eyes to Liran.

Along with a shocked expression, Liran held his hands against his chest. "Me?" But then his expression shifted to one of comprehension. "Do you think he'd believe me?"

Achem appeared pleased that Liran was on track with him.

"You said you felt the pull of the staff when you confronted him at the park."

"What? Wait...you felt it, but it didn't kill you?" Nichole couldn't deny the relief she felt that Achem didn't intend to use Jerad as a decoy—she would have had to completely disown him.

Liran appeared reluctant to share a secret. "No...Eben and I are descendants of Aaron. The Levitical heritage is in our blood."

Jerad jumped into the stream of understanding. "And that gives you the ability to control the staff."

Achem scrunched his features into a partial frown. "To some degree, it seems. Eben's desires are self-centered, thus creating harm. But Liran..."

"I only want to get it away from my brother, not use it."

Achem rose to his feet. "But if you can convince Eben you're having a change of heart..."

"And mind..." Liran nodded as if making a decision with himself. "I'll do it. I'll convince Eben I want to join him."

THEY'D LEFT THE STRAUSS FOUNDATION THE SAME WAY THEY came so as not to be seen. But Liran could tell by the look Nichole's security officer gave them that he wasn't happy about it. And Achem hadn't said much once they established the situation was not in their hands. She appeared more relieved than anything, but who could blame her? She finally had what she wanted—to be left out of the efforts to attain the staff and the dangers it presented.

And once his brother knew he would get what he wanted, the pressure coming from the press would likely ease up as well. Seemed like a true bargain all the way around.

Now all he had to do was pull it off.

Achem stopped on the stairwell and rested a hand on his shoulder. "I know you're concerned about convincing Eben you want to join him, Liran. It goes against your belief that the brother you once knew is still there and can be brought back around."

"What's wrong with that?"

"Nothing at all." He put his other hand over Liran's heart. "Your heart always believes the best of people. Your brother knows that too. So you don't have to change your stance there. Just make him believe that since you encountered the power of the staff, it's made you reconsider its value to the world and you want to help him accomplish that the right way."

Liran dipped his chin to see Achem's hand and the ring he wore signifying his position as Natsar leader. Just a simple star of David with the cross of Christ in the middle. Would he ever wear that ring? "What if I fail?"

"You won't, Liran. Don't forget that Yahweh is on your side. As am I. You're not alone. Together, we will get the staff back where it belongs."

He allowed a tight smile to reach his lips. "You would make a great motivational speaker, Achem."

Achem chuckled. "Perhaps in my next position in heaven, Yahweh will allow me that pleasure. It certainly would be less stressful."

His mind wanted to pick apart Achem's words. Why did he sense yet again that Achem held something back; as if he had knowledge about the future?

Achem continued down the stairway. "We'd best get in touch with Mira and make a believable plan."

The mention of her name shifted Liran's focus. "Do you think we should?"

Achem paused at the basement-level exit. "Should what?"

"Tell Mira about this part of our plan? Would it be better if she didn't know? Make it more believable?" Would she even believe it herself? That would be a good test. If she believed him, Eben most likely would too. But she'd hate him for it. That thought alone created a most uncomfortable feeling in his chest.

"I see what you're saying. And you might be right."

"I'm just thinking, if I can convince Mira, then I can convince Eben."

"Can you live with that, Liran? That's quite a sacrifice. I can see how you've both come to care for each other."

"Yes, but isn't this part of what we've been called to do? Make sacrifices for a greater cause?"

Achem's eyes grew moist as he spoke. "Yes, my son. You are exactly right."

CHAPTER TWENTY-FOUR

Jerad wanted to do more to help Achem and Liran prevent a global disaster. He'd prepared himself to jump in, whatever the cost; because he was usually the one exposing conspiracies and lies. But now he and Nikki had been sidelined.

She seemed relieved. He felt cheated of a chance to make what little time he had left matter—in a big way. Although he had to admit, seeing Nikki more relaxed did matter. A lot. He'd made a commitment to himself to do whatever he could to help her with whatever time he had left.

He shook that thought off, keeping Nikki's face front and center in his mind. The rest was gravy on the chicken fried steak, right? Still, he wished for more time...

His phone vibrated in his hand, startling him. Stone Abrams's name showed on the screen. He'd contemplated what to do about the situation many times since the conference. Despite Nichole's reservations, and fear even, the possibility still resided in the back of his mind. And now in light of his latest prognosis—God love his doctor—and the situation with the staff, maybe he needed a Plan B. A backup plan. Something to give him hope that he might actually have a little bit more time on this planet to spend with Nikki.

He hit accept. "Stone, you picked the perfect time to call."

"Really? Did you and Nicole make a decision?"

"Yes, actually. I'd like to move forward. As long as you don't have a problem with Nichole not being part of the equation."

"I take it she's not on board?"

Jerad paused a moment, considering the best way to answer. "Not really. And she has a lot on her plate right now. I'd rather not add to it."

"I understand. And no, that doesn't change my determination to help you and see you healed."

"Good...then what do we do next?"

"That's up to you, Jerad. We can move at the pace that works for you, but I do think it needs to be sooner than later. Especially based on the progression of your condition."

Jerad tried to recall exactly what he'd shared with Stone at the conference and the conversations before that.

"What about this week? Let's get the ball rolling and see what happens."

He refocused his train of thought on Stone's question. Why wait to see what the staff could do? As Stone said, the sooner the better. He'd need every ounce of strength to play his part in Achem's plan.

"Tell me when and where and I'll be there."

NICHOLE SET HER PHONE BACK ON HER DESK. TALKING TO Robin's daughter had been brutal. The guilt she carried for walking out of the hospital alive that day doubled in light of what her daughter just shared.

She was expecting her first child. A child that would never meet his or her grandmother. She buried her face in her hands. If she had the power, she would go back in time and swap places with Robin. Shoot, if she had that kind of ability, she'd roll back time five years ago and make sure Leah didn't succeed in killing herself. Then Jerad would never have left. And maybe, just maybe, they'd be married and expecting their own kid by now.

"Ugh, this is awful."

"What is?"

She jumped at the sound of Jerad's voice. "When did you get here?"

"Just now. What's so awful?"

"I just got off the phone with Robin's daughter. I wanted to see if she needed help with the funeral arrangements. She told me she just found out she's pregnant."

He dropped onto the couch. "Wow. Yeah, that's awful."

Nichole left her desk to sit by him. She wanted to feel safe in his arms, even if it was just for a few moments. "I feel so guilty."

As she snuggled in against him, he wrapped his arms around her and kissed her head. "Why?"

She stretched her neck up to see him better. "Because I'm alive and that baby's grandmother isn't."

The look in his eyes melted the last bits of her strength. She buried her face against his chest and let the sobs come. All of them. Even the ugly ones.

When her tears reached the end of the deep well of her grief, she pulled away to blow her nose, grateful she kept a box of tissues on the table. As she added her last tissue to the pile she'd made on the table, Jerad pulled her against him and into a deep kiss.

After a few moments, she pushed away because of her clogged nose. And the man knew how to take her breath away.

He cupped her cheek and stared at her with impassioned eyes. "I missed you."

A rogue tear slipped down her cheek. "I always miss you."

In a sudden movement, he pressed his lips against hers in a kiss that held the urgency of the moment and the fear of what was to come.

THEY'D RETURNED TO THEIR RENTAL FLAT TO FINISH DISCUSSING their plan of action and to secure travel arrangements for the return to Jerusalem. The more details they worked out, the more confident he felt in their plan. And he trusted Yahweh to protect them.

Now all that remained to be done was up to Liran. He would call his brother and convince him that when he returned, he fully intended to switch sides, that Achem had no idea and wouldn't realize until after he'd given Eben access to the vault at *Natsar* headquarters.

But one unknown factor kept rising up in his thoughts.

Liran came of out the kitchen with a tray holding two plates of food and set it on the table. "I don't know whether to eat before or after I make the call."

"I know what you mean." Still somewhat distracted, Achem ran a hand over his mouth. "My one concern is Artemis Tombs. Will he fully believe you've changed sides?"

Liran sat down at the table. "I had the same thought. What can you tell me about him so I'm better prepared?" He took a bite of his sandwich.

"Well, for one, I don't believe Artemis Tombs is his real name."

"Who would?"

Achem laughed. "I had my first run-in with him shortly after we found the Ark. He started sniffing around in Egypt, asking questions. I caught wind and set our best people to find out who he was. He simply doesn't exist."

"No background or history?"

"Not that I could find. Although I did find a connection to another name—Tobias Rickman. But I couldn't tell if they were the same person or not. Whoever he is, he's buried his true identity deeper than I could dig."

"That says a lot coming from a man with a Ph.D. in archeological history and research."

Achem stifled his laugh. "A lot of good it's done me lately." He waved his hand to brush off his words. When did he start speaking before he considered his words? "Oh, don't mind the grumbling of an old—older man."

Liran pushed his unfinished sandwich away. "What's going on, Achem? You don't seem yourself lately."

"I'm fine. Just a bit weary perhaps. We barely had time to recover from the manna jar before the staff appeared. I dare to say that once we have the staff safely interred, the stone tablets will make their appearance."

"Why do you think that?"

"It's no accident that the elements have appeared in succession."

"You think someone is purposely revealing them?" Liran leaned his arms on the table.

"Yes. Yahweh."

"But why? Seems like it would be easier for them to remain hidden."

"But then they'd remain in darkness and become tools of the enemy—the devil himself."

Liran laughed. "Don't you think that's already happened?"

"Not directly, but I've no doubt he's exerting his influence."

Liran dropped his gaze to the table. "So it would seem."

Achem rested his hand on Liran's arm. "I'm sorry. I don't mean to imply Eben—"

"No point in dancing around the truth. He's not the man I once knew." Liran cleared his throat. "That will make what I'm about to do a little easier."

"I'm sorry, Liran. I never imagined Eben capable of this."

"Neither did I."

More than anything, Achem hated to see Liran in this position. Brother against brother...not at all what he'd imagined years ago when he began grooming the two boys for leadership. Despite their father's betrayal, he never doubted what they carried. Or their potential.

Had he done enough for Eben? Where had he fallen short? His phone buzzed on the table, showing Mira's name on the screen. "Time for the show to begin." He tapped accept. "Hello, my dear."

"Are you both there?"

Liran leaned toward the phone. "Yes, I'm here."

"Good. I have to say, I'm getting bloody tired of all the cloak and dagger shenanigans."

Achem chuckled but noted Liran's frown of concern. "Are you being careful, my dear?"

She expelled a noisy breath over the line. "Yes, no worries there. But I called to tell you things are quite astir here. Large sums of money have been and are being moved around."

"Funds for what?" Liran moved in closer.

"As far as I can tell, for private services. A large number of them."

Achem sent a questioning glance at Liran. "What kind?"

"Independent special ops and mercenaries. Some in the US and other large countries but mostly here in Jerusalem. Almost as if they're postponing themselves."

"Mira, you've done a great job, but I think it's time for you to disengage from CBS for good. I'm concerned for your safety." Achem sent a knowing look at Liran. "Liran and I leave in the morning to come back to Jerusalem."

"You may be right. I'll make up an excuse as to why I can't be there for a few days. If I don't show up, it might set off alarm signals to them."

"Good point. Just stay safe."

"I'll be fine, but I'm not sure it's safe for you to return to your offices."

Achem smiled at how she avoided using '*Natsar* headquarters' over the phone. "I agree. Do you think you can find us a secure location to use temporarily?"

"Yes, I'll get on that right away. I'll make contact as soon as I have more details." The connection ended.

Liran groaned as he sat back in his chair. "This part will be harder than I anticipated."

"I know, but it's best if we don't tell her everything. At least until we're there and can gauge better what we're dealing with right away. Right now we need to get back on home ground."

Moses and Aaron did just as the LORD had commanded. He raised his staff in the presence of Pharaoh and his officials and struck the water of the Nile, and all the water was changed into blood. —Exodus 7:20

DESTRUCTION

"Did you share our...proposition?"

By agreement or by force, he would possess the Ark and its treasures. And the world would know about them. Just as it should be. He would show people everywhere the goodness of his mercy and kindness. But also with a firm hand, his control.

Yet fools never fully understand the complete corruption of power. Or its destruction of the one who wielded it.

"Yes, in complete detail." Artemis didn't exude his usual confidence. "But I don't expect that they will agree to our terms."

"Most likely not. But it doesn't matter. One way or another the Ark and jar will be ours. The staff of Aaron will make sure of it."

"I've given them time to think it over."

"Waiting has never been my strong point. If we don't hear something by the end of today, I will have to make my next point."

"What are you planning?"

"A surprise, Artemis. Something that will convince them the Ark and its precious elements belong to the world."

CHAPTER TWENTY-FIVE

"I guess now is as good a time as any." Liran picked up his phone and prepared in his head what he would say to Eben.

Achem put his hand over his phone. "You can do this, Liran. You've been in contact with him and know his mental state better than anyone."

He let loose a guttural growl. "I don't have a choice, really. I can't even imagine what could happen if the Collective got their hands on the Ark and the manna jar. Along with the staff, they'd be a nearly unstoppable force."

"Let's not forget Yahweh's role in all this. Nothing's impossible for Him, right?"

"That's what I keep telling myself."

"Good. Then trust Yahweh and call your brother."

Liran nodded as he picked up his phone. A text sat there from Mira.

I will make sure to have Babka for your arrival. Miss you...

He started to reply then stopped. The only way he could keep this from her successfully would be to not communicate at all.

Hopefully, she'd forgive him when she learned the truth. He tapped his brother's number.

Eben's recorded messaged came over the line. His brother was rejecting his call. Liran hung up and dialed again.

"Liran...I'm surprised to get your call."

Liran allowed the knot in his emotion in his throat to affect his voice. He had to be believable to pull this off. "*Ach*...I can't stop thinking about what you said."

"Which part, Liran? I can't stop thinking about some things you said as well." His tone exposed his offense.

"I'm sorry, Eben. I was wrong. I felt the power of the staff, and I've thought of nothing since. You were right. There's so much we can do to help this world." He knew that would appeal to his brother's pride.

"We?"

"Yes, if you'll still have me. I want to help you."

"You mean be my moral compass. You always tried to be when we were young." His tone lightened with his words.

Liran's confidence grew a little more as his brother seemed to open up to him. "Whatever you need, *achi*."

"What about Achem? What have you shared with him?"

"Nothing. I haven't talked to him about any of this. You and I both know where he stands. As did our father." He cringed as he said it, but he knew that would also touch a need in Eben.

When Eben remained silent, Liran felt the urge to keep talking but resisted. He had to give Eben time to process or he'd feel manipulated.

"Why should I trust you, *achi*. You seem quite cozy with Achem."

"Not anymore. You were right about Achem shooting our father. Achem admitted to it. I don't know if I can trust him anymore. We fly back to Jerusalem the day after tomorrow. Let me know when you're ready, *achi*. I'll help you get the Ark and manna jar."

Dawn had barely broken the hold of the night, but Jerad didn't want to risk running into Nichole and losing his nerve. Better to leave her a note. She could chew him out later.

If this worked—if Stone Abrams could really do what he promised—he and Nikki could plan that wedding and start their life together. Maybe even a family. He didn't like going behind her back, but if there was even a chance that Stone could really heal him, he had to try. If he couldn't, then Jerad would be no worse off.

And he sent up his own silent prayer for God to heal him. In his research on Stone, he'd wound up watching a few sermons by fairly known pastors. They seemed to believe God still heals. So, why not join the ranks? He'd have one heck of a testimony.

After rummaging through her drawer, he finally found a sticky note pad on her desk. He scrawled a message telling her he went to see Stone. He could just imagine the livid expression on her face when she saw it, but he had to do what he thought was best.

He looked around her office, trying to figure out where to put the note. Her desk was a clutter of paperwork with sticky notes all over them. His would get lost in the shuffle. Then he saw the postcard from Stone's conference sticking out from under a stack of magazines. He'd stick it on that and put it right on her seat. She'd see it right away.

Before he put the card down, he kissed the note for good luck, then shook his head at himself. Did he think that would really buy him some grace with Nikki?

But if he came back healed, she'd be too happy to be mad.

Please God...

Nichole pulled into the back parking lot, relieved to see the reporters had cleared out. Did that mean Liran had made the call? Tombs said they would make it go away if they made a deal. The thought made her shudder.

She checked her phone to see if Jerad replied to her last text about joining her for breakfast at the office. Nothing. The man was up to something, she just didn't know what. His unpredictability added to her growing concern. At least now they weren't in the middle of the whole staff retrieval thing. Maybe they could have some peace for once.

After collecting her laptop and the stack of files she'd taken home with her last night, she entered the building.

Benny rose from his station. "Your friends showed up again. I let them go upstairs but I didn't let them into your offices."

"Thank you, Benny."

"Is everyone okay, Ms. Strauss?"

She redirected her path to his desk. "As good as they can be. Why do you ask?"

He tilted his head. "I've been in this business a long time. I recognize the type, you know," he gestured to himself, "like me. They've seen some action."

"I think we all have, Benny. We're just trying to prevent more of it." She smiled at him. "But thank you for asking. If I need help, be assured I will let you know."

"Good."

When the elevator doors opened on the top floor, Achem and Liran stood there waiting. She felt like Madam Secretary arriving at the White House, except Achem and Liran didn't have a coffee and muffin to hand to her.

"Hi, boys. What's up?"

Achem turned and walked with her to the outer doors of the Strauss Foundation. "We're on our way to the airport to catch a flight back to Jerusalem. We wanted to say goodbye before we left."

She had just inserted her key into the lock but paused, looking at Liran. "You made contact with your brother?"

Liran nodded but remained silent. He didn't need to say anything. The expression on his face said it all.

"I'm so sorry, Liran. I can't even imagine what this is like for you."

He attempted a small smile but said nothing.

"Is Jerad coming up as well?" Achem listed his brows in question.

She unlocked the door. "No, I've been trying to reach him but he hasn't replied. I'm hoping he's here already, surprising me with breakfast. Like he did the other day."

Liran and Achem followed her in. She glanced in the direction of her office but didn't see him. Nor was he in the conference room. She walked into her office, but the couch was empty as well. "He's not here." She put her things on the chair in front of her desk.

As she rounded her desk to her seat, she found the postcard and note. Flashes of the vision blasted through her mind along with memories of the conference. She sat before her legs gave out on her. "Oh no, he did NOT do this."

Achem stood by Liran in front of her desk. "Do what?"

"He went to see that healing evangelist I told you about. I asked him not to pursue it. The whole thing freaked me out. The man who does this is the same one I saw in that vision the day we got the manna jar back."

"I remember." Achem moved closer to her desk.

Nichole pulled off the note and held out the postcard with Stone's face on the front. "That's the guy."

As Achem took the card and brought it closer, something guttural erupted from Liran's throat.

Achem put the card down, looking more shaken than she thought he ever could.

She darted her gaze between the two of them, fighting the panic rising up from the sick mess in her stomach. "What? What am I missing here?"

Liran looked ashen. "That's Eben. My brother."

CHAPTER TWENTY-SIX

The image of his brother stared back at him, composed and smiling like a real estate agent ready to sell someone their next dream home. Not a man out to prove himself to be a god.

Next, registered the name. Stone Abrams. His brother had always loved his games.

"Eben is Hebrew for Stone. Abrams points to 'of Abraham.' The father of nations." He threw the card down on the desk. "My brother's idea of a sick joke."

Nichole had leaned over and pulled the trash can closer. Her breathing appeared distressed. She retched into the can.

Achem crouched down in front of her. "I'm right here, Nichole. Do you have any idea where Jerad would have gone to meet him?"

She gulped more air, shook her head. "No. Give me my phone. Please."

Achem spotted her cell on the desk and handed it to her. He lifted his gaze to him. "Get a bottle of water."

Liran jogged over to the conference room and grabbed a bottle of water from the mini-fridge. His shock from seeing his brother's alternate persona faded some, allowing his brain to process. But he couldn't make sense of any of it. Once back in the office he handed the bottle to Achem, who held it in Nichole's line of sight.

"See if you can drink some of this."

After wiping her mouth with a wad of tissues, she sat back in her seat and gulped down more water. "He's not answering his phone or replying to my text." She shot up from her chair. "We have to find him."

Achem grabbed her arms and helped her to sit back down. "We will, Nichole. We just need to think it through first."

Liran began to pace the room. "Why would he do this now that I've told him I would help him? Did he not believe me?"

He had to do something to stop his brother. His mind raced to find something he could do right now. He stopped and pulled his cell phone from his pocket.

Achem strode to where Liran stood. "Are you texting him?"

"He's lost his mind. I have to get him to see reason."

Achem held his wrist holding the phone. "He's not going to listen to reason right now."

Liran lowered his phone. "Then what do I say to him? He's become a raving maniac who's determined to make himself known as the savior of the world."

"Then that's who we speak to." Nichole swiped the tears from under her eyes. "At the conference, he was all about the show. The emotional impact. And I'm convinced he even put some kind of hallucinogenic in the fog makers to mesmerize the crowd. He wants an audience to praise and acknowledge him."

As much as it sickened him, Nichole was right. His brother had always been that way on some level—an attention seeker as a boy, hungry for power as an adult. That need ultimately forced Achem to discount him as a future leader of the *Natsar*. The staff must be amplifying his need to the point of madness; like the golden manna jar had done to Soren Umberger.

After shoving his phone back into his pocket, he dropped down on the couch and held his head in his hands. There had to be a way to tap into Eben's weakness and use it.

Nichole said he'd had an audience at the conference...

He shot to his feet. "He's going to want an audience for whatever he has planned for Jerad. So let's give him one."

"How?" Nichole frowned.

Liran narrowed his gaze to Achem. "By giving him the audience of the one person he needs to impress the most."

Achem lifted his brows. "That's quite brilliant actually. But how do you propose we persuade him to tell us where he is?"

He pulled his phone out again. "I'll tell him I know what he's about to do and that Achem wants to find him. If he'll tell us where he is, we can watch our father's murderer pay the price for what he did."

Nichole sent a frown to Achem. "Wait. What? You murdered his father?" She lowered her chin as she finished her words and looked at him from under her brows.

Achem frowned at him before focusing on Nichole. "It's a long story. I'll fill you in later."

She sighed, looking wearier than ever. "We're like one of those broken families on a reality show."

Achem's frown shifted to a sad smile at her words. "I promise it's not that bad."

Liran held the phone up to Achem. "How does that sound?"

Achem scanned the words. "Send it."

Liran tapped the send icon. Almost immediately the three dots showed up that he was replying. Then the message showed up.

> Nice try, *achi*. But if you really want to know where I am, ask Nichole where Leah would go to pray.

Liran scanned the reply three times. "He replied, but he's not making sense. Who's Leah?"

Nichole snatched the phone from his hand, staring at the screen. "She was Jerad's sister." She darted her gaze between the two of them. "I know where he is."

❦

JERAD HADN'T STEPPED FOOT ON CAMPUS SINCE LEAH'S DEATH. Even when he returned to San Francisco, he had no desire to come back and face his demons. But maybe it was time. Stone said the Stanford University chapel would be an ideal place for them to meet. He had even mentioned something about reconciling Leah's death would be part of it.

That he didn't understand, and he had questions. Stone had reassured him he would explain once they met. As he walked toward the campus from the parking lot, he reached for his phone but realized he left it in his car. He stopped, considered whether or not to go back to his car but decided against it. He'd call her when he was finished, hopefully with good news.

She'd be livid at first, but if he could show her he was fine—healed—she'd be too happy to berate him for agreeing to meet with Stone despite her request that he stay away from the man.

He hoped he didn't regret his decision.

One of the double doors to the chapel stood open. He leaned in first to get a glimpse of what he was walking into.

"Jerad! Please, come in." Stone wore a white, cotton button-down shirt tucked in a simple pair of faded jeans. Not the pressed slacks and tailored shirt he'd worn when they met and at the conference.

Jerad followed him into the sanctuary area and down the center aisle. He'd only attended service a couple times because Leah had begged him to come. Now he wished he'd come more often. The chapel reminded him of the old churches he'd seen in Europe. The arched architecture, the murals around the stained glass windows behind the pulpit, and the stonework—all amazing.

As they reached the steps leading up to the pulpit, Stone stopped and turned around. He gestured to the front pew. "Let's sit and talk for a few minutes before we get started."

Jerad sat down, looking around the cavernous room. "I'd forgotten how beautiful this place was."

Stone sat a couple of feet from him, but turned sideways to face Jerad. "Your sister loved it here."

There it was. The proverbial two-ton elephant he didn't want to get trampled under. "You mentioned Leah's death as being a part of this. If you mean unforgiveness, I've mostly dealt with that already. I know Leah never meant to hurt anyone. She was just in too much pain herself."

Stone nodded. "Yes, she was. And that's why I need you to forgive me, Jerad."

"For what? You were her friend. You tried to help her."

Stone turned and stared at the image of the crucified Christ on the center stained glass panel. "Yes, but I failed. I didn't save her."

"I don't think that was your job, so I don't understand why you need me to forgive you."

He smiled and dropped his chin. "Maybe not, but it's a burden I still carry.

"Then if it helps, I forgive you. Thank you for trying to help her."

"Good. Thank you for that. Because healing you is my chance to make things right. I failed Leah, but I won't fail you."

"You keep saying you failed her. I don't understand."

"I was convinced I had healed her, Jerad. So was she, until she got worse. And then I walked away, told her I couldn't do anything more for her." Stone rose from the pew as he finished what he was saying.

"Wait." Memories of Leah's journal entries flooded his thoughts. "She referred to someone in her journals as 'E.' You're him?"

Stone nodded, then waved someone over. "Yes, my real name is Eben. I'm Liran's brother."

Artemis Tombs walked out of the shadows carrying a jacket over his arm and a long, slim, black case in his other hand.

Jerad jumped to his feet as the pieces fell together. He knew what that case held. Knew what it could mean for him. And he didn't want to hang around to find out for sure. He climbed over the pew to get away from them both only to see three men dressed in black fatigues and gun holsters.

Jerad turned around. Every part of him vibrated with an odd tension. He fisted his hands, ready to go out fighting at least. "I changed my mind. I don't want to be healed. And forget about what I said about forgiving you for Leah's death."

Stone took the jacket from Artemis and slipped it on. "I'm sorry to hear you say that, Jerad, but it doesn't change my plans. I will heal you to make amends for Leah's death, but for now, I'm taking you with us as a bargaining chip."

He nodded over Jerad's shoulder to the two lugs behind them.

Jerad lunged but not fast enough. Stone's goons grabbed and held him on both sides.

Stone pulled out a syringe from his pocket. "Hold his head still."

Jerad tried to twist away but the lug on his right had the advantage. He didn't see the needle go in but he felt the prick.

"There, that should make you more comfortable for our journey."

As Stone stepped back, Tombs placed the case on the first step, flipped the latches, then lifted the lid.

"What are doing?" Jerad's words slurred and his head felt too heavy to hold up.

"We have to leave a trail for your friends to follow, don't we?"

Jerad felt mesmerized. Or was that the drug? The thick shaft of the staff seemed to glow. Branches with leaves had sprouted near the top.

Stone lifted the staff from the case, which released the branches. Flower buds formed, then opened. "Stunning, isn't it?" He shifted his gaze to Jerad.

His mind screamed at him to run, but he couldn't move and he couldn't look away. The drug had immobilized him. Or was that the staff's doing? He couldn't think straight anymore.

"I couldn't heal your sister, Jerad. But I can heal you."

Jerad felt like he was watching one of those films played at high speed to show how a seed turned into a plant as he watched the flowers age, drop, and grew almond pods in their place. As Stone walked by him down the aisle, the pods split and almonds still in their inner shell dropped to the carpet.

The room turned hazy. Stone...Eben...whoever he was, turned around at the end of the aisle and walked back. He continued to speak, but the sounds became garbled as if Jerad were underwater. His body felt heavy and weak.

He fought the desire to sleep as long as he could until he lost the battle and succumbed to the sweet peace of darkness.

CHAPTER TWENTY-SEVEN

Never in her life had she wished more that flying cars were a reality. Traffic filled the three lines to a snail's pace already with rush hour traffic. The slow pace was agonizing, but the images of Jerad succumbing to a plague tortured her even more. Would they get to him on time?

Liran expanded the GPS on the screen, which showed red lines for miles. As they approached another exit, he pulled off. "We can reach the university through back roads. I remember Eben taking them once when I visited him years back."

Nichole thought she'd start crying again. "Thank you."

He nodded as he glanced at her.

From the back seat, Achem leaned forward and patted her shoulder. "We'll find him."

She squeezed his hand but could say nothing. That would let loose her panic and fear in a torrent of tears.

When they reached Stanford University, Liran parked the vehicle as close as possible. Nichole released her seat belt and shoved her door open in one fell swoop, slammed the door shut as she launched into a run. If she remembered right, the chapel was near the middle of the campus.

Her heartbeat whooshed in her ears, almost blocking out the

sound of Achem and Liran's footfalls behind her. Students gave them strange looks as they ran by, but she didn't care. Only one thing mattered. Jerad.

As they reached the front of the chapel, she headed toward the partially open double doors at one of the entrances. When she launched herself up the steps, a crunching sound came from where her foot landed on the steps.

Achem grabbed her arm to stop her. "Let us go in first."

She nodded, then knelt down. Almonds littered the step. The outer shell of the ones she crushed revealed the inner meat of the nut. "Why are these here?"

Achem grabbed her wrist. "Don't touch them. They came from the staff. We have no idea if they may spread the plague as well."

Liran rushed him past them, pushing the door open.

She stayed behind Achem as she followed him inside. As her eyes adjusted to the interior lighting, she took in the arches and murals. The scattering of almonds continued down the red, carpeted aisle leading to the steps and stage area.

Nichole ran ahead of Achem. "Jerad!" She spun around when she reached the steps to look behind them. The place appeared empty. Her eyes burned with the angry tears she refused to shed yet. He had to be here somewhere. She turned to Liran. "Where are they?"

"I don't know." He stared at her, but the message in his eyes sent her over the edge.

"No, it's not too late. Jerad has to be okay. I'd know it if he wasn't." She sat down on the carpeted step.

Liran stooped to pick up a piece of a branch with two leaves and an almond pod on it. "We know they were here."

A cell phone vibrated. Nichole pulled hers from her back jeans pocket. A blank screen met her. "It's not mine."

Liran had his phone in hand. Achem leaned in. Nichole jumped to her feet to join them.

Another text from Eben had joined his earlier one.

> I do so hope you found the gifts I left behind for you, *achi*. I've decided home ground is a better place to negotiate. And Jerad has decided to join us.

"Home ground?" Nichole sat back down on the stairs.

Achem nodded at Liran, then sat down next to her.

Liran walked down the aisle toward the doors as he held his phone to his ear.

She turned to Achem. "Is he calling his brother?"

"No, my dear, he's arranging a way for us to get back to Israel as soon as possible."

Nichole fought against the panic threatening to steal the air from her lungs and decimate her heart. She had to stop Eben. She had to get Jerad back. She had to breathe.

She grabbed Achem's hand. "I'm going with you."

He nodded. "Yes, I know."

She closed her eyes, tried to form a prayer but nothing would come. As she opened her eyes, tears streamed down her cheeks. "Pray with me?"

Achem squeezed her hand. "Yes, of course."

He couldn't move his body. Was this what death felt like?

But then a sensation like floating up from the bottom of a pool spread from his head to his feet. And as he drew closer to the surface, a roaring sound penetrated his ears and light pierced through his eyelids. Jerad cracked one open but immediately had to squint at the brightness.

Sensation slowly returned to his body. He was sitting, that much he could tell. He moaned as he lifted his head. Everything ached. He tried to cradle his head in his hands but something tugged at his wrists.

"Mr. Nebal, would you like some water?"

The voiced sounded female. He braved opening his eyes again. A petite woman in a dark skirt and white shirt held a plastic cup with a straw dangling to the side. The promise of what the cup held brought his intense thirst front and center. "Yes, please." He sounded more like a grumpy bullfrog.

As soon as the straw hit his lips he gulped down the entire cup.

"I'll get you some more." She moved away, causing him to squint again as the light she'd blocked flooded in.

"Jerad, good to see you awake." A figure leaned in front of him.

Jerad's blurred vision began to focus on Stone. The ceiling above him looked curved. He was on an airplane? He tried to move, but his body felt like an old punching bag and his wrists were bound to the arms of his seat.

"Seriously? In this condition, you think I'm some kind of threat?"

Stone straightened and signaled to someone behind Jerad. One of the men he remembered seeing in the chapel came over and cut the zip ties holding him. Once finished he returned to wherever he came from.

Jerad strained his neck to look around as he rubbed his wrists. Both lugs sat in the seats behind and to his right in what he could see now was a private jet. "Glad to see they're not dead from a plague. I assume your side-kick Tombs joined the party too?"

Stone laughed and sat in the seat facing Jerad. "You didn't think I'd hurt them, did you?"

"You killed people at a hotel in Denver and a children's hospital in Palo Alto."

Stone glanced away as he picked at something on his jeans. "I didn't fully understand how to control the staff then. Now I do."

Jerad tilted his head. "Your revelation, as great as that is for you, won't bring back a dear friend of mine and Nikki's."

Stone stopped fidgeting with a thread on his pants and met Jerad's gaze.

He continued his rant. "Who by the way, has a daughter who just found out she's pregnant with her first child."

Stone pushed out of his seat and headed toward the front of the plane.

He shouted over his shoulder. "You took away someone's mother and grandmother, Stone. I mean Eben. Whatever your name is. Can you live with that?"

Only the constant hum of the jet engines answered his question. At least the maniac had some remorse. Otherwise, he would have just laughed at him again.

The petite woman returned with a tray. "I brought you more water and a sandwich in case you're hungry."

Jerad thanked her as she handed him the tray. "Any idea where this thing is headed?"

She frowned at him. "Israel. Jerusalem specifically."

"Jerusalem?!"

The woman jumped back.

He hadn't intended to shout. "I'm sorry. I—"

The thug who cut his ties moved into view. "Is there a problem here?"

Jerad noted the zip ties he held up like a threat. As he gave the man a meek smile, he grabbed the water in one hand and the sandwich in the other. He needed time to assess his situation and preferred to do that with free hands.

The woman diverted her eyes and made a beeline to the back of the plane. Whoever she was either worked for Stone or for a private charter company that kept strict privacy clauses. Either way, she knew what was going on and would keep her mouth shut. He'd have to find an ally some other way.

The lug with the zip ties returned to his seat by his partner. Jerad eyed the water and sandwich. He still didn't have a clue if what he experienced in the chapel was the staff or the drug. Since he was clearly still alive, it must have been the drug.

One thing he knew for sure. Dead or alive, he was now their bargaining chip.

CHAPTER TWENTY-EIGHT

JERUSALEM

When they got off the jet, Nichole inhaled the sweet scent of wisteria floating on the night air. The private airstrip afforded them the invisibility they needed right now. Kudos to Liran for arranging their trip so quickly. She'd begun to appreciate the man's ability to step in and get things done.

Liran took the bag she'd quickly thrown together for the trip.

As he started to walk past her toward a vehicle she assumed to be their ride to some unknown destination, she touched his arm. "Thank you."

He gave her a small smile that didn't touch the sadness in his eyes.

Achem came alongside her and matched her stride. "He's very burdened."

"I can't even imagine." She wanted to ask him about Liran's father, but the timing just seemed wrong.

Liran stood by a Jeep, holding the passenger side door open. Nichole slid in first, then Achem. A dark-haired woman with a long braid sat behind the wheel.

She nodded to them. "Good evening."

Liran shut their door before climbing into the passenger seat. He turned to face her. "Nichole, this is Mira." He paused as he shifted his gaze to the young woman beside him. "She's the newest addition to the *Natsar*."

The look that passed between them shouted that their connection was more than business. Nichole covered her mouth to hide her smile. Another area of curiosity that she'd have to question and explore at a better time.

She sighed as she buckled her seat belt, taking in her first yet limited view of Jerusalem. How had this become her life? She wanted to blame someone but in reality, how could she blame anyone? Not even herself. They all seemed to be at the mercy of the consequences of other people's actions. First Soren, and now Liran's brother Eben. Even Liran and Achem shared the same proverbial boat with her but at least they chose to step into it. That's what they did.

But she'd had enough of the chaos and catastrophes. She wanted her quiet, peaceful life back. She wanted her father back. She wanted a normal life with Jerad.

However, could she really return to that after all she'd seen? Was that even possible? She'd heard others say trials change you. Even made you a different person sometimes. She thought of Frodo from Lord of the Rings and how he knew he could never return to the Shire and be happy.

Was that her fate too? Discontent in her own little shire?

They'd only driven about twenty minutes when Mira steered the vehicle onto a dirt road that crossed through a smaller wooded area to another small road. Grass and weeds grew up through cracks in the aged and faded tarmac, making the ride bumpy.

She turned right at what barely looked like a road and drove through a small tunnel nestled in the side of a hill. The interior of the vehicle grew even darker until they emerged on the other side and drove up to a cluster of Quonset huts huddled around one end of a crumbling tarmac.

She leaned forward in her seat. "What is this place?"

Mira parked the vehicle in front of the first building. "It's an old airstrip base the Israeli Military abandoned close to fifty years ago. My family purchased it two years ago with a plan to develop the area into a park and a neighborhood."

Halfway out the door, Liran stopped and twisted around to face her. "When do they plan to start construction?"

"No idea. You'll have to ask my father that. He's always coming up with new ideas."

The ever-present grief over her father squeezed Nichole's heart a little tighter. "My father used to be like that."

"Used to?" Mira tossed her braid behind her back.

"He died about a year ago."

Mira's eyes grew round. "That's got to be super painful."

Nichole blinked back tears as she nodded. She'd just met Mira but felt a connection to the young woman already.

Once Liran and Mira entered the structure, Nichole stopped Achem. "You mentioned Mira's name before, but who is she?"

"She was engaged to Eben several years ago. When he became withdrawn and secretive, she came to me with her concerns."

"About the relationship?"

He shook his head. "No, about what he'd involved himself in and what it would mean to the *Natsar*. She's a very observant young woman."

"Sounds like she was meant to be one of you."

Achem smiled. "I think so too."

He started to head to the structure, but she stopped him again. "So what's this thing between her and Liran?" She knew she was just being nosy, but in the big scheme of the mess they had all landed in, she wanted a full picture.

"That remains to be seen."

"That must be awkward since she was once engaged to his brother."

"Perhaps, but I don't think she ever fully gave her heart to Eben."

Liran leaned out the door. "Are you coming?"

Achem waved at him. "Yes, just discussing something. Be right in."

Liran paused, looking at them before he ducked back inside.

Achem tilted his head and raised his brows in the direction of where he had stood.

She made a silent 'oh' with her mouth. "Liran?"

"It would seem so."

"WHY ARE THEY TAKING SO LONG?" MIRA STOOD WITH HER hands on her hips, much like Nichole tended to when she took charge.

Liran tried to stifle his laugh.

"And why are you laughing?" She dropped her hands to her sides. "I see nothing humorous about any of this."

He approached her with his hand out in an attempt to calm her down. "I'm sorry. You just remind me of Nichole when you get miffed."

"I'm not miffed. Concerned is more likely."

"I'm sure they'll be in any moment." Liran took the opportunity to look around. The interior looked sturdy enough. A mishmash of carpets covered the floor, clashing in color as harshly as the array of dated furniture scattered around. And no dust...

"Did you set this place up yourself?"

"For the most part. I did enlist my brother's help with some of the furniture; but be assured, we can trust him."

"How is Isaac these days?" He remembered meeting her brother a couple times while she and Eben dated. The thought of his brother stabbed him in his heart. Achem was right. He'd tried to believe the best about Eben for so long that he'd become blind.

"He's quite well. Still a computer nerd." She let out a soft laugh. "He's hoping Achem will enlist him now."

"We may have to."

She fiddled with the end of her braid. "I hope you're not hurt."

Liran turned around. "Why would I be hurt?"

"That I didn't tell you more about what I saw happening with Eben." She took a step forward as her words tumbled one into another. "Perhaps if I'd said something sooner..."

"We all wanted to believe the best of him, didn't we?"

"Especially you." Her gray eyes seemed to see into the deepest place of his pain.

Which made him want to run at the moment. Swallowing down the knot of emotion in his throat, he stepped away to scan the room. Several cots lined one side of the sloping roof. A small sofa, coffee table, and three chairs of various designs and sizes filled the other side to create a sitting area. Water bottles and several boxes of dry goods sat on a table set up against the back wall. "Very impressive."

Mira lifted one of the storm lanterns. "No electricity but the water pump for the well works." She set the lamp down as her voice dropped. "I hope Nichole doesn't mind." She glanced toward the door. "What's she like?"

"A lot like you actually." He moved closer to where she stood. "Strong, determined...impassioned."

A blush spread through her cheeks as she looked down.

He lifted her chin, which hooded her eyes, making her even more attractive. He wanted to open up to her but didn't quite know how to yet. "We have a lot to talk about."

As she lowered her arms, she lifted her gaze to his. Long black lashes swept over dark brown eyes.

He tried not to look at her full lips but everything in him felt drawn to her.

"Yes, we do. I—"

The door creaked as it opened. Liran took a quick step back and spun around. Nichole and Achem filed in and looked around.

Achem clapped his hands together. "Mira, I'm impressed."

Liran sauntered over to the supplies and took a bottle of water. "My exact words."

Nichole took a bottle as well and raised one brow at him. She held the water up to take a sip but not before mumbling, "Is that what that was?"

Liran felt his face grow hot as he turned away.

Mira gave him a shy smile.

Achem held his finger to his mouth, lost in thought.

Liran dropped into one of the larger chairs that suited his long legs better. He stared at his water but kept Mira in his periphery vision. Somehow she seemed different to him. The thought sent a thrill through him then twisted his insides. He gulped down more of his water. Would they get a chance to explore the growing spark between them? Or would Eben always be a barrier between them?

Nichole and Mira both went to sit on the sofa, then stopped to make allowance for the other. They finally laughed and both sat down. The two women chatted for a moment about Jerusalem and seemed to connect easily.

For some reason, Liran found it...enchanting.

Mira moved to the edge of the couch. "What now?"

Achem crossed his legs as he settled back in his seat. "For the moment, get some rest and figure out our next move. Tomorrow I will reach out to some older contacts and call in a few overdue favors. We may need to build an army of our own for this confrontation."

"Will that be necessary?" Nichole's evident tiredness did nothing to diminish the passion in her tone.

"I'm afraid so. Based on what Mira discovered, our adversary is building reinforcements. And not just here."

Mira nodded. "Exactly. We're grossly outnumbered."

Achem gave her a tired smile. "No one can outnumber the army of Yahweh. We may have to deal with a confrontation, but I do believe we will prevail. Somehow."

Liran leaned on his knees as weariness settled into his body. "Maybe I can still convince Eben I can get him what he wants."

"Do what?" Mira's braid fell off her shoulder when she jerked back.

Liran ran his hands over his face. "I tried to convince Eben I would help him."

"Might have worked if he hadn't decided kidnapping Jerad might work better." Nichole's voice sounded sleepy.

Achem rose from his chair. "My friends, let's get some rest. I dare say our answer will present itself in the morning. One way or another."

CHAPTER TWENTY-NINE

OUTSKIRTS OF JERUSALEM

Eben left the solitude of his residence and headed to the business side of his secluded estate. He burst into Artemis Tombs' office. "Any surveillance updates?"

Artemis gathered the pages in front of him, then tapped them into a neat stack before setting them to the side. "Nothing significant yet. They didn't take a commercial flight so we can assume they made private arrangements. They're most likely hiding and will reach out at any time to negotiate something with us when they realize they have no choice."

Again they had to wait. His impatience grew unbearable with each passing minute. Breaking into Achem's offices would be easy. Overriding the security system to the lower levels of the *Natsar* headquarters would be slightly challenging but doable—he had resources readily available to deal with even that.

But the vault? For that they needed Achem, and that drove him near the edge, to need the man for anything when he'd worked so hard to be free of him. "It's been almost twenty-four hours. I won't wait much longer. I want this done and over with."

"We've found someone who may be able to tell us where they're hiding."

"Who?" He stopped and turned around.

"Isaac Kohen." Artemis raised his brows above his spectacles.

His breath caught in his lungs and stayed there. He grabbed hold of the bookshelf to his left. "Mira's brother? Are you sure?"

"Quite. A two-man team is on the way to bring him in for questioning."

Eben reined in the fury threatening to erupt from his core. How could she betray him like this? He drew in a deep breath through his nose and release a steady flow through his mouth. Perhaps she didn't know of his involvement. "How deeply is Mira involved?"

"She's been giving Achem information about some of our...dealings."

"How long has this been going on?"

"Several weeks, but when we examined her logins more closely we saw a pattern. But I believe she only recently figured out your part in the Collective."

"Why didn't you tell me sooner?"

"Seemed irrelevant. Until now."

"And now?"

"It's useful." Tombs adjusted his glasses.

Eben didn't realize he'd clenched his jaw so tightly until pain shot through his jaw. "I want to deal with her myself."

Artemis nodded. "I assumed you would."

"And her brother." He rolled his shoulders to tug his shirt away from the sweat on his back. "As soon as they get here, let me know. I'll handle his interrogation."

He strode out of the room without waiting for Artemis's reply. The thought of Mira's involvement stirred something deep that even alarmed him in its intensity. His pulse sped. He clenched his fists at his sides against the bubbling fury trying to take over his hold on reason. He thought he'd let go of that part of his life completely, but perhaps not.

Eben walked into his quarters and shut the door. Until the team arrived, he'd spend time in meditation to recenter his mind and prepare for Isaac's interrogation. He needed to free his mind of the past. None of that mattered at the moment.

Yet the harder he tried to push it away, the harder it pushed back. He picked up the glass of water he left on the side table and gulp down most of the contents. A guttural sound erupted from his mouth as he smashed the glass into the fireplace.

The long case sat open on a long credenza he'd cleared of everything. As he drew closer, the staff beckoned to him. He lifted the staff with reverent hands. Its power surged through him and brought him to his knees.

THE NIGHT HAD PASSED IN FITFUL SPURTS FOR ALL OF THEM. THE one-room Quonset hut did little to mask the sounds of their restlessness. Liran's cot had creaked quite a bit with his tossing and turning. Plus, he'd been acutely aware of Mira's presence in the cot near his. Perhaps a bad choice on his part, but he found himself feeling more and more protective of her.

As he continued to prep the Jeep for the supplies they would need, Achem and Mira walked out of the hut. Liran waited for them to finish their conversation before approaching her. Before they left to implement the first stages of their plan, he needed to say something to her. Tell her things she needed to know. Just in case.

As he approached, Achem nodded at him before going back inside.

Mira turned around to face him. She wore her hair loose, and as she moved, it cascaded over her shoulder and caught the morning light. "Liran, I thought that might be you."

"Oh?" He tilted his head, curious to hear her explanation and found himself eager to hear her voice. He fought the urge to capture a lock of her hair to see if it felt as silky as it looked.

She glanced away, as if suddenly shy. "Yes, I've come to recognize the sound of your footsteps."

Her words left him speechless for a moment. How could the recognition of his footsteps sound so...intimate?

She giggled behind her hand. "And you're the only one outside."

A wave of heat crept up the back of his neck. He cleared his throat. "I...I wish we had time to figure things out."

"We will as we go. Achem has—"

He moved closer to her. "No, I mean us. We haven't really had a chance..."

She kept staring up at him with those dark eyes.

He took her hand and led her around to the other side of the Jeep in an attempt to gain some privacy and prevent another commentary from Nichole. "I want you to know..."

A small smile turned up the corners of her mouth, tucking in the corners of her lips. "Yes?"

He did a quick sweep of their surroundings to make sure the others were still inside before tugging her closer. Words just wouldn't work for him right now. He lowered his head and captured her lips with his.

Nothing prepared him for what hit him next. He'd never believed in soul mates, as that could only work in a world that operated perfectly. But kissing Mira could convince him otherwise. She felt so familiar and comforting. He pulled away before the kiss became much more.

She blinked at him, almost as if surprised.

Had she felt what he had? Maybe kissing her was a huge mistake. He ran a hand through his hair. "I didn't know how else to express what I was feeling. I'm sorry."

"I'm not." She leaned in to initiate another kiss.

Just as their lips touched, the sound of Achem clearing his throat shot them apart faster than opposing magnets.

"I left my phone inside." Mira dashed into the hut.

Achem moved closer to him. At least he was smiling. A little. "I see you and Mira are progressing."

He turned his back to the Jeep and leaned against the door. "Yes, sorry about that. I know the timing is off, but I didn't want to lose my chance to tell her...in case..."

Achem patted his shoulder. "Everything will work out fine, Liran. You'll see. And then you and Mira can figure out what you mean to each other."

He nodded.

Achem went to the back of the Jeep to load the satchel he carried.

Liran followed him, recognizing the bag as the one Achem used to carry currency when they needed cash on hand—most likely US Dollars and Israeli Sheqel this time.

Liran lifted the bed covering in back to stow the satchel out of sight. "Do you think it's possible for her and me to..."

"Have a relationship? Yes, of course. You two are already figuring that out."

He paused as he found the words he needed. "Yes, but will Eben always be between us?"

Achem straightened from what he was doing and faced him. "Yes, but that's up to you two to decide if you're willing to let go of the past and embrace the future."

Liran nodded again before walking back to the Quonset hut to retrieve what he needed. In light of what lay ahead, he dearly hoped they'd have a future to embrace.

Mira stood by the table holding the food supplies, staring at her phone. "Isaac sent a text. He has more supplies for us."

Achem stood just inside the door. "I didn't realize Isaac was aware of our location."

She smiled. "Yes, he helped me set this place up. He should be here any minute. I'll go out and wait for him." She headed back out the door.

Liran had started to follow her but stopped. "Isaac helped her set this place up."

The sound of tires on the rough ground met his ears, then grew much louder. More like several vehicles.

Achem's expression shifted to alarm.

Nichole jumped up from the couch. "Oh no..."

"Stay inside!" Liran rushed out after Achem just as multiple vehicles skidded on the broken tarmac in front of the hut. He grabbed Mira's arm and pushed her back inside. "Stay with Nichole."

Several black SUVs surrounded them. Uniformed men jumped out, semi-automatics up and ready. As Liran counted eight of them, his brother climbed out of the middle vehicle. When Eben opened the door, Liran caught a glimpse of Artemis Tombs too.

Eben stopped in front of Liran. "*Shabbat Shalom*, *achi*."

"What are you doing, Eben?" Liran clenched his fists at his sides. Everything ceased to exist except for the six-foot gap between him and his brother, which he wanted more than anything to eliminate in a launched attack. He'd never liked to use the word 'hate' but at the moment nothing else fit what vibrated through his every cell. He no longer faced his brother, he faced his enemy.

"I got tired of waiting." Eben signaled to one of his men. "Bring out the two inside."

Mira's protest came from behind. "Let go of me, you big buffoon."

Nichole's voice came from his left. "Where's Jerad?"

Eben gestured to the SUV farthest from them. "He's quite safe, I assure you. In fact, if you'd like to join him, he's in the last vehicle there." He darted his gaze to one of the guards. "Put her with the other ones."

"What are you doing?" Nichole fought against the guard trying to bind her hands behind her back. She looked at Eben. "Seriously?"

Achem took a step toward her, but one of the guards behind them pulled him back and bound his hands behind his back as well. "*Shalom*, Nichole. All will be well"

She nodded before letting the guard lead her away.

When he opened the vehicle door to help her in, Liran caught a glimpse of Jerad and Mira's brother, Isaac.

Mira jumped forward and cried out. "Isaac!"

Eben caught her wrist and yanked her around. "You brother agreed to tell us where you and your friends set up your makeshift base if we promised not to hurt you. And I intend to keep that promise, Mira. I'm a man of my word. And I will make that same promise to you. I will do nothing to harm your brother as long as you cooperate."

Liran charged his brother, but two of the guards grabbed him and pushed him to his knees, wrenching his arms behind him at an awkward angle.

Rage blazed over Mira's face like an inferno as she tried to twist away. "You're acting like a maniac."

Eben yanked her toward him. "Is that all you have to say, Mira? After all, we haven't seen each other for over a year."

Liran struggled against his captors, but only succeed in causing pain to shoot through his shoulders. "Let her go!"

"Stop fighting, *achi*. You've lost this battle." Eben nodded to the guards, who then lifted Liran to his feet and zip-tied his wrists behind his back.

Mira yanked away from Eben's grasp. "What would you like me to say? Thank you for walking away from everyone who cared about you? Or how about this. Thank you for betraying Liran and me."

His eyes narrowed. "You and Liran?"

She glanced at Liran.

Eben darted his gaze between the two of them. "You care about him, don't you?" He laughed. "Imagine that. My little brother has swooped in and rescued my ex-fiancée."

Mira sneered at him. "I never needed rescuing, Eben, except maybe from you. So, let me thank you right now for leaving and saving me from making a *huge* mistake."

He shoved her toward one of the guards. "Bind her and put her with the others. Put these two in the middle vehicle. I'm done playing games."

As guards holding Liran led him past Eben, he dug his heels into the ground. "What are you doing, *achi*?"

For a moment his features softened, reminding Liran of when they were boys. "Going home, of course. To *Natsar* Headquarters, which will belong to me now. As will the contents of the vault."

"Don't do this, Eben."

"This is my destiny, little brother." He tossed a glance toward Achem. "And nothing will stand in my way."

CHAPTER THIRTY

"I'm ready to go home." Nikki nestled into the crook of Jerad's shoulder as the SUV made its way to whatever unknown destination their armed chauffeurs had orders to take them to.

He kissed the top of her head. "I know. Me too."

Mira and her brother Isaac sat in the seats facing them.

Isaac, who looked to be maybe twenty years old if that, appeared crestfallen. "I remember when Eben would hang out with us." He shook his head. "I don't know who he is anymore."

Mira gave him a wan smile. "I know."

Isaac kept his gaze on his sister. "Any idea where they're taking us?"

Mira leaned toward the window. "I'm guessing *Natsar* Headquarters. For a final showdown."

She sent Jerad a telling look before facing the window again.

They rode the rest of the way in silence. But not for long. The vehicle came to a stop. The driver and his partner slid out and shut their doors.

Silence filled the SUV again. Then the doors opened, flooding the vehicle with light. The guards helped them step down to a gravel-covered back road. The other two SUVs sat nearby, already empty.

The guards took them through a back gate that led into a beautiful garden courtyard.

Nichole let out a small gasp. "It's gorgeous here."

Mira nodded. "One of my favorite places here. Achem's too."

Once inside, the guards took them down a hallway with random doors on both sides. The architecture reminded Jerad of early twentieth-century design, especially the transom windows over the doors. He knew Achem presented an image of an archeological consultant with ties to the Israel Antiquities Authority as a cover. But neither Achem nor Liran had ever really described their 'headquarters.'

They turned left and went through a door that led to a stairwell that spiraled down at least three levels by Jerad's estimation. The lower they went the danker the air turned. Must be going underground. One of the guards took lead and opened the single door there.

The smell of damp earth grew stronger. An underground tunnel stretched ahead with large stones lining the walls and an arched ceiling that must be twelve feet high, much like the images he saw from the underground Templar tunnels in the city of Acre.

Could they be connected somehow? He'd have to sit down and have a deep conversation with Achem when they reached the other side of this nightmare. If they made it through it alive. He didn't want to say anything to Nikki while they were in the SUV, for her sake and Isaac's, but he and Mira both seemed to have doubts as to whether they would live past the day.

As they drew closer to what appeared to be a large opening to another underground area, he caught the sound of voices.

Achem's rich voice seemed amplified by the catacombs. "What makes you think you can really control any of the relics, Eben."

"I've already proven that, old man."

The guards herded them into the room off of the main tunnel. More like a meeting hall in a way. The ceiling spanned upward even higher than the tunnel and looked hewn out of stone, almost like an underground cistern. At the far end stood an ominous door, roughly ten feet tall and eight feet wide. A long handle ran down the right side with a keypad and screen next to it.

The Vault.

The thought that the Ark of the Covenant sat behind that door did weird things to Jerad's brain.

Eben stood at the back of the room, along with Artemis Tombs. Six more uniformed men stood guard, three on each side. Tombs signaled to the guard closest to them. "Cut their ties."

Once freed, Mira rushed over to where Liran sat bound to an ornate chair, just like Achem.

As the guards release them, Jerad leaned toward Nikki. "They're an item now I see."

Eben bent down and lifted the staff of Aaron from its case.

She opened her eyes wider. "I think we have bigger things to think about right now."

NICHOLE CLUNG TO JERAD. HER BREATH CAUGHT AT THE SIGHT of the staff in Eben's hand. She remembered the description in the Bible of when it budded and bloomed, but never imagined she'd see it in person.

Eben stood in front of Achem, silent in his consideration. As he looked down at Achem, a battle of uncertainty played across his features.

Did he doubt his decision?

Tombs stood just behind him, watching Eben.

Nichole still couldn't figure out who was really in charge here, Eben or Tombs. And what did Tombs hope to gain from all of this?

Anger twisted Eben's expression as he bumped Achem's foot with the bottom of the staff. "Wake up, old man."

"I wasn't sleeping. I was praying." Achem shifted in his chair.

"Good, because you'll soon stand before judgment."

"Why?"

"Because you're a liar."

"I'm not a liar, Eben." The cadence of his voice remained calm.

"You kept what you did to our father a secret." Eben seemed even angrier at Achem's lack of offense.

"Only because your father asked me to. I honored his wish."

Eben sneered at him and started to turn away.

"And I kept him out of prison."

Eben spun around, his face contorted with rage as he lifted the staff as if to strike Achem.

"No!" Liran's cheeks had turned red from his shout.

Eben lowered his arm as he faced Liran. "If you play his defender you will have to face judgment too."

Liran shook his head. "It's true, *achi*. Our father took a bribe to help the thieves going after the Ark. Achem had no choice. Nichole would have perished in that fire as well had he not taken action."

Nichole gasped. "Are you saying..." A sob broke her train of words. She strode closer to where Eben stood, shaking free of Jerad's grip when he tried to stop her. Tears made the anger in her eyes glitter. "Is that what all this is about?"

Eben's expression turned cold. "In part. It's about restitution." He nodded at Tombs who signaled the guard standing behind Jerad. "Bring him."

"No, no, no!" Nichole lunged forward, holding onto Jerad, but another guard grabbed her from behind. "Please, you can't do this. The staff kills people. You can't use it on Jerad."

Eben took measured steps to where she stood. The leaves on the staff rustled with his movement. The sweet scent of the blossoms filled her nose. The green leaves were the most beautiful green she'd ever seen in nature. The wood of the staff appeared richly oiled and full of life.

"Don't be afraid, Nichole. I will use the staff to heal Jerad, just as the children were healed."

She shook her head and tried to squelch her tears. A knot of desperation lodged in her throat, making her words sound hoarse.

"No, they weren't. Please, I'm begging you." She shook her head. "Please don't take him away from me."

Eben ignored her, returning to where he stood before. The guard still held Jerad in place in front of him.

Liran strained against his bindings. "Eben, don't do this."

When Mira pulled at Liran's ties, one of the guards yanked her back. "No, let me go!"

Both hands holding the staff, Eben closed his eyes and began to hum. Soft at first, the sound took on a life of its own, growing in resonance until Nichole felt the vibrations break through her sobs and spread through her entire body.

And that meant she would die too. She welcomed it. At least she wouldn't have to live without Jerad. She closed her eyes against the blinding light exploding from the staff and waited for death to claim her.

Peace settled over her. A soft and comforting voice seemed to pierce her heart.

Shalom, Nichole, all will be well.

CHAPTER THIRTY-ONE

Liran fought against the ties holding him as the sound of the vibrations reached a deafening level. He gritted his teeth and grunted as he tried to scoot the iron chair along the stone floor. He had to stop Eben from killing Jerad and releasing more of the deadly plague.

Opposite him, Achem struggled yet managed to break one hand free.

Liran pushed harder. Broke his right hand loose and reached for the staff just as Achem launched himself between Jerad and the staff.

An explosion of light and force pushed his body back against the chair, while every wish and desire he had about his life exploded in his mind like a slide show.

The past.

The present.

The future.

He tried to hold the images but the pain in his head grew in intensity and then it stopped. Like an image playing in slow motion, he watched his brother thrown back into the wall. Achem fell to the ground. Jerad crumbled to his knees.

❦

Nichole blinked. At first she could only see the image of the last thing she saw, like when she looked at a bright light and then closed her eyes. The horrific scene of Eben and Achem engulfed and Liran flying in between them. Then everything went dark.

She inhaled deeply against the tightness across her chest before realizing it was an arm. She lifted her head. "Jerad?"

The guard next to her groaned.

She pushed his arm off as she sat up.

She was alive?

She was alive!

As her vision cleared, she crawled to where Jerad lay as fast as she could. "Jerad?"

She crouched over him and sobbed his name. "Jerad, please be okay."

He groaned.

She covered her mouth with her hand as she laughed. "Are you okay?"

He blinked several times. "I think so. Can't see much though."

"Give it a minute." She turned to look around the room. Most everyone appeared passed out on the ground, including the guards.

Mira and her brother had managed to get Liran free and lowered him to the ground. Yet even he seemed to be coming back to consciousness.

She searched the back of the room. Achem lay in a heap, unmoving. Something deep in her gut rose up and snatched her breath away. "Achem?" She crawled toward him. "Achem."

When she reached him, she nudged his shoulder, but he didn't respond. She felt his neck for a pulse but found nothing. She drew closer and turned him onto his back. His head lolled to the side, his lips a deathly blue. She started CPR as Jerad came to help her.

She didn't know how long they tried, only that Jerad stopped her at one point. Still crouched at his side, she lay her head on his chest. A sob broke with her words. "Achem, please, please...come back."

Jerad held her shoulders and lifted her to her feet. She turned and sobbed into his chest.

He stroked her hair. "I'm sorry, Nikki."

She lifted her face to his. Tears streamed down his cheeks as well. She cupped his face between her hands and pressed his lips against his, grateful he was still alive, praying he would remain so.

"Achem?" Liran's voice broke into a sob as he knelt by Achem's body.

Mira crouched by Eben's lifeless form, his head at an odd angle to his body against the wall. "His neck was broken." She went to Liran and stood next to him with her hand on his shoulder.

The guards were rousing and looking around, disoriented and then confused when they could find neither of the men in their command. Artemis Tombs was nowhere to be seen. He must have fled while they were still unconscious.

Liran pushed to his feet, then crouched before his brother's body, as if to pay his respects. He picked up the staff as he came back to where the rest of them stood waiting.

No leaves or flowers remained. The wood looked old, dry, and ancient now. He held it across his palms, staring at it a moment before lifting his head. "I'll put it with the Ark, as Achem wanted." He glanced over his shoulder at his brother. "It won't fall into the wrong hands again."

Tears burned her eyes again. She couldn't stand to look at Achem laying there, so lifeless. "I think he knew he was going to die today."

Jerad tilted his head down to look down at her. "You think so?"

She nodded. "I saw it in his eyes when he spoke to me. He wanted me to be at peace with it."

He pulled her into a full embrace. "I'm so sorry, Nikki."

She rubbed her face against his shirt. "I'm glad you're okay." She leaned back to see his face. The dark circles she'd grown accustomed to seeing under his eyes weren't there and he didn't look exhausted. "Are you okay?"

He looked away for a moment as if he needed to think about it. "I think I am. The constant headache is gone."

They both shifted their focus to Liran as he left the room, carrying the staff to the vault. He leaned forward until his face was level with the screen. The lock released with a loud click.

"Do you believe...?" Jerad searched her face with a hint of awe in his expression.

Her heart clenched as she gave him a trembling smile. "Yes, I believe."

CHAPTER THIRTY-TWO

JERUSALEM, TWO WEEKS LATER

Liran had chosen the courtyard garden to hold Achem's celebration of life ceremony. Achem would have loved it as it was his favorite place in the whole compound that made up *Natsar* Headquarters. The natural flora and fauna added their own touch of beauty and meaning. He thanked Yahweh for a perfect day, weather-wise.

Many colleagues Achem had connected with from various archeological digs came to pay their respects. Liran had greeted each one with the care and concern he imagined Achem would. And for those who asked, he explained that Achem's heart had just given out. The medical examiner had declared it a fatal heart attack due to the stress of the situation. Liran preferred to think of it as a fateful heart event. He liked thinking of Achem sitting with Yahweh and asking Him all kinds of questions.

Tomorrow he would bury his brother. After giving the Israeli police the details of what had occurred, minus the staff, they'd ruled it a hostage situation and were investigating Mira's employer and their connection to dealings with Artemis Tombs, who seemed to have disappeared without a trace of his existence. Mira's former employer would soon be on trial for his part, though Liran suspected the man hadn't had a clue as to what he'd involved himself in.

Now as the day waned, just a few close friends remained. For that, he was most grateful. To see Nichole and Jerad together—and Jerad looking healthier than he had since Liran first saw him digging wells in Africa with Nichole.

Mira and her brother stood to one side of the garden, talking in hushed tones. Liran couldn't imagine walking through the last two weeks without this petite fireball. And he'd started to think he might be falling for her in a big way. But would she be involved with the *Natsar* after what had happened? He did not want to make a decision between love and duty.

Love? His chest tightened. Was he in love with Mira? He walked over to join them, just as Nichole and Jerad strolled over.

Nichole dabbed her eyes with a tissue. "I think this would have made Achem very happy, Liran."

He tucked his hands in his trouser pockets. "I think so too." His right hand hit the small bag he'd tucked away and had forgotten about. He pulled it out and held it out to Nichole. "I found this in Achem's jacket. There's a note inside."

She covered her mouth before reaching out to take it, slipping out the contents. As the bracelet sparkled in her hand, she gasped. "It's so beautiful." She unfolded the small slip of paper. More tears fell down her cheeks. She covered her mouth as she handed it to Jerad, nodding at him to read it aloud.

"Shalom, Nichole, all is well. Achem."

Jerad pulled her against him. "That's beautiful."

As dusk made its first appearance, Liran glanced around the garden to see they were the only ones left. A peaceful hush fell between them.

Mira glanced at her brother, Isaac, who gave her an encouraging nod. She swung her gaze to Liran but hesitated to speak.

"What is it, Mira?" He wanted to take her hand but with so

many eyes, he didn't want to make her uncomfortable. He'd let her take the lead on what kind of future she wanted with him.

"I never had the chance to tell Achem that I found something else of great interest while at CBS. Artemis Tombs had some other transactions outside of his direct dealings with the company. One, in particular, had to do with two artifacts found not far from the Nile outside of Egypt."

A surge of energy and expectation shot through Liran. "That can't be a coincidence. Do you remember the details?"

She gave a sheepish smile. "Yes, I swiped the data."

He allowed himself to laugh. He wished Achem had been part of it as well, to see the culmination of his lifelong mission. But somehow discussing it here after the celebration seemed fitting and honoring to the man he was.

Liran brought his attention to Jerad and Nichole. "Looks like we may have another adventure ahead of us. Care to join us?"

"Sure." Jerad grinned.

Nichole laughed and then playfully slapped Jerad's chest. "I think we have a wedding to take care of first."

Again, Liran glanced around the garden. "This seems like an ideal place for a wedding too."

Nichole's eyes and mouth turned into perfect circles. She shot her gaze to Jerad, tears filling her eyes. "Are you game?"

He pressed his lips to hers in a quick kiss. "Always."

As Liran headed inside, Mira slipped her hand into his. He stopped and looked down into her gray eyes. "Are you sure you want to be involved with the next *Natsar* leader?" He kept his tone light but the weight of his question came from the deepest of places of his soul.

Mira put her hand on his chest. "As long as I get Liran Dakarai first."

Sign up for my newsletter and get a free copy of my novella, The First Encounter.

(written as Dineen Miller)

He's fighting with his past. She's sent to show him a future. Will Lexie succeed in her mission, or will Elliott stay trapped in the torment of his previous life?

Want more stories by Neena Roth?
Check out **CONVERGENT REVOLUTION**
on KindleVella.

**Two worlds. Two unlikely heroes. They're about to meet for the first time...
or die trying.**

A NOTE FROM NEENA

Dear friend,

If you enjoyed *Staff Dominion*, please share it with your friends and write a review on Amazon so others readers can enjoy this second installment of the Treasures of the Ark thriller series. Book three, *Stone Sovereignty,* is in the works!

You can also check out my Prophetic Arts Thriller series written under my author name, Dineen Miller. *The Soul Saver* is book one.

Thanks for reading!

-Neena

Find me also at Neena Roth Books on DineenMiller.com.

Sign up for my newsletter to get the latest updates on future books, news, and giveaways too!

And please connect with me on these social media platforms:

facebook.com/DineenMiller.AuthorGraphicDesinger
goodreads.com/dineenmiller
twitter.com/dineenmiller
instagram.com/dineenmiller
bookbub.com/authors/neena-roth

CONVERGENT REVOLUTION: SAMPLE

EPISODE 1: WHAT IF...

Convergent Evolution is the independent evolution of similar features in species of different lineages.
— Wikipedia

Convergent Revolution is the merging of two parallel realities into one, resulting in either complete destruction or the salvation of all.
— Sage Bendari Bekene

The Bendari Prophecy

The great emergence will stir the waters.
The great waters will birth the bridge.
The great bridge will span the gap and join two lands.
And great will be the new day that is revealed.
The bride and groom will meet,
and the inheritance of the generations
will be seen in the filling of the pools.
And this will be the beginning of
the Convergent Revolution.

PROLOGUE

The path welcomed her, beckoned to her. Morning dew still coated the hard ground and leaves scattered by the night storm. Their tips curled gently upward, creating tiny pools of rainwater that reflected the overhead tree branches and clouds in miniature.

Sunrise had peeked over the horizon, bathing the trees in a subtle glow. Cool air lingered and welcomed her into its embrace. Reyna inhaled the scent of the earth washed and refreshed by the summer showers. She closed her eyes and smiled. That familiar, peaceful sensation never grew old. Kept her grounded and solid.

When she opened her eyes, she no longer stood on her beloved path. A dark opening to the woods loomed ahead of her. She spun around. Her house stood in its usual place, as well as the rest of the horse ranch.

Yet...something was different.

The life that hummed about the place in a constant flow of activity was absent. And the colors...the red stones of the house and barn looked darker. The bright green of the new grasses resembled the old pines in the deep, old woods. Even the rocks and boulders along the hillside in the distance appeared starker than normal.

Horses grazing in the field whinnied and burst into a run, their chestnut and black manes waving as they scattered in several directions. A black undulating mass pursued them, then redirected toward her. Out of the dark cloud emerged animals similar in shape to a dog, teeth bared and snarling.

Mountain wolves.

The rumors were true. She hadn't wanted to believe them anything more than scare tactics her grandmother used to frighten her and her older brother when they were little. Mountain wolves rarely came down from the higher regions and if they did, never more than one or two at a time.

Yet the black mass moving toward her numbered at least two

dozen if not more. She glanced side to side. Nothing to protect her. Reyna turned and bolted into the dark woods, searching for a high perch to escape.

The thundering rhythm increased behind her, accompanied by faint snarls. Every tree she ran past held the age of the ancient trees she knew well from the northern country. They stood tall and wide with no lower branches, not even one she could jump to reach.

Her leg muscles began to burn and ache along with her lungs. How much longer could she outrun the pack? They lived miles from their neighbors and even further from town, isolated from everyone.

But this didn't even feel like her woods. Nothing looked familiar.

Reyna dared a glance back. The dogs gained on her. As she turned back around, a branch smacked her shoulder, knocking her to the ground. She jumped up and grabbed where it met the trunk and hauled herself up.

The wolves circled the tree in a frenzied, writhing mass of black fur and white teeth. She looked back in the direction she came—nothing but trees. She'd have to climb higher, figure out a plan of rescue. Glancing upward, she fingered her red floral scarf. If she could get high enough, maybe she could signal for help.

As she reached up, the tree began to vibrate, then shake. She threw her arms around the trunk in a desperate hug. Below, the wolves squealed and parted in all directions. One floundered in a crack in the ground that widened and seemed to swallow the animal in a single gulp.

She needed help. She started praying as Gamma had taught her as a young child.

The tree swayed, knocking her feet loose. Reyna yelped, legs flailing. She managed to hook one knee over a branch and pulled herself tighter against the tree. Ahead of her, some of the trees began falling to the side, opening a clear view of what lay beyond. A fog seemed to be rolling in from the sea.

A young man emerged from the mist. He had light brown hair and wore a tunic-like shirt that buttoned down the front. As he drew closer, he reached out toward her as if waving or calling out to her, but she heard nothing but a growing roar like that of a tornado.

She ripped her scarf free of her neck and waved it. "Help! Please!"

The mist thickened and overtook him, completely shrouding his form. In the distance, the ocean churned like she'd never seen before. Not like the waves on the shore she remembered playing in as a child when her family made the two-hour trek on horseback.

No, the great span of water boiled, churned like an angry mass. Shafts of water broke free of the violent dance and shot into the air. A dark, rocky mass emerged from the chaos and grew.

An explosion filled the air, knocking her right arm and leg loose. The branch in her left hand snapped. She tumbled backward, glimpsing the blue sky over her and the green and brown of the branches rushing past her.

They'd never find her because the wolves would find her first.

EPISODE 2: FEARFUL DREAMS

Reyna James watched the seeds sail from her hand and sprinkle the ground like the first snowflakes of the winter now gone. This section of their small flower garden would soon be filled with sunflowers and dahlias by the summer. She loved their big bold heads of color that stood tall and unaware of their vulnerability to the winds that swayed and at times knocked them over.

Another handful peppered the ground. She worked her way from the front of the garden to the back, careful to keep her back to the forest. She didn't want to be reminded of the dream...the nightmare. She'd looked forward all winter to walking her favorite wooded path in the freshness of spring, but the images kept tormenting her heart.

Why would she dream such a thing? Again? Wolves hadn't been seen in the area for years. Nothing had happened locally to spark such fears in her sub-conscience. Why couldn't she shake this lingering feeling?

She started to turn her head to look behind her but stopped herself. What if the dream meant something more? Her Gamma had had dreams in the past that had proven significant. Did she have the same gift?

Reyna lifted her head. Her grandmother stood at the end of

the garden, her skirts in her hands as she tip-toed through the loose dirt barefoot.

"Gamma! It's still chilly out and the ground is cold. You'll catch a cold." Though she'd long ago learned to pronounce her r's, she still preferred her childhood nickname for her grandmother.

Gamma waved her hand as if to shoo away Reyna's words. "I'm fine. It's you I'm concerned about."

"Why?" She glanced up at her grandmother but continued to distribute a fine layer of seeds. The last frost had passed so her days would become busy again helping with the family horse ranch.

"Sometimes things aren't what they seem, Rey."

With a soft laugh, Reyna tossed another handful of seeds. "And what makes you say that."

Though her grandmother had long ago lost any of the honey tones to her hair, her grayness did nothing to diminish her great beauty. In fact, it only enhanced it. Along with a wisdom she wore in the crinkle of her eyes and the way her lips tilted in a knowing smile.

"A dream can be an opportunity for the Holy One to show us something we need to know, even if he didn't send it."

"I don't know what you're talking about." She kept her head down. If she didn't talk about it, the nightmare would go away, and no one would die.

Gamma stood in front of her now. She wrapped her hands around Reyna's seed-filled hand. "I heard you cry out last night. Doesn't take a genius to figure out you had a nightmare again. Same one?"

Head down, she fought the tears, just nodded. "I thought they were gone. I haven't had one since I was a little girl...right before Granddad died."

"I know." Tears crept into her gray-blue eyes for just a moment. She took a deep breath. "You know, the enemy tries to steal our joy by disrupting the things that bring us peace."

Reyna searched Gamma's face and found some hope. "Then is it a warning to protect me?"

Gamma wiped away the one tear that escaped down Reyna's cheek. "Perhaps. Or is it the enemy's attempt to hide something from you that terrifies him?"

"Like what?"

"Something wonderful." She patted Reyna's hand before turning back the way she came. "I'm making buttermilk biscuits for breakfast. Come grab a few before you head out."

Head out? Where? Reyna glanced behind her, stared at the opening in the woods that seemed to beckon her back to her favorite path. Her heart longed to go and explore, to see the forest coming back to life after the hibernation of winter. Did she really think she could stay away?

She turned back around, quickly spreading the remainder of the flower seeds. The rest of her chores could wait until she returned. Just a short walk would restore her peace and relieve her fears, surely.

Reyna draped the seed sack on its hook in the barn and made her way back into the house to get her hiking boots and satchel. Maybe she could extend her walk a wee bit to sketch a few of her favorite spots. Once in her room, she donned her boots and reached for her floral scarf then paused. She studied the gauze in her hand, fighting the memory of the nightmare.

Did she dare the trip, take the risk? She tossed it on the bed and then stuffed her sketch book and pencils into her bag before heading back downstairs and to the back door.

Gamma met her there, handing her a baggie filled with warm biscuits and kissed her on the cheek. "Take your time. The rest can wait." She cupped Reyna's cheek. "Go before your parents wake up and put you to work."

"Thanks, Gamma." Reyna stepped off the porch, nabbing a biscuit to munch on her way. The doughy smell made her smile. Her mouth watered and her stomach gurgled in anticipation of the buttery goodness that defined her grandmother's baking skills.

She reached the opening in the woods behind her house. The path called to her like a lost love. Not really a path though. More like a natural break in the dense forest. For as long as she could remember the trail had been there. The constant tread of her booted feet only enhanced it.

Reyna glanced back at the James' family ranch. All stood as it should. The sun now rose high enough to fully illuminate the house and barn, highlighting the red stones and glinting off the paned windows. The horses grazed in the pasture on the west side of their property. Just as it always looked.

Bright. Comfy. Home.

Not a single thing to be afraid of.

She turned back to the path and stepped into the woods.

EPISODE 3: JOSHUA'S MISSION

His father handed him another apple for his supply sack. Sunlight streaming in through the picture window created a warped reflection in the shiny red skin. Soon the distortions and deceptions of the past would be set to right. The prophecy would be proven true. The time had come. He was certain of it. With a nod, Joshua Taylor tucked the apple into his bag with the rest of his supplies.

"You know, *you* don't have to do this?" His father's eyes held the weight of the world in a single glance, yet even Joshua, who hadn't lived in his twenty-five years half the life his father had, somehow knew he did. They'd waited long enough. They needed to know.

He *wanted* to know. "But we both know it's time. The signs are there."

His father nodded and turned away. His shoulders slumped.

Joshua studied the man who'd raised him since the age of seven without his wife—Joshua's mother. At the very least, he would find a way to settle the question of what happened to her. Why she hadn't come back when the Great Emergence failed to happen.

"Your sister is at the dock, waiting to say goodbye." His father turned around, cheeks wet.

Joshua slung the strap of his satchel over his neck before

walking over to his father. "I'll be back soon. It's just like any other coastal survey assignment. I'm just going to keep alert to anything else...significant."

"You seem so sure you'll find something."

"I am."

His father pulled him into a hug. Joshua inhaled the familiar smells of his father's pipe and wood stain from his workshop. "I've never regretted teaching you about the prophecy, son." He pulled back and held Joshua at arm's length. "Until now."

"But you won't in the end." He picked up the supply bag.

His father nodded and patted him on the shoulder. "That's what I'm afraid of."

Though he understood what his father feared, he chose not to acknowledge and give it life. His father believed their mother's disappearance and the last failed occurrence indicated her death. Joshua believed the recent signs said otherwise, that there was a chance she could still be out there somewhere, destined to fulfill her role in the Great Emergence.

He headed toward the door. He wouldn't let fear eclipse the very thing they'd hoped and prayed for—believed in—for two generations. Their region had diminished radically the last five years and the outskirts of Cape Sempler barely existed. These days orders for his father's handcrafted furniture came from more populated areas like Billington and larger cities further east.

When he had compared the coastal surveys he'd done over the last year to the ones done just ten and five years earlier, he'd begun to see a pattern. And the last two years alone showed a significant acceleration in the changes happening to coastal lines and inland water basins. Once livable lands were now barren and decimated, as if the ground were dying from beneath.

Joshua didn't know how he knew, but something major was about to shift. An urgency pushed him to find evidence to prove to the High Council that they needed to face their fading reality of prosperity and figure out what needed to be done.

He headed out the front door, glancing behind to wave at his father who remained on the front porch. His sister Jessie stood barefoot at the end of the pier, her sandy hair loose and blowing free in the breeze, looking more like the little girl she used to be instead of the young woman she had become. Bluey's white fur undulated in the wind, his blue eyes squinting against the sun as he panted. He kept his usual place next to her as a faithful guardian.

Joshua's little, not-so-little-anymore sister didn't remember their mother, didn't fully understand what was taken from them. He at least had seven years with his mother whereas Jessie barely had three. That also spurred him on to find out the truth as to why the prophecy still hadn't come to fruition—why their mother hadn't fulfilled her role and was still missing.

He tapped Jessie gently on the shoulder.

She spun around and wrapped her arms around his chest. "What am I going to do without you?"

He hugged her, then gently pushed her back. The redness around her eyes told him she'd been there for hours, worrying. "You'll do just fine, Jessie. You practically run the place on your own."

She dipped her head down before lifting her chin. "I know, it's just that..."

"Just what?"

"I'm used to you being here most of the time. Even when you're annoying. Your other trips didn't last near this long." Tears welled up in her eyes, pleading with him to stay.

He smiled and didn't even try to hold back the tears pushing into his own eyes. Over the last year, she'd bloomed like the wildflowers she loved to grow behind the house. He gently tapped her nose. "I'll be back soon to annoy you again."

"Promise?"

"I promise." He studied her face, waiting to see if she believed him. He would do everything in his power to keep that promise. But he knew the risks, didn't he? His father's words stirred an uncertainty deep within. He bent over and rubbed Bluey's soft ears. "Besides, you've got Bluey here to keep you company."

She took his hand. "What are you supposed to be looking for?"

"I don't know, but I'll know when I see it." He kissed her on the forehead then climbed into the boat he and his father had built together three years ago.

"Wait! I have something for you." She knelt down on the deck and tugged a small book out from under her jacket. "Here. In case you get lonely."

He reached up to take the book she held down to him. "What's this?"

"Something to remind you of home."

He flipped through the first few pages. Photographs filled them along with short quips and sayings she'd embellished in script or calligraphy. "These are—"

The picture on the last page stopped him.

"Where'd you get this one?"

She tucked her hair behind her ear. "Dad gave it to me. I asked him for one of her pictures."

"I'm surprised he let you have one." Joshua stared up at Jessie. "You know, you look a lot like her."

"That's what Dad said." She took a deep breath and exhaled a sigh. "I wish I could remember her better."

"You were so young." He tucked the book into his inside satchel. "Thanks, Jess. I'll look at it every night." He stowed both bags inside the sleeping compartment just inside the door alongside the rest of his gear he'd loaded the day before. "And I'll be back before you know it."

"You better be. This place can't run itself." She stood with her hands on her hips. "Dad has orders to fill so that leaves the rest to me."

"You're more than qualified." He winked at her.

Bluey barked then jumped into the boat.

Joshua crouched down next to him. "Not this time, buddy. You need to stay with Jessie and help her keep the chickens in line."

"Come on, Bluey." Jessie patted her leg as she called to him.

Bluey pawed Joshua's leg and whined.

"See? Even he doesn't want you to go."

He didn't miss the tears she fought. If he got out of the boat to hug her, he'd have to wait until tomorrow to leave. "Go on, Bluey."

The dog jumped back onto the dock and sat next to Jessie.

After untying the boat, Joshua turned over the engine. He kept a slow pace as he steered toward the mouth of the bay. The sensation of being watched drew his backward glance. Jessie and Bluey stood at the end of the pier. His sister waved.

A pang hit him in the gut. He waved back, pushing on a smile he hoped she could see. Should he have told her what was at stake? Their father understood. But Jessie...she didn't understand the prophecy yet.

Nor the role she may yet have to play to save them all.

Want to find out what's about to destroy Reyna and Joshua's worlds?
Read more episodes on Kindle Vella!

Made in United States
North Haven, CT
06 May 2023